ONE OF THE GOOD GUYS

ONE OF THE GOOD GUYS

by

Reverend Joanna Z. Ray

Copyright

© *2008 by Joanna Ray. All rights reserved.*

First published in 2008 for and on behalf of the author by Lulu

website: www.lulu.com

email: RevdJoannaRay@aol.com

All rights reserved.
Unorthorised duplication
Contravenes existing laws.

ISBN 978-1-4092-2406-8

Published By Lulu
Printed and bound by Lulu

Registered with the IP Rights Office

Copyright Registration Service

Ref: 282341529

CONTENTS

Introduction

Chapter One: Getting To Know Them

Chapter Two: The Flashtechno syntamic

Chapter Three: One of the Good Guys

INTERLUDE: PART 1

Chapter Four: The trumpet sounds the Final Offensive

INTERLUDE: PART 2

Chapter Five: The Sikaran Court

Chapter Six: Sikaran Telepathy

Chapter Seven: The End of the Space War

Epilogue

Introduction:

Hi, the name's Joe Marsh and I am the narrator for this book and it's the twenty-fourth century using the Earth calendar and not the Galactic Year count, in case anybody decides to read this book five hundred or so years from now. I begin the story as a soldier on the Security Team of the *Interspace* starship, the I.G.S. *McBride*. This was a supplies grain ship that had been converted to a war vessel, as there was a severe shortage of space battle cruisers on Earth. That is because we were losing the space war, right up until two years ago when the Sikaran Empire, who were allied to the Gloshan Empire, suddenly decided to break their treaty with the planet *Gloshos* and change sides just in the nick of time for us humans. Siding with us has altered the balance of power and now we may have half a chance of winning.

Before being on the I.G.S. *McBride*, I was an Earth Special Forces soldier for two years, until I could not stand it any longer. The things that we were made to do on missions went against all that I believed was right in life, all my principles were shaken up and turned on their head and I didn't appreciate it. Because of this, I signed up with a front line starship, which was in the thick of all the action against the Gloshans and their allies. The starship was captained by Sir Lawrence Grey: an Englishman who was also from a line of English aristocrats going back a thousand years or more. A friend of mine helped me write this book and so it is mostly written in the third person. I felt that I had to write this to share my experiences of getting to know the group of Sikaran soldiers who joined the *McBride* to be transported to the *beta*-Naiobi colonies to boost the security there.

The *beta*-Naiobi colonies were essentially human colonies and were the last outpost before you reached Earth, so they were vital to any of our enemies. If the Naiobi colonies were captured, it would be easy to launch a full-scale space attack on our planet Earth. An elite group of twenty-two Sikaran soldiers who belonged to the *Isithan* came aboard in order to travel to the *beta*-Naiobi colonies, where they were going to help protect the colonies against attack by Gloshan forces.

The Sikaran Empire lay near the rim of the galaxy just beyond a place called *Kaloris,* which shares borders with the Gloshan Empire. Let me tell you something about the Sikarans who came aboard the *McBride*. Sikarans are very similar to us humans, except their skin colouring is pale purple, almost violet and their features are very slightly feline; the tips of their ears are a little catlike and to an extent so are their eyes. Otherwise, they are the same as humans.

The older men have sleek-looking shoulder-length black hair streaked with a small amount of golden-coloured strands and the younger men usually seem to have black hair, not a mixture of both. According to the women, the Sikaran men who came aboard are extremely handsome and amazingly attractive. Of course, we could see that for ourselves, and it really irritated us human men and it sparked a lot of rivalry between us and the Sikaran guys. Mind you, it didn't bother me too much as I had a steady girlfriend at the time. That first evening in the canteen, after the Sikarans had embarked, we were talking together in the Security Team and Morrison remarked, "Gentlemen, listen up. We have to plan a careful strategy here. We have some strong competition that's just walked on board. Did you see the way our women were looking at them Sikaran guys?"

The Sikarans are physically humanoid and so are able to have compatible relationships with human women or with any other humanoid species in the galaxy, for example, the Gloshans, Lasoans and Kalesians. Marayshan, Avernyi, Navaronschyia and Devthanyi appear to be the older men in the group and look middle-aged. We did not know, at the start, that the Sikarans are strongly telepathic people. They are touch telepaths and this is a significant difference between our two species and took some working out when the Sikarans began to develop close relationships with human women.

Chapter One: Getting To Know Them

When he first arrived in the *beta*-Naiobi colonies with the group of Sikaran *Isithan* soldiers, Joe Marsh spent a lot of off-duty time talking to Captain Maitland, telling him about the many good things that had happened with these soldiers aboard the starship *McBride*. Maitland would invite him into his office as he was keen to learn more about the Sikarans. One of the things Joe related to Maitland happened four days after the Sikarans had boarded. No one knew them, so everyone was frightened of them. No one except a few of the senior officers had ever met Sikarans before, let alone soldiers who were from the legendary Sikaran *Isithan*: a martial arts society, which translated into Galactic as '*The Brotherhood of the Sword*'. There were many rumours about them of course but no-one really knew what they were like.

It was breakfast time in the noisy, crowded canteen. The security team usually sat at tables together and now they included the Sikaran soldiers, as they would be working closely with the Security Team. The aroma of bacon, eggs, tomatoes and hot, buttered toast filled the place and caused Pete Walsh to really long for his meal after missing supper the previous night. Pete joined the breakfast table, rubbing his hands together and said,

"Hey, you guys, have you heard about Gloria Kincade? Gloria's up for it, if you get my meaning. Pay her a visit and she'll oblige. I heard a guy talking about her yesterday in the cargo bay."

"Oh get lost, Pete," Joe Marsh said as he tucked into his breakfast with great gusto. "That is so not true. Leave Gloria alone. Look, she's had some difficult times: her first boyfriend treated her real bad, so why don't you just leave her alone. Let her get over it in her own time, you hear me, kid?" He piled more food onto his plate after revolving the centre of the table around in order to collect the items that he wanted.

"Okay Joe, okay. You can't blame me for trying though, can you?" Pete replied.

"Shut up Pete," said Saunders waving his fork at him. "You're getting on my nerves. Why don't you get yourself a steady girlfriend?"

"You're just jealous, Saunders, because you're married and I'm free. I'll bet these Sikaran guys agree with me. Isn't it more fun to mess about than to be married to just one woman all the time? Avernyi? Deva? Marayshan? What do you think?"

"I don't agree with you. Being in a stable relationship is much better," Avernyi replied to Pete's surprise. The Sikarans spoke with accents that sounded rather Slavic perhaps even Hungarian.

"I think that marriage is a great honour for any man," said Deva seriously, examining the food in the table centre dishes with some curiosity, pushing it around with a spoon.

"It is wonderful to really get to know one woman," said Marayshan starting to fill his plate with bacon, tomatoes, and toast. "We three have all been married, but now we are widowers."

"Pete, I don't think the Sikaran guys agree with you," said Kelly laughing at him.

"Very funny, Kelly. I always thought that Sikaran men would like sleeping around. I heard them tell that they'd make love to anything that moves," he said.
"Ohh ... no ... Pete, that is an awful thing to say to anyone," said Heinrich. "Just awful. You should say sorry for that one, pretty damn quick if I was you."

Heinrich had noticed the subtle change of expression on the Sikaran soldiers' faces.

Sitting opposite Pete, Deva reached across the table, grabbed hold of the human by the wrists in a steel-like grip, and pulled him towards him and fixed him with a look.

"When we get to the security training centre later, I am going to make you pay for zat remark, young human," he said, in a very cold voice.

"Yeah?" said Pete attempting to sound braver than he felt, but he was pale and trembled badly.

"Yes," said Deva, "I promise you."

"Hey, fight, fight, fight!" Heinrich laughed, trying to lighten the mood, "We're gonna have some fun later, gentlemen!"

"Peter, can I ask you something?" said Marayshan then. "Deva, let him go. Let him go. He is young and foolish. Now listen, I have something to say. Why do you say things like 'Gloria Kincade is up for it' or the things that you said about Sikaran men just now? They are not very nice things to say. It is very unpleasant."

Pete coloured heavily, ashamed now, and said, "I'm sorry okay? It was a joke, that's all."

"Peter, I don't think you realise how much you have insulted my friends and I. In our culture, it is a grave insult to say something like that. If you were a Gloshan soldier, we would have visited your quarters tonight and beaten you. As it is, we are giving you some leeway because you are human, and we believe that you are better zan Gloshans."

"Geeze, I said I was sorry, didn't I? And you're talking about beating me? Where are you guys coming from?"

"Next time, think before you speak!" Deva said sharply.

Pete became silent and kept his eyes fixed to his plate.

Heinrich shrugged at Marayshan,
"Pete's like that sometimes. He kind of says stupid things, before he thinks, and he doesn't really mean them. He's the youngest guy in security, so you need to make allowances for him. We all kind of treat him like a younger brother, the way you and your friends do with Chalek."

"I will not make too many allowances," said Deva ominously.

Pete's hand shook and he dropped the food off his fork then became tearful. "Look, I said I was sorry. It was a stupid thing to say. I said it without thinking, that's all."

"Deva," Marayshan spoke to him in Sikaran then said, "Peter, we accept your apology and we will forget all about it, all right?"

"Thanks Marayshan," Pete replied. Wiping his eyes, he looked over at the Sikaran and Marayshan nodded and smiled at him.

"It is okay, we are all friends again. This breakfast is very good. Tell me, what is this here, Peter?"

"It's called a tomato," Pete replied. "They grow on Earth. My ma used to grow them in our garden back home."

"Well, we used to grow a lot of fruit and vegetables on my parents' farm back in my home also, and we kept much livestock too. It was a very good farm," Marayshan replied, taking two hard-boiled eggs, cracking them on the table and peeling the shells rapidly until they were clean enough to eat.

"You don't seem to mind eating human food, Marayshan," said Kelly.

"No, of course not. My friends and I eat human and Gloshan food, but sometimes we found that Gloshan food was hard to digest for us. But, they do make a good vegetable soup though. It is very nutritious. I got the recipe from one of the cooks before we left the Gloshan camps. I have it here somewhere. Let me see."

He put on a pair of spectacles he often used for reading. "Ah yes, here, it says, *Cho d'ruk, g'va chanush, dru isak*."

"If that's *Gloshanese*, none of us speak the language, Marayshan," Heinrich replied.

"Well, then I will translate. To make one litre of soup, you need two *cho*, four *chanush* roots, and a small piece of *dru*."

"What in heck is a *chanush* root?" asked Saunders.

"Oh, well, let me see. I will draw one for you. See, this is what it looks like."

"Oh that's just like a carrot or a turnip, kind of," said Connors.

"Do you speak fluent *Gloshanese*, Marayshan?" Joe Marsh asked.

"Yes, we all do," Marayshan said, "we also understand a lot about Gloshan weaponry. We must teach you. It will give you an advantage in situations of combat."

"Marayshan, listen," said Connors. "If you know Gloshans so well, can you explain to us why they do the awful things they do to alien prisoners. Why do they commit such atrocities?"

"I cannot answer that. I do not understand it myself," Marayshan replied seriously. "All I can say is that I think they are a little crazy, from ze way they are brought up in zeir culture. We tried to tell them that what they are doing is wrong. That it is despicable and dishonourable. We said it so many times, but they would not listen to us. That was the main reason why we changed sides in ze space war. We were so disgusted by their continued ill treatment of alien prisoners. They always go against the galactic *Treaty of Naforek* which protects prisoners of space war. Zey I mean *they*, never listen to anyone."

"We're kind of glad your people changed sides," said Saunders, in a matter of fact way.

"That's about the understatement of the millennium, ain't it, Saunders?" said Connors. "Without the Sikarans' help, these past two years Earth would have been invaded by Gloshan forces ten times over."

Marayshan went quiet and looked grim.

"Geeze, what's wrong, Marayshan?" Heinrich asked.

"It is just that my friends and I know what Gloshans plan to do to your Earth and your people if they ever were to take control." There was an ominous silence as the security men looked at each other.

"Would you like to tell us what that is?" said Saunders.

"No," Marayshan replied, looking at them over the top of his spectacles. "I do not think I wish to tell you. It is really not very pleasant. I don't think I would enjoy ze rest of my breakfast if I did tell you," he said and continued to eat. And there the conversation ended. The security men exchanged glances again.

On the fifth day that the Sikarans were aboard, they were still not yet on active duty with the security team as they had been given some time by the Captain to get to know the ship and to settle in. Marayshan, disliking inactivity, made his way down to the cargo bay to see if he could help with moving supplies around and unpacking. In the starship's cargo bay, supplies were forever being sorted, logged in and out, requisitioned and distributed. The catering team were there twice a week, replenishing their supplies for the ship's kitchens.

When Marayshan turned up, he asked if anyone needed any extra help.

A call came from the catering team. "Hey, soldier, over here, we're short-handed," said one of the men. "We need to get supplies to the kitchens. We're part of the catering team. I'm Terry and this is Steve, Ken, Angie, Marcie, Alison and Tim. When we break, you're welcome to have coffee with us, and then to have lunch in the kitchens with us when we finish down here."

"Thank you and hello. My name is Marayshan. I am pleased to meet ze catering team as I really enjoy cooking. Maybe you can teach me how to make some Earth dishes and I can teach you some Sikaran ones." Marayshan replied. Trying to sound as unthreatening as he possibly could, he realised that all the humans aboard appeared to be frightened of he and his friends. Some even seemed to be terrified.

"Of course we'll teach you," said Angie smiling at him. "Now, let me explain what we do in the cargo bay. We drag those containers from there, and fill them up over there. They are colour coded so that no one can go wrong, except for Ken, of course, so we all have to help him. When all the containers are full, we load them onto a transport trolley and, somehow, we manage to get it into one of the cargo lifts and take it to the kitchens. We're always here in the cargo bay twice a week on a Tuesday and a Friday from 9am to 11am and we could always use extra hands."

"I will help you when I am able, Angie. But when my friends and I begin work with ze security team, I may not be able to help very often." Marayshan replied. He then lifted a container and carried it over to where it needed to be filled.

Ken went over with him, dragging another container and said, "Hello, I'm Ken. Can you help me? Which colour does this go with, please? Angie told me that I have to ask someone to match the colours before I fill the container."

"Oh, zat colour is green, and it matches with zis tank. See, Green and green."

"Thank you, what's your name? I've never seen anyone who looks like you before. Not being horrible, but your face and arms and hands are a very funny colour." Ken said.

"My name is Marayshan, but you can just call me Shan, if you like. It is easier. I am not from your home on Earth. I am from another place, a long, long way from Earth, so my people look a little different to your people. Do you understand?"

Ken shook his head. "No, but I like you anyway, even if you look strange," Ken said smiling at him.

"Ken, for goodness sake. Leave Marayshan alone. He doesn't want to be pestered while he's trying to work," said Tim.

"I wasn't pestering him, Tim. I was just being friendly," said Ken.

"Tim, it is okay, really, I have no objection to Ken speaking to me while I work." Marayshan replied.

"What's that, Shan?" said Ken, pointing to Marayshan's *Isithan* wrist bracelet.

"It is a communicator. If I press it, I can talk to all my friends wherever they are on the ship."

"Oh, that's clever, Shan. That's very clever," said Ken. "Do you know I used to have a pet dog at home called Rover, but I had to leave him there with my mum and dad when I came here with Angie and Tim and Alison. I miss my little dog, I loved him lots and lots."

"Oh I am sorry you had to leave him behind, Ken," Marayshan said. "Can you describe to me what your pet looks like, because I am not sure there are dogs where I live."

"Oh well, Rover is brown with black spots, and has four legs and wags his tail a lot and barks like this, 'woof woof woof.'"

"Oh yes, I know now. We do have dogs, then, but we call them a different name, we call them '*Virrath*' in my language. You see where I live we speak a different language to where you live. I used to have some pet dogs also when I was at home."

"Oh did you, Shan, that's really good, I really like you," said Ken.

"I like you also, Ken," said Marayshan, "now look that is red, and matches with zis, you see, red and red. Green and green and red and red, you see; green and green and red and red. Can you remember that?"

"Green and green and red and red, green and green and red and red," Ken repeated the words several times as Marayshan pointed to each colour on the container and the tank as he said it. Ken's face lit up and he hugged the Sikaran and clapped his hands. "I know it now," he said. "Tim, I know it now. Angie I know it now. Shan taught me. Shan taught me."

"Yes, of course you know it now, Ken, until next time," Tim said smiling at him and sighing. "Thanks for trying to teach him, Marayshan."

"It is no problem," Marayshan replied, smiling at him.

"You know what, Shan? I always want to be able to juggle, but no one can teach me how. Nobody knows here. Do you know how? Will you teach me, please?"

"Yes, I know how to juggle, and I will show you at lunch time, okay? Now we should do some more work, yes?"

Ken nodded. "Yes. I like you," he said.

"You're really patient with Ken. Thanks for helping him," Alison said later when they were sitting down to coffee and cakes.

"Oh this cake tastes very good, what is the flavour?" Marayshan asked.

"The flavour is called vanilla," said Terry, "I'm one of the chefs. I baked it."

"Terry bakes all the cakes, Marayshan. He is just fantastic, aren't you, Terry."

Terry smiled his thanks at Alison and raised his coffee cup to her.

"Well, tell us something about yourself, Marayshan. We're dying to find out everything about you and your friends. None of us has ever met any Sikarans before," Alison continued.

"Well, let me see," Marayshan said. "I was not always a soldier. I used to be a farmer at first. I am from ze *Arakiarth* Valley on the first world of our Empire. There are nine planets all togezer. My village is called *Kirai*. When I became a soldier, I spent a lot of time on one spaceship or another. I have two good friends with me here. Their names are Avernyi and Navaronschyia. We are all three from the same village of Kirai."

"Are you married? Do Sikarans have families?" asked Angie.

"Yes, of course we do. And I have been married, but now I am a widower. I still have my parents and five sisters in Kirai."

"Five sisters?" laughed Angie.

"Flaming heck," said Terry. "I had two sisters and that was bad enough." Marayshan laughed with them.

"They were not so bad. Usually we got on well. My parents loved children. That is why they had so many of us. It was easy to bring us up on a big farm. There was room for everyone and we did most of the farm work too. We all enjoyed it. We were fortunate to grow up in the *Arakiarth* Valley. It is a good place to be. You would like it. Although we were poor, it did not seem to matter there, because most people were from low or middle clans in the *Arakiarth* Valley. It was only when I left that I came up against the High Clans and Royal Clan. It was not always easy for me."

"I'm sorry to hear that," said Alison sympathetically. "So, they're the rich ones who don't know how lucky they are. We've got people like that too on Earth. Those kinds of people usually think they're better than everyone else just because they're born rich. One of the officers on board is like that, Commander Nicholas Carter. He won't give you the time of day. Captain Grey is aristocracy too, but he's different. He's more approachable. They're both Lords or Earls or something from England, a country on Earth."

"The last spaceship I was on was ze Flag ship *Voran* and the Captain and most officers were Royal Clan. All the men in zis group except for Harith and Chalek were there with me. Do you know the royals went and hired a top class chef from a really exclusive hotel? My friends and I could not believe it."

"Actually, our catering group are from a very good hotel in London, England. It's not an exclusive hotel, but still very good. We put in a bid to do the catering on this starship and we won. Mind you, there wasn't much competition, not to work on a frontline starship like this. People thought we were fools to do it, but someone's got to, haven't they?"

"You are all very brave to be on this starship when you are not crew or soldiers. As you say, it is very much frontline in the space war," Marayshan replied.

"It's not a bad life here on the *McBride*," Alison continued. "Most folk are friendly like us. D'you think it will take your friends long to settle in? We heard they're a bit jumpy and spiky, a bit unapproachable. Not meaning any offence or anything, but if they could be a bit more friendly, it would help. Could you have a word with them, Marayshan? It's difficult enough being under threat from Gloshan attack all the time, without extra problems on board. Will you talk to them, please, for all our sakes?"

"Of course I will talk to zem, Alison," Marayshan replied, "but perhaps I need to say something in zeir defence. For a time, all of us lived among Gloshan soldiers in their camps. Camp *K'Taak* was the last one we were in before the treaty was broken with zem. The Gloshans really got on our nerves. I mean seriously. When our High Council asked us to consider living among humans and help to protect zem from Gloshan attack, we assumed zat humans and Gloshans are very similar. So we decide we will treat humans as we did the Gloshans. We have to be tough and aggressive with Gloshan soldiers or they don't get the message. Now, we are here among humans, we begin to realise a little zat you are different to Gloshans. But we have only been here a very few days. It will take a few weeks, I think, before my friends adjust to being here. I will talk with them and tell them what you have said, and I will bring them here to talk with all of you."

Alison nodded then folding her arms said, "How could you and your friends ever imagine we would be as bad as Gloshans? I can't understand that, I just can't. Poor Pete Walsh from security yesterday got on the wrong side of your group, didn't he? He's just a foolish young man. You shouldn't take what he says so seriously. None of the rest of us do. Your friend scared Pete half to death, and then someone else told him that if he had been Gloshan he would have been beaten for insulting you all. Don't you think that was just a bit over the top?"

"It was I who said it because it is true, but because we have not known humans for long, we gave Walsh the benefit of the doubt and, of course, he did not understand that what he said to us was a grave insult in our culture."

"You still haven't said why you thought we're as bad as Gloshans," said Angie, but was interrupted by Marcie doubling up with pain and crying out,

"Angie! Alison! I think the baby's coming! Ohh … someone help me please."

"Oh no, the baby can't come now, Marcie, it's too soon, and not in the cargo bay! It will take the paramedics forever to get down here to us. Somebody call them quick! What are we going to do?"

Marcie collapsed onto the floor.

"I will help, I have done some nursing," said Marayshan.

"But you surely don't understand about human women. You've only been with us for a few days," Alison said.

"No, but you look the same as Sikaran women, and I am sure I can help. I have delivered Sikaran babies before. Someone get me water, if you can and something for her to lie on, quickly. She is in urgent need of help."

He went to Marcie and said calmly and quietly, "I will help you. I have done nursing and delivered babies before, so just relax."

"Oh thank goodness," Marcie replied, and screamed again.

Marayshan washed his hands quickly as Steve and Terry brought water in any container they could find, and he began to help her.

"Alison and Angie please come and hold her hands quickly. She needs you to give her courage," Marayshan said.

They came and did as he had asked. Quite a crowd gathered.

Angie shouted at them, "Oh please, give Marcie some privacy! If you must watch, stand back! Stand further back!"

Marcie kept screaming.

Marayshan washed his hands again, and rested one hand on her chest while the other he placed on her forehead, then concentrated.

"What's he doing?" whispered Alison.

"I don't know," Angie whispered back.

Marcie went quiet, breathing normally and looking very relieved.

"Thank you, I don't know what you did, but it's helped so much and the pain has gone – it's all gone." Marcie said in amazement.

"It will stay so for only a little while I am afraid, but it will give you some respite. I cannot do more than zat. Are you ready to let me help you to give birth now? Will you try now?"

Marcie nodded.

Marayshan worked on delivering the baby. At last the baby was delivered and Marayshan got a round of applause from the group of humans standing nearby.

The baby began to cry with a good healthy pair of lungs and Marayshan washed the little boy then gave him to Alison to hold.

"I need to help Marcie again, she is in a bad way, Alison," he said.

He reduced her pain until the paramedics worked their way down to the cargo bay and finally arrived. They did as much as they could to stabilize her condition.

"That's it, she's going to be all right," said one of the paramedics. "How did you help her with the pain, if you don't mind my asking?"

"No, I don't mind," Marayshan replied. "It is the Sikaran way of helping – we are telepaths through touch."

The humans were silent now and looked at each other.

"I could only help her for a few seconds at a time, but it gave her enough respite to keep going until you arrived."

"Yes, I believe that we would have lost her if you hadn't done that. It's lucky for Marcie that you were here on hand and that you acted so promptly, otherwise we would have lost her and the baby. Here, you can use these to clean up a little until you can get to your room and change."

"No, listen – we'll take Marayshan to our catering rest room – he can put on a pair of Terry's overalls," said Angie, "Terry will show you to the catering department. By the way," Angie kissed Marayshan, "that's to say thank you for helping Marcie. We're all so grateful to you for saving our friend."
Alison kissed him too.

Marayshan smiled at them and went with Terry.

The paramedics put through a report to First Officer McKye. It read:
'A Sikaran soldier has just delivered a baby in the middle of the cargo bay, without any help or medical equipment. The mother is a civilian named Marcie Jones from the Catering Department.'

McKye rubbed his eyes twice, wondering if he was seeing things due to another sleepless night and then called sickbay to double check that the report was not a hoax. It was actually confirmed by Dr. Grafton himself.

McKye let Captain Grey know right away. He had been asked to keep the Captain informed of anything relating to the Sikaran soldiers.

That night, a large group of security men were gathered in the leisure suite with some of the Sikarans, where they were all playing a noisy game of cards together.

Heinrich paused for a moment, frowning and said, "Marayshan, I heard this weird rumour from Angie in catering today. Angie said that this morning you delivered a baby right in the middle of the cargo bay. Now some of the guys and me, we've been taking bets that Angie's going space crazy and that you never did any such thing. Now come on, we're taking bets on this so tell us, did you or didn't you deliver a baby in the cargo bay?"

"Yes I did," Marayshan replied. "I have done some nursing. The mother is Marcie from catering."

"You did *that* in the middle of the cargo bay? Are you serious? Can you really deliver babies?"

"Well yes, Sikaran babies mostly, but I have delivered a Gloshan baby and now a human baby, but I have to admit, that the middle of the cargo bay was not ze best place I would have chosen to do that."

"Angie says you saved Marcie's life and the baby too. I think that's really something," Saunders said.

"The poor woman was in a bad way, but she is in sickbay now."

"Kelly, ain't you got nothing' to say to Marayshan about all this?" said Saunders.

Kelly shrugged as Marayshan looked at him and he said quietly,

"Thanks for doing that. I'm the baby's father."

"If you are the father, why are you not in sickbay with Marcie? She is in a very bad way. She is in intensive care."

"I think Kelly wants to be there, but I don't think Marcie would want him to be," said Saunders. "There's been trouble between them."

"I still love her, I still love her, why doesn't anybody ever believe me?" said Kelly in a subdued way.

"You got a damn strange way of showing your love, Kelly, the things you done to her," said Connors.

"Look, things got out of hand – we were on a date and I drank too much – remember how stressed I was after that mission we'd been on the day before? I spent three months in the brig for it and I said I was sorry to her. I still love her, damn it!"

"The guy's nuts, that's what I think." said Saunders, "Kelly, you can't do that and expect Marcie to go on loving you. I don't understand why in this galaxy you think she should still love you? You know, Kelly, you are ruining my card game."

"Kelly, look, I am about to go to visit her in sickbay, so why don't you come with me? If Marcie will not see you, at least you can see your newborn son."

Marayshan took Kelly with him.

"I don't know why Marayshan is bothering with the guy," said Connors.

"Marayshan is like that. He cares a lot about people," said Avernyi.

"Well, that's for sure, Avernyi," said Saunders. "I gotta say it took us all by surprise. If you want the honest truth, we never expected a Sikaran soldier to give a damn about how humans feel about anything."

"Actually, Saunders, we all give a damn, not just Marayshan," said Avernyi. "Otherwise we would not be here."

"I thought you were sent here by your High Commander or something," said Connors.

"No not really, your Earth president asked for more help on ze *beta*-Naiobi colonies as it is ze last station before Earth, and if the Gloshans captured it, zey could easily get control of Earth. Other Sikaran soldiers who volunteered are already there, and we will join them and all work as Peace Officers in ze Naiobi Police Force. We were asked to consider going to Naiobi as we are part of the *Isithan,* which is an elite force. No one said we have to go. We are volunteers."

"I never realized that," said Heinrich. "You must care about us a lot to want to travel all the way to Naiobi, so far from the Sikaran Empire."

"We do care – we all do – even Harith," said Navaronschyia. "We are sorry if we have been rather unapproachable and aggressive since we got here, but we are used to living among Gloshan soldiers and zat is how we had to behave towards zem. We have realized now that you are not at all similar and we are very relieved."

Two mornings later at breakfast, Chalek and Ilashon, two young Sikaran soldiers, were having an argument. Sitting beside each other they started hitting each other's shoulders, staring intently at each other.

Marayshan looked up from his breakfast and said, "Chalek and Ilashon, what do you think you are doing? Stop it right now. Don't make me come over there."

Heinrich smiled at Marsh and said, "The guy cracks me up."

The two young men went quiet for a moment then the argument began again.

"Stop!" said Marayshan. "Ilashon, come here, and you too, Chalek. Tell me, what is going on between the two of you?"

"He took my comb!" said Ilashon, "Without asking me! He took it."

"Chalek is this true?" asked Marayshan.

"Ilashon took my comb last month and did not ask me!" Chalek replied.

"So Ilashon started this, is zat what you are saying, Chalek?" Marayshan replied.

Ilashon made a dive at Chalek and hit him.

Marayshan held up a hand for silence.

They stood absolutely still and to attention.

"Now, that is enough from both of you. I mean it," said Marayshan.

"Sir, if I am going to be beaten and not Chalek, it will not be fair!" Ilashon said, angrily. "You always take Chalek's part, always!"

"I will pretend I did not hear that, Ilashon," said Marayshan. "No one is going to be punished this time. I want you both to say sorry to each other. Say it and mean it."

After they apologized to each other, Marayshan said, "If this happens again, you will both be beaten, do you hear me?"

They nodded, looking crestfallen.

"Now sit down and eat your breakfast in a decent fashion."

They sat and sulked heavily, much to the amusement of the human security men.

After a time, Marayshan looked up over the top of his reading glasses. He had been reading the weekly starship news bulletin.

"Will you two stop sulking? I have a job for you. I want you to find this list of places on the ship today and describe to me exactly where they are." He handed a list to Ilashon.

"Yes sir," Ilashon said quietly then smiled at him. "Come on, Chalek, hurry up so we can get started," he said.

"Oh, I am glad to see you are both friends again," Marayshan said beginning to read the bulletin.

A few days later, the Sikaran soldiers were to go out on their first ground mission with the human security men. Commander Baillie was already in the Security Training Area waiting for his men to get ready for the ground mission. The disarray of the inexperienced human soldiers amazed Marayshan; they were still talking and pulling on protective armour and weaponry, taking them off again and trying to adjust them.

"Good morning, Commander," Marayshan said, saluting him. "Is everything all right?"

"No, not really," Baillie replied. "Things have been difficult since one of my men was captured by Gloshans recently, tortured and sent back to us. Marayshan, it was an awful sight. It's really unsettled them. I was planning on going through Gloshan weaponry with them soon to try and boost their morale; they're all so rattled, I can almost feel it."

Marayshan sighed for a moment and said, "The Gloshans are a little crazy, I think and it makes them commit these atrocities. Look, Commander, maybe my friends and I can help. We can do our warm up session in here instead of planet-side and zat may distract your men – also we understand well about Gloshan weaponry. We could demonstrate them if you wish."

"That would be a great help, thank you, Marayshan. Will Harith agree do you think?"

"Yes, I think so." Marayshan replied. He called to Harith and spoke in Sikaran for a few moments.

Harith replied and the whole Sikaran group moved to make a circle in the centre of the gym and spread out.

Harith sang out then, "*E-lar-an*! *Isi-than*!"

They all replied, "*Hai! Hai! Hai!*"

Marayshan went to join them.

Harith then sang out, "*Isi-than*! *Kai – ithan!*" and the soldiers called out, "*Cheh! Cheh! Cheh!*"

The human soldiers turned to watch what was going on. There was a moment of silence and Harith began a song, which sounded to the humans like, "*Kare-Var-darth, thyi-akie, thyi-akie, Kare-Var-darth, ilyashin,*" and continued.

The others joined in and began to do a martial arts work out, moving slowly around in the circle at first and then the pace picked up and they fought the person beside them and then in threes, fours and sixes.

Harith suddenly clapped his hands and shouted, "*Itharie! Itharie! Hai!*" and got an answering call of, "*Itharie! Itharie! Cheh!*"

He then began to chant, "*Itharie! Gloshanyi! Itharie! Gloshanyi!*" with a tone of menace in it, repeatedly and softly and the rest joined in.

There was disbelief on the faces of some of the humans, and they exchanged glances with each other. None of them had ever come up against the *Isithan* in their battles with Gloshan ground troops before, and so this came as something of a shock to them that the Sikaran soldiers were such expert fighters in the martial arts. They had heard rumours about the singing soldiers of the *Isithan,* but had never witnessed them in action.

"Geeze, aren't they something. It's good to have them on our side now, sir," said Joe Marsh to Commander Baillie.
"Yes, Marsh," said Baillie, "we really need them. They really are vital to the safety of this ship."
"Yes sir," said Saunders. "You know, Marayshan's an okay guy. Pete Walsh just told me that he went to see Pete this morning in sickbay and talked him out of his fit of the terrors."
"Yes, I have a feeling that he is going to be a good man to have around in the team, Saunders. Anyone who can boost Walsh's morale like that has got something about him."

"Yes sir, I copy that," said Kelly. "I think he's a real nice guy. I noticed him helping someone yesterday in the canteen."

Baillie smiled at his men, beginning to feel that things were at last taking a turn for the better. Anyone who could improve the atmosphere of fear and depression that had settled recently on his team was a real bonus.

The warm up ended. Marayshan came back over to Baillie and said,

"Commander, my friends and I are very good with armour and weaponry. We are very experienced soldiers. Shall we help your men to prepare for the battle?"

"Please do, Marayshan, go ahead," said Baillie.

Marayshan saluted him again and waded through the heaps of body armour, padded boots and all kinds of weaponry that were strewn across the floor and said, hitting Heinrich's arm, "Heh! Heinrich! Look at you! You are such a mess! Come on, I will help you."

Marayshan helped him to adjust the armlets, chest and back shields, then the leggings and boots, adjusting everything carefully until it fitted him well.

"Say, thanks, that's just great! It's the best fit I've ever had from these damned things. They're usually so uncomfortable!"

"Well, now you can fight in comfort. You will be invincible, Heinrich!" Marayshan said and called over to his friends. "Deva, Nava, Avernyi! Come and help, everyone is having problems today. This armour is really hopeless. Joe, are you okay?"

"Do I look okay, Marayshan," Joe replied exasperated by some leggings.

"No, you are a complete shambles. You should look in a mirror sometime. Really, I don't know what your girlfriend would say if she could see you now."
He got a laugh from everyone including Commander Baillie.

Just then, Joe Marsh said, "Okay, Marayshan, so where's the armour you and your friends are going to wear? I don't see you or your friends putting any on. There's plenty to go round and you can't go on a ground mission without it." He indicated the spare equipment with a sweep of his arm.

"Oh, we have our own armour, Joe," Marayshan replied. "Deva is carrying it in that container. Deva, why don't you distribute the armour?"

Deva opened the container, and took out small rolled up balls of metallic material and threw one to each of the Sikarans calling out their names. They each unrolled the armour and wore what looked like a chain-mail vest with long sleeves, which was silver-coloured. They placed it beneath their jackets.

"Is that all there is of your armour?" asked Joe, greatly concerned.

"Our clothes are lined with a special protective Sikaran material woven from fine strands of *urstallian*, Joe, so we will be okay. It is special *Isithan* armour, only our groups are able to wear such armour." said Avernyi.

"*Urstallian*, isn't that a metal only found in the Sikaran Empire?" Connors said, falling over as he tried to balance on one leg whilst putting on a pair of boots.

"Yes, that is right, it is a Sikaran metal. Back home we have mountains which are covered in *urstallian*." Avernyi rubbed the chain mail tunic several times before he put it on.

"Oh, you don't have to mine the metal ore underground then. I'm only asking because I've studied a bit of geology," said Joe, interested.

"We do not mine it, no. We remove it in thin layers, from the tops of the mountain peaks. It is very easy for us to remove, because we ask it nicely if it would not mind coming with us. If it agrees, zen we roll it up and take it." Nava said which caused no end of laughter from the security men.

"They're goddamn comedians," said Peterson smiling at Marsh.

"Ah, geeze, it's really great having you and your friends with us, Nava," said Saunders, "you've certainly cheered me up."

"Me too," said Heinrich, "don't go away, will you, at least not before we get to Naiobi."

Nava wondered what the humans found so amusing about what he had said about communicating telepathically with the *urstallian* metal. He puzzled over it for a while and realized how much the human soldiers needed to laugh, as they were in such a state of gloom and despondency and felt sorry for them. Once the battle began, there was no time to think about anything else except how to keep the inexperienced human soldiers safe and to stop them from being snatched by Gloshan ground troops.

What surprised the humans about that first mission with the Sikarans were their excellent skills in the martial arts. They were amazed however by the way the Sikarans' chain-mail armour crackled, shimmered and emitted small bursts of lightning as they fought. It made them look like mythical people from a bygone age.

After a few missions, however, the human soldiers grew accustomed to the lightning phenomenon and besides it certainly succeeded in frightening the enemy, causing some Gloshan soldiers even to run away whilst yelling, "*Ayeeei! Isithan! Isithan!*" when they realized that the Sikaran soldiers were present.

Joe Marsh soon realized they certainly lived up to their reputation as the elite of the Sikaran forces. They were amazing combatants, and Joe realized too that the Earth Special Forces soldiers would be no match for them, were they ever to meet and try out their skills against one another. Joe himself had been in the Special Forces for two years, but withdrew because of the relentless pace of the training and the dreadful things they were often required to do on missions, things that went against his conscience.

Deva fought beside Connors in this first battle and, at the last minute, two Gloshans grabbed Connors by the arms in a grip that was impossible to escape from and were about to take him prisoner when Deva sensed the human's terror behind him and heard him cry out. He turned quickly and snatched Connors away, then fought off the two Gloshan soldiers.

Connors lay on the ground trembling, unable to continue fighting but the battle drew quickly to a close anyway and the remaining Gloshans ran back to their waiting transport craft.

Deva sat beside Connors, who had been hit by the realization that he had almost been the next victim of Gloshan brutality. He could not stop shaking and buried his head in his hands.

"Connors, it is all right, you have not been taken," Deva said quietly. "All is well you are safe you are safe." Deva put an arm around Connors' shoulders and rested his other hand on Connors's chest then spoke to him in silence through a telepathic surface link.

Connors did not know what was going on and gazed at him in disbelief.

"How did you do that? What happened just then? Was that telepathy?" he whispered in trepidation.

"Yes, of course it was," Deva replied, smiling at him. "You do not need to fear it. We would never use a deep link with non-telepaths without zeir permission."

"I wasn't afraid, exactly, Deva," Connors replied. "It was just an unusual sensation, that's all. Thanks for saving me just then."

"Well, are we not friends? You said yesterday that we were," Deva replied, "How should I not save a friend?"

Connors embraced him for a moment and clung to him. "You don't know how grateful I am. I owe you one." was all he could say.

They returned to the starship soon afterwards, having achieved their objective of destroying a Gloshan communications tower.

Commander Baillie did a debriefing session when they returned, and asked for any recommendation for commendations.

The human soldiers began calling out the names of the Sikaran soldiers, and each one was called several times.

"Commander, I have some names of security men," said Deva, "Marsh, Saunders, this man, I am sorry I do not yet know your name, and Heinrich, Morrison and Dayton."

Dayton was named by practically all the Sikarans along with Marsh, Saunders and Heinrich.

"Thank you. That's very helpful. I am proud of you, all of you. Now that the first joint battle has been fought, I can safely say that I consider the Sikaran soldiers to be fairly and squarely a part of this team, and they will not be excluded from anything to do with my team. I hope that's clear to everyone."

Affirmative replies followed. Connors however remained silent sitting slumped with his head leaning on his hands.

Baillie said then, "Connors, what's wrong? You look mighty shaken up."

"Two Gloshans grabbed me, sir, and they were about to take me prisoner like they did Grafton, when Deva saw me in time and pulled me back. I've already thanked him for saving my life, for saving me from what happened to Grafton."

"Thank you, Deva, we're all grateful for what you did," said Baillie.

"Captain Grey will have a list of commendations and citations by the end of today. You have all done extremely well. I'm proud of you, all of you."

Harith stood, then saluted Baillie and thanked him for what he had said about the Sikaran group. He also said something else that Baillie found interesting. "Most of us, we do not yet understand your culture and are accustomed only to Gloshans. If we have offended any of you in these past few days, we ask that you forgive us and believe that, in time, we will learn your ways."

"That's a two-way thing, Harith," said Baillie. "The same goes for my men and me. We have to learn about your culture too. We will all have to try to be tolerant towards each other until we do get to know each other better. Everyone dismissed!" Baillie ended the session.

The Sikarans all stood, and then saluted Baillie along with his men.

Chapter Two: The flashtechno syntamic

Extracts taken directly from Security Lieutenant Joe Marsh's diary:

I began this mission to capture a new Gloshan communication device in good spirits. I had just received news of my promotion to Security Lieutenant and everything was just fine. I had fallen out with one girlfriend and found another in the space of two days, so what more could I ask?

The mission we were embarking on was such a high level of priority that Captain Grey himself was going to go down to the planetoid in order to meet up with someone from Interspace intelligence. There were Gloshan ground troops swarming all over that planetoid. Maybe I am exaggerating a bit, but you know what I mean.

Now Commander Baillie, our security chief, picked his twenty best men for the mission, and asked for four Sikaran soldiers to go with them. We were the most experienced of the security team so on-one was giving orders: we were all roughly equal to each other in seniority. We had to rely on our instincts and experience. We all knew it was going to be a tough assignment.

This mission took place after we found out that a Sikaran soldier, named Marayshan, was a Fourth Dan in martial arts; a real expert. We all made a big assumption that, because he did not train with his Sikaran buddies in the gym, he could not do all the first class martial arts stuff they could do.

He used to sit around in the gym with us and chat during our recreation times while the rest of his friends put themselves through their paces. He would eat, drink tea, and look at whatever magazines we brought in. We assumed that he was not up to their standard of excellence, and that he was just a soldier like the rest of us. We got that one wrong. Still, it was understandable, because he's a really nice guy. In fact, people started bringing in magazines, just for him to read.

The more members of the crew got to know him, the more popular he became, especially after seeing how he helped Cheryl Masterson. He was so gentle with her. Cheryl had been through a bad time after being captured by Gloshans.

Who hadn't these days? After being rescued, she was trying to get back into the swing of things, doing half time on duty and went into the Recreation Lounge. There she began to collapse. Quick to respond, Marayshan was the first to notice and caught her as she fell, and helped her to a seat.

Anyway that's beside the point, so when exactly did this top priority mission start going down the tubes? When we attempted to capture the Gloshan *flashtechno syntamic* equipment, that's when everything went wrong. Lance Dayton almost had it in his grasp when he was spotted by ground troops and taken. The rest of us retreated silently. There were too many of the enemy there and no way that the nine of us could do anything. The other ten were way back covering our tracks.

We managed to lay low and circle around without attracting attention because everything was focused on Dayton. They were going to have a field day with him, poor guy. So we returned to base camp, which was in a labyrinth of caves. I was never so glad to get back as I was then. I shivered and pulled my jacket more tightly around me. The caves were vast with numerous patches of coloured crystal over their walls, causing them to sparkle in the light from our illuminators. Water dripped somewhere further inside into a pool, and the noise of it echoed around the caves with an uncanny sound; the presence of the water made the air humid and left us feeling cold and damp. We were fortunate that our uniforms were so well insulated otherwise I am sure we would have developed rheumatism. My left shoulder was already beginning to ache.

We were all angry and depressed by then and the Sikarans quickly seemed to notice how bad we were feeling. Nava spoke first. "Peterson, what is wrong? What has happened?"

"It's Lance Dayton. He's been captured by Gloshan ground troops, Nava, and we didn't even get the *flashtechno syntamic* device we want so badly."

"Oh no, I am sorry, Peterson," Nava replied.

In a few minutes, after consulting with his friends, Marayshan went up to Captain Grey and said, "Captain, my friends and I will go and see if we can rescue Dayton and get the *flashtechno* device for you."

"Look, Marayshan," said the Captain, voicing my thoughts, "there are only four of you. What is the point of getting yourselves killed? We need to stay together here now that everything has gone wrong, so that we can survive the next thirty-six hours. It is imperative that I meet up with my Interspace Intelligence contact: who is planning to come to these caves. We are expecting the contact to be a Gloshan woman. Besides, I don't give a lot for Dayton's chances, do you?"

"Listen Captain, because we have lived among Gloshans, know their habits and speak zeir language, we have a strong chance of reaching Dayton, under cover of darkness. If we have not rescued him in six hours, I promise you, we will return. Do not concern yourself about my friends and me. We are experienced soldiers and have electronic blanking devices, so we can take care of ourselves."

"Good luck to the four of you then," Grey said.

In a moment, the Sikarans had collected their packs and began to leave the caves. As they walked past, I said, "Guys, give me a few minutes and I'll go with you to rescue Dayton."

Marayshan sat on his heels beside me and said, "Joe, thank you for the offer, but you seem to be just as exhausted as the rest. Why don't you stay here? I think it would be better." I nodded, not needing a lot of persuading and said, "Okay. Take care of yourselves, you hear me?" By now, I looked on all the Sikarans as my friends.

"Of course," said Marayshan, and squeezed my hand for a moment.

The Sikarans were always doing that. It didn't matter if the person was a man or woman, it was a Sikaran thing and surprised us, at first, until we got used to it. They also touched the cave walls. On the way out Avernyi and the others rested their hands on some of the crystals and I could have sworn that the crystals responded in some way by sparkling more brightly. Each time any of the four Sikarans went near the crystal deposits, the minerals seemed to gleam with an incandescence that was entrancing to me. It might just have been my imagination of course, but I do not think that it was.

Later Avernyi told me what happened when they rescued Dayton. They succeeded in getting him into a land carrier, packed it with supplies, somehow snatched the '*flashtechno syntamic*' device and drove back here and brought Dayton inside. Somehow they had managed to keep him alive because he was in a bad way.

"Oh God," Peterson said, shaken up to see his friend in such a state. "Nava how can I help him?"

"Peterson," Marayshan replied. "We will all help him. Come on, you and Avernyi, get the supplies from the land carrier and bring them here. And Morrison, get anything else that anyone can spare to make him comfortable, and do it quickly!"

I offered my jacket along with those standing nearby.

Marayshan took them and covered Dayton.

Peterson and Avernyi returned several minutes later with enough to make Dayton very comfortable and Marayshan began to move him onto the bedding that had been brought from the land carrier, but he awoke and began to cry.

"Hey, old buddy," I said. "Glad to have you back with us."

Marayshan began to see to his injuries as much as he could then searched through the emergency supplies finding various things that could help.

"You look as though you know what you're doing, Marayshan," I said.

"I have done some nursing, Joe," he replied. When Dayton was finally comfortable, Marayshan gave him some water to drink, but he could not drink it at first. He then finally managed to take some then began shivering and crying out, but then he calmed down when Marayshan talked to him.

After a time Marayshan said, "Now that the Gloshans know that Dayton has escaped, they will be furious and will be searching for him. All of you need to go outside and be on the look out for ground troops. But before you do, let me tell you about two Gloshan ground troops who are friendly. We knew them in Camp *K'Taak*. Their names are Junath and Ancho. We recognized them and spoke to them in secret and asked them to come to these caves and bring what they could to help us to survive until we would be picked up. They will each say these words to you in Galactic when they meet you, '*The Ivthalyin is singing again: at last it is dawn*'. Bring them here under guard just in case they are impostors. Now, you all have special night-visors. Go and use them very carefully and don't take them off. Morrison, if you get bored and are tempted to stop using your visor, just remember what happened to Dayton and be careful. Watch out for yourself. So go out and look for Junath and Ancho and please do not shoot them."

"Hey Marayshan, who put you in charge of the mission?" demanded Carrington, kicking his rucksack angrily. "I don't take my orders from you, damn it!"

"Carrington, I am a very experienced soldier, much more than you. I know what I am talking about. So you had better listen to what I say and *get outside and do your job*!" Marayshan finished with a spark of anger in his voice.

"Just because you walked into a camp swarming with Gloshan ground troops, rescued Dayton and captured the *flashtechno* device, you think that gives you the right to order us about?"

"I think you should listen to what Marayshan says," said Avernyi confronting the other soldier.

"So do I Carrington. May I suggest you follow his advice," said Captain Grey pointedly.
Taken aback, Carrington left without another word.

"I see that there is another side to you, Marayshan," Captain Grey said, walking over to join him.
"Yes there is, Captain." He replied, then said, "You know, if Dayton recovers physically, he may not recover mentally. He has been much abused."
"In that case, he will have to be sent back to Earth." Grey replied.
"How will he manage? Who will look after him?" Marayshan asked.
"He will be well looked after in a home for retired soldiers," said Grey.
"That is good. We have similar facilities on my home world, but the Gloshans leave their soldiers to beg for money and food if they are deemed unfit for duty."
"How dreadful,. I think that is absolutely appalling," said the human captain.
"Most of what the Gloshans do to each other is appalling, let alone what they do to alien prisoners. Do you know something else that is appalling? They allow soldier cadets to fight on the front line and to fend for themselves and Gloshan officers, like Captain Kaleen, terrify their men into obedience with the threat of over-harsh punishments."
"That would perhaps explain the atrocities that they so often commit," replied Grey. "Did you manage to bring anything with you in the land-carrier in the way of food supplies? Our emergency rations aren't going to last too much longer."

"We managed to bring a huge container of soup and some bread. Gloshan soup for their army is nutritious and palatable, more than anything else they eat. We got their bowls too. They will be so angry when they realize this." Marayshan laughed a little and Grey joined in.
"I shouldn't really laugh at a time like this, but it would be marvellous to see the looks on their faces when they find out," said Grey.

"It is always a good time to laugh," Marayshan replied. "And by the way, here is the *flashtechno syntamic* device. In all the commotion with Dayton, I forgot about it. Here. It is for you."

"All this fuss about such a little thing," said Grey, scrutinising it.

Commander Connors interrupted and asked to see the device.

Marayshan said surprisingly, "This is for Captain Grey and no-one else. I think I will keep it safe for him."

He took it back from Grey and replaced it in his jacket; Connors tried to grab it, but Marayshan hit his hand away.

"If you weren't nursing Dayton so well, I would kill you for that!" said Connors, hitting him back.

Marayshan pulled out a dagger and said, "Two things, commander. First, do not threaten me and secondly, I have seen you somewhere before in disguise. You were an Interspace spy, weren't you? You were in Camp *K'Taak*, posing as a Lasoan trader. I did not bother you because you seemed harmless enough. What were you doing in Captain Kaleen's office when you were there? Why did you speak to him for so long?"

"I was never in his office!" he replied emphatically denying it.

Marayshan grabbed Connors by the jacket and shook him. "You were with him for over an hour! You are a double agent, aren't you? Aren't you?"

"I am not saying anything!" Connors shouted back then regained his equanimity.

"Connors, is this possible? Surely you cannot be working against Earth. Please say it isn't true." Grey looked desolate.

"The Gloshans are going to win the space war, aren't they? So why shouldn't I pick the winning side for once? But actually, I am *not* a double agent. While I was in Camp *K'Taak* with Kaleen, he was beside himself with rage, because another set of Earth prisoners had escaped and someone in the camp must have helped them to get out. He suspected that it might be Sikaran *Isithan* soldiers, but he never had any proof, and I gathered that he was very afraid of these soldiers himself. It wasn't your group, was it, by any chance, led by a Shield Lord of the *Isithan*?"

"Actually, yes, it was," Marayshan replied.

"You and your friends helped dozens of humans to leave there, didn't you?" Captain Grey said with a new respect in his voice.

Marayshan nodded at Grey whilst keeping hold of Dayton.

"The Earth president should know about this. You all deserve medals for what you have done."

"Do you know why I was really there in disguise?" Connors said. "I was there to rescue my sister, only to find that you and your friends had already rescued her, for which, of course, I am eternally grateful. Please do not misunderstand my seeming disinterest and coldness, being in espionage one has to be this way. This was the only time I allowed personal considerations to get in my way. I went to find my sister Eva. I was going to try to bribe Kaleen to let me take her away."

"I remember her. Eva was a very beautiful Earth woman." Marayshan said. "We helped her. Your sister was losing her grip on reality so we got her out and back to our empire, and then allowed her to meet with an Earth ship to take her home."

Connors nodded, then turned to Grey and said, "Captain, Eva told me a very curious story. I didn't know what to make of it at the time. Eva said that Sikaran *Isithan* soldiers brought extra food to the women prisoners and it was the soldiers' own food that they shared with the women, who I might add were practically starving. Then they stayed and talked and sang songs to them and were always kind. One of them was exceptional as an extremely caring man with a very gentle nature. I didn't believe Eva. I thought she had drifted into a fantasy world, until I met Marayshan. One thing Eva said was even stranger was that the extremely caring man seemed to be the leader of the *Isithan* group. Eva said that she had never met anyone like this man before, and that he was someone quite special."

"Eva's memory was becoming very fragmented, Commander and, as you say, she lived in a fantasy world most of ze time." Marayshan replied.

Four security men came in then and said to the Captain that they had worked out a series of shifts amongst themselves.

"If you men want soup, it is in that container," Marayshan said. "And bowls are in that bag."

"Bowls?" said Morrison, "I can't believe you brought bowls too, Marayshan."

After a while he said, "This soup tastes really good. I thought you said Gloshan food was awful."

"It is, all except za soup. That is good and nutritious. It will make you stronger."

"Yeah?" Morrison smiled. "I could do with a bit of a tonic. Those Gloshan soldiers are too darned tough."

"Later I will show you a place where you can kick them. That really gets their attention," said Marayshan and everyone laughed.

Dayton looked around him, clutched at Marayshan and said shakily, "Everything all right now?"

"Everything is all right now Dayton, everything is going to be fine." Marayshan responded, "You are safe now, everyone is safe now."

"Good, good. Marayshan, I feel so weak, why do I feel like this? What's happened to me?"

"You are ill, Dayton, that is all. You are ill and I am looking after you. Soon you will feel better. Soon you will recover. You will be sitting up and then walking again, and everything will be fine."

"Do you think so? What about being a soldier? Will I be able to fight again?"

There was a pause then Marayshan said, "I do not think it would be a good idea. I think you should, let me see, do all the things you're really enjoy doing: read, listen to music go on long holidays in the sun. Go back to your home on Earth. Rent a place by the sea where it is peaceful and where you can watch the seabirds circling overhead. Sit and relax, and listen to the sounds of the sea. With a glass of brandy in one hand and a good book in the other, you will be very content."

"It sounds wonderful." Dayton replied. "I can almost hear the sea now. I wish we could go there."

"If you give me your permission, I can bring pictures of the sea to you," Marayshan said.

"How can you do that?" Dayton asked.

"Through telepathy: Sikarans are touch telepaths, but we don't use our telepathy with non-telepaths unless we have their permission."

"You have my permission," Dayton said. "I trust you completely."

"Thank you for your trust." Marayshan replied, and contacted him by placing a hand on Dayton's chest.

"I can see it! I can see it!" Dayton said. "I can see the shore and the cliffs and the seagulls. Captain Grey, it is amazing, it's wonderful!" Dayton then drifted into a peaceful sleep.

"He will rest now and hopefully feel better when he wakes," Marayshan said.

"I wish I were on those cliffs, looking out to sea," said Grey, smiling at Marayshan. "Thank you for helping Dayton like that, we all appreciated what you did for him."

Connors spoke then, "My sister, in one of her more lucid moments, when I first saw her on her return to Earth, told me that one of the Sikaran soldiers helped her on a particularly bad day when she thought she could not go on any longer. He spent the entire day with her, and pulled her through that particular bad patch. Eva told me that this man was named Marayshan. Might that have been you?"

"It was me, yes," Marayshan replied.

"In that case, I have to think of a way to repay you for everything you did for her. Eva is now completely well and back among her friends, living a normal life. She told me that she has you to thank for that, and I have long wanted to meet you and thank you in person. I have a debt of gratitude to pay to you and I don't quite know how to pay it."

"If you are serious about it, then I can think of something you can do for me," Marayshan replied. "The youngest member of our group, Chalek, needs a few things. Chalek is from a very poor family and I would appreciate it if you could help him."

"Of course, it's the least I can do," Connors replied. "But what about you, is there nothing you would like?"

"Two new shirts would be fine, and maybe a bottle of Sanvrian brandy."

"I was going to give you a lot more than that," said Connors.

"I did not help your sister with the hope of a huge reward, I helped her because she was in great need at the time," Marayshan replied.

To Grey's surprise, Commander Connors was close to tears. He held out a hand to Marayshan who took it.

"Thank you," he said. "I hope you never think that I'm a double agent again. If we ever get out of here, you'll get your shirts and brandy."

"We will only get out of here if Morrison stops eating long enough to do some work," Marayshan said. "You have had three bowls of soup already, Morrison. Leave some for the rest of us."

"Sorry, sorry, I was real hungry, Marayshan, and that container of soup is massive!"

"Well, now you have finished your three helpings. Would you like to fill bowls for the rest of us? We would appreciate it. I personally have not eaten for over twenty-four hours. Unless I get some soup soon, Morrison, I am going to get very unhappy and you would not like that."

"Sure, sure, I'll get you some soup," Morrison replied, filling a bowl and bringing it to him.

"Thank you. You know, every time I speak to you aboard ship, you are eating.

"What is it with you?"

Morrison laughed and said, "I just gotta have food and lots of it, that's all. I need it. I need it. I'll eat anything, even that overgrown rabbit I saw in one of the caves down there."

"What rabbit? What colour is it and how big is it?" Marayshan said.

"Well, the animal's about four feet tall, with pinkish fur. Darned beautiful, it is, actually, with green stripes, and it makes trilling sounds."

"That is not an animal, Morrison, that's a female Alkastian trying to communicate with you. Only the ladies have green stripes. For Var's sake, don't you dare frighten her."

"Dang, an Alkastian lady, do you mean to say that giant rabbit understands what I'm saying?"

"That giant rabbit is a very intelligent and sensitive creature. Alkastians are rare, they only inhabit this area of space," Marayshan replied.

"Dang," said Morrison. "I'm sure relieved you told me about her."

Four more soldiers came in, of which one was Avernyi, who spoke in Sikaran to Marayshan.

"Hey gimme that, Henson," Heinrich Klauss lunged past the other man and grabbed the bowl out of his hand.

"Heinrich, where are your manners? Your captain is here in the same place as you but look how you behave!" Avernyi said.

"I always behave like this, Avernyi. You know that," Heinrich replied.

"Heinrich!" said Marayshan.

"Oh all right! Sorry I ain't behaving as I should be, Captain Grey, sir. Will that do, Marayshan?"

Marayshan sighed. "Did anyone ever teach you any manners, Heinrich?"

"No sir, they did not. I taught my self everything I know. I look out for me. Ain't no one gonna look out for Heinrich. How's Dayton, by the way? He's mighty quiet. Is that a good sign or a bad sign?"

"That is a good sign," Marayshan replied.

"That's great news. You're a darned good nurse you know, Marayshan."

"Thank you Heinrich, I was a senior nurse when I left to be a full-time soldier. Actually I prefer to help people than to be a soldier."

"You shouldn't ever have left nursing. Why did you leave? It is numb brains like me and Morrison that get to be soldiers, but you can do other things."

"You are not a numb brain, Heinrich. I have told you that before. Just because you have not had a good education, it does not mean that you are stupid."

Heinrich smiled at him.

"Thanks for getting the soup. I bet them Gloshans was hopping mad. It's great soup. Avernyi, how in heck did you get Dayton out? There were so many ground troops."

"Well, I suppose it was easy in the darkness, and we speak *Gloshanese* very well, so they all thought we were Gloshan in the shadows. We just walked in and took him. Also we are not afraid of the ground troops as you are."

"Are you saying you think we're cowards, Avernyi?" Heinrich asked, sounding hurt.

"No, of course not, Heinrich, you have good reason to fear them, but we understand them and also, they fear us, so it is easy for us, you see."

"I see, but why do they fear you? You're really nice guys."

"Well, you see, once we found out how badly they treated alien prisoners, we lost all respect for them," Marayshan replied. "Also, the only way to resolve a disagreement with them was to slap zem. It was the only thing they understood. You cannot reason with them."

"At the start of our time in the camps," Avernyi took over from where Marayshan had left off, "whenever we wanted supplies from the stores, we used to go to the stores huts. But the men in charge would always say no to us, no matter what we requested—always, and then they would swear at us. This happened once, twice, and then we got fed up, and slapped them. It never happened again. So we got many things that way for the women prisoners. For your sister, Connors, we got a reading lamp and books and writing materials, as she enjoys writing so much."

"Really, I can't believe it," Connors replied shaking his head.

"So you see, Heinrich, ze ground troops fear us, and not ze other way around."

"Because you slap 'em around a bit, no, I don't think so, Marayshan," Heinrich replied, smiling at him. "There's got to be other reasons for that."

"We must find a way to stop Kaleen and his henchmen from carrying out atrocities," said Captain Grey. "And the only way we can do that is with the help of your people, Marayshan. But even after two years with the Sikaran Space Force on our side, it doesn't seem to be very easy defeating the Gloshans."

"The Gloshans have an extremely powerful space force," said Marayshan with gravity. "But they are being kept at bay beyond *Kaloris*, by Sikarans. Our space force is keeping them as far away from your Earth as possible. Captain, you do not realize the fierceness of the battles that have been taking place on behalf of your Earth and her allies, just beyond *Kaloris*. The Sikaran Empire is the only thing now that stands between your people and a Gloshan full-scale attack. It will probably take another two years to deter the Gloshan war mongers sufficiently to stop the space war."

Grey and Connors exchanged glances then Connors said, "You sound as though you are quite an authority on the subject, Marayshan."

"It is common knowledge in our Empire. Only we do not boast to the galaxy about our successes as the Gloshans do," Avernyi said.

"Avernyi, should I be calling your friend '*Ivthalyin*'? Is Marayshan a Shield Lord?" asked Connors, but Avernyi did not answer.

"All right, all right, Commander Connors," said Marayshan sighing. "I am *Ivthalyin Isithan*. I did not want to tell anyone because I wished to have a break from being a leader whilst aboard the *McBride*. It is not an easy job, you know, being a Shield Lord. Just for a while I thought I would relax."

"I knew it!" said Connors. "I knew you were the Shield Lord in the group! I had a feeling."

"I would prefer it if we could, for the time being, keep this between the few of us who are here, if you do not object, Captain Grey."

"I have no objection. The rest of you, please keep this to yourselves," Grey replied, then turned back to look at Marayshan and said, "No wonder you managed to rescue Dayton so smoothly. I feel privileged to be meeting one of the legendary Shield Lords of the *Isithan*."

"Me too," said Connors, "but I never thought to meet a Shield Lord outside the Sikaran Empire. What brings you to a human starship?"

"Oh I don't know. I wished to live among humans, I suppose, to get to know them, as I have lived among Gloshans. I have been asked to make sure that all is well, that we are doing the right things to help our new human allies. You see, your Earth president keeps contacting us."

"It's very good of you to want to do the right thing by your new allies," Connors said, holding Marayshan's gaze.

Marayshan smiled and said, "Commander, you are a deeply suspicious man."

"It pays to be, when you're like me and have spent your whole career in espionage, *Ivthalyin*," Connors replied. "You know, two years have passed since the signing of the Treaty, and there have not been any visits to us humans from high ranking Sikarans at all, until now. Not one visit and now suddenly, well, we have a Shield Lord of the *Isithan* in our midst. After two years. Not that I'm complaining of course, but what does it all mean, I wonder?"

"It means whatever you wish it to mean, commander," said Marayshan, then yawning.

"I hope it means that the Sikaran Empire is thinking of giving us more help, in a military sense."

"It can mean many things." Marayshan replied cryptically.

"It can also mean that you might decide to break your treaty with Earth," said Grey.

"No, it does not mean that," replied Marayshan.

"You are very definite about that, Shield Lord," said Connors.

"I am very definite. The High Council will not go back on their treaty with humans. We are here to stay, whether you like it or not."

"I like it," said Heinrich. "Anyone who's looked after Dayton, the way you've done, has got my vote, ten times over."

"Thank you, Heinrich, your words are appreciated," Marayshan replied. Heinrich smiled.

"You're an amazingly good nurse for a Shield Lord," said Grey.

"Marayshan is an amazingly good nurse and an amazingly good soldier, Captain Grey," said Avernyi. "He is very versatile."

Just then, the entrance of a beautiful Gloshan woman limping badly and shivering, clutching a document case interrupted them.

"It's the Gloshan spy who has been helping Interspace!" said Captain Grey. "Miss Chiret, thank heavens you've got here safely."

"Captain Grey, this is for you. Interspace has agreed that I can leave with you aboard your ship *McBride*," the woman replied, handing him the document case then sinking to the ground, exhausted.

"Chiret!" Avernyi exclaimed. "It is good to see you again."

"Oh Avernyi!" Chiret looked round then said, "Marayshan too! My gods have rewarded me this day." Chiret shuffled towards them, but Marayshan went to her, helped her to her feet, and then embraced her.

"Oh Marayshan, it is so good to see you again," Chiret said after kissing him several times with what little energy she had left.

"Hey, Avernyi, were they having a relationship in the Gloshan camps?" asked Heinrich interested.

"No, they are just old friends." Avernyi replied.

Chiret turned to look at the human, who had spoken and said, "That human is so beautiful. Later I will dance for him."

Heinrich looked startled.

Marayshan said then, "Heinrich, Chiret has never had a relationship with any of us. I think Devthanyi would have developed such feelings for her, but he was married at the time. I am not sure how he feels now you would have to ask him. After all, two years have passed. If, however, Chiret does not find anyone soon and feels she needs support, all my friends will look after her, if that is her wish." He smiled at Chiret who wrapped her arms around him again, leant her head on his shoulder and fell asleep. He shifted position, took off his jacket, put it on the ground and let her head rest against it.

"Even though they might get married later?" asked Peterson lowering his voice.

"Yes, Chiret has been a good friend to all of us and has been through a lot. Also, she is an extremely courageous person and we, of the *Isithan,* honour bravery above all else. We will look out for her no matter what. I believe that if she wishes, Deva will agree to marry her. Chiret used to care a great deal about him."

"Why couldn't Chiret find a Gloshan man to marry?" asked Connors.

"Chiret and Shkiru were not taken seriously by many Gloshan men, because their ways are not tough enough. They are gentle. Gloshan men prefer tougher women and only use Chiret and Shkiru, but will not marry them."

"But she's so beautiful. She's really beautiful." Heinrich murmured.

"Yes, but more importantly, she is a lovely person," said Avernyi, "very warm and good-natured. You would really like her if you got to know her, Heinrich. You should try. I could teach you about Gloshan ways, if you wish."

"Sure, I would like that, Avernyi," Heinrich replied. "I'd really like to get to know her. Thanks for helping me out."

"There are twenty hours to go before we can be collected by a transport," said Commander Connors. "A lot can happen in twenty hours. We may never get out of here."

Marayshan spoke then. "Elaan and Avernyi left a few surprises for the Gloshan ground troops while Navaronschyia and I rescued Dayton. Soon they should be kept very busy and it will take their minds off looking for Dayton and the rest of us."

"We are all extremely grateful to you," Captain Grey replied. "I have a feeling that we are going to be thanking you for keeping us alive."

"Well, I hope that we can keep Dayton alive also until we return," Marayshan replied.

"Whether you do or not, he will have had the best help I know of," said Grey.

Chiret awoke and leaned once more against Marayshan as though imbibing strength from him. Marayshan spoke to her in Gloshanese for a time and she replied quietly.

In a while Elaan and Marsh brought in two Gloshan ground troops and Marayshan stood to greet them.

Junath and Ancho knelt on one knee to him and bowed and said, "Shield Lord, we come to serve."

"Captain Grey, these are our two friends from Camp K'Taak. This is Junath and this, Ancho. Did you manage to bring anything that can help the humans, Junath?"

"Ah," Junath replied, "first I speak of joy at seeing the Shield Lord again, "ah, ah, bright, bright!" He held out his hands to Marayshan who took them and then Ancho did the same.

"Now, we give the human soldiers *techno* things to help them." They took several pieces of equipment and handed them to Connors.

"You have risked much to come here to help your enemies," said Captain Grey.

"When the Shield Lord asks, we obey," said Ancho. "He does not have to command, only to ask. He does not have to threaten for us to obey. We do his bidding out of respect."

"Shield Lord, I Junath must speak. Permit me to speak."

"I permit, Junath," Marayshan replied. Captain Grey looked at him.

"Shield Lord, there are many of us, those from Camp *K'Taak*, those who knew you and knew of you. They still speak about you and some have written ballads to remember your deeds. There are many ground troops who are angry with the war and wish to have peace. There are many, many who wish for a good leader, a special leader. Shield Lord of the Sikaran *Isithan*, I have been charged to deliver these words from over three thousand ground troops and many, many ordinary soldiers. If you call, we will come to you. If you call, we will fight for you. If you lead, we will follow you. If you ask, there is nothing we will not do for you. We plead that you help us to find a way to peace. These are their words. If you speak now in answer, I will record your words for them."

"Junath, ah, bright, bright, bright," Marayshan replied with enthusiasm. "Say this to your friends who knew me in Camp *K'Taak*. They honour me greatly. I will try to help them. Soon I will summon the *Isithan*. Soon we will fight together against Commodore Shtol and against Captain Kaleen and all those like them. Soon a new dawn will come, when Humans, Gloshans and Sikarans and all the people of the galaxy will know peace. Soon the trumpets will sound for the final battle when the *Isithan* will ride forth. You must keep your courage and be strong until that time, soldiers of *Gloshos*. You will hear from me when the time is right. Do this for me. Try to be successful on *Gloshos,* so that you can gain influence in your society. Leave darkness and shame behind you.

"My friends: be proud soldiers. Only do deeds of valour. Only those who are true at heart may fight alongside the *Isithan*. Do this for me. Look after your women. Do not let them be degraded. I know you will not understand this, but try, be kind to them. Honour all people, all women, not only your wives. Alien prisoners, that you take, must be valued also. Become advocates. Argue on their behalf. Do not allow them to be mistreated. Allowing this brings shame to your Empire. The people of the galaxy look at your people and point fingers and ask why? Why do you treat your prisoners so badly? My friends from Camp *K'Taak*: try to do all this for me."

The humans looked wonderingly at Marayshan as he spoke.
"Soldiers of *Gloshos,* you who are brave and strong, rally to the banners of the *Isithan*! Ride with us into a new day when all will know peace. Listen for the trumpets that sound the final battle. Hear the war cry of the *Isithan. Elaran! Isithan! Isithan! Kai-ithan! Hai Cheh!*"

He nodded at Junath to stop recording and the Gloshan turned off the small machine. Tears streamed down his face. His friend Ancho trembled with emotion. Grey and Connors looked at each other and the security men stared at Marayshan.

"I thank, I thank, Shield Lord, now at last we have some hope," he said quietly, clutching the machine to him. "We must depart soon." He wiped his face, pulling himself together, embarrassed that he had broken down in front of the humans.

"Before we go, I must tell you good news, Shield Lord! My woman Mocharu has given birth to a son for me, and he is named Kiroth, but in secret. Mocharu and me, we have given him a Sikaran name. We have named him Marayshan after you, our special friend, to honour you."

Marayshan slapped his chest with the palm of his left hand and said, "You do honour me! Junath! Mocharu! Both give me greatness! Tomorrow and tomorrow and tomorrow I will remember! Ah. Ah."

Junath took the Sikaran's hands then and held them to his forehead. "We go now," he said. "Come Ancho! Humans, luck to you! Gods go with you, Chiret, ah, ah."

"Junath, ah, ah, say Mocharu me! Ah! Ah!" Chiret replied clasping her hands, and then waved as he left.

"Shield Lord, you speak bright words. The soldiers will listen." Chiret continued, "They always will listen when you speak! They will be ready when you call. You will see. All is bright again. My gods reward me much today."

Marayshan smiled at Chiret and said, "All is bright for you from now on. No darkness will touch you again whilst Captain Kaleen is not near you."

Chiret smiled joyously and her heart felt glad and full of hope for the future.
"Avernyi, do you know how this Gloshan equipment works?" Connors asked, after puzzling over it for several minutes.

"Yes I do. I will help you," Avernyi replied. "It is blocking equipment and will ensure that all of us remain hidden here until we can return to the ship. All in this place will be shielded once we switch it on. Now, there, it is working, Connors. Peterson and Henson, tell the others outside to come in here quickly as they will be safer."

"Are you sure it's working, Avernyi?" said Henson.

"I am sure," Avernyi replied.

"Captain Grey, what should we do? Should we all come inside?" Henson asked.

"Do as Avernyi says, Henson," said Grey. "I believe he knows what he is talking about."

The blocking equipment worked well and kept us safe until we were able to return to the starship *McBride*.

Later Henson told me that Commander Connors was having quite a conversation with Marayshan and gave me the gist of it: Henson was nearby attempting to sleep when Connors went to sit beside Marayshan, who was trying to get some rest himself.

Connors began the conversation. "How will your Sikaran Empire stand against evil men like Captain Kaleen?"

"It is possible," Marayshan replied. "You have seen that we now have numerous Gloshan ground troops and ordinary soldiers on our side."

"Do you really believe they would be loyal to you? In your heart of hearts, do you really believe it?"

"I believe that most of them will, commander, because they are ordinary men, who are desperate to escape the darkness of men like Kaleen." Connors shivered. "The *Isithan* offers them some hope of escape. We offer them a lifeline. We have shown them another way, a better way. Do not step over to Kaleen's side, Commander."

"How did you know? How did you know that I was contemplating becoming a double agent that time I was in Camp *K'Taak*?"
"I saw it in your eyes." Marayshan replied. "You must not follow such a path, for your sister's sake, for your Earth's sake."
"But the Gloshans have such power, such incredible power. I could have a share of that, Marayshan. You could have a share of that too."

"You would not have a share of anything. Kaleen is completely treacherous. When he finished using you for his own gain, he would destroy you. It is a difficult thing for me to say to you, but there is no place for humans in his empire, Commander. I know Kaleen very well, and no matter how helpful you were to him, he would not embrace you as an equal when the day was done."
"And you would? You would embrace me as an equal?"

"Why do you ask such a question? Is what I did for your sister not proof enough, as well as what I have done for Dayton?"

"I'm sorry I shouldn't have said that," Connors replied. "It was very bad of me. Please, will you forgive me?"

Marayshan looked at him for a long moment then said, "I am not sure. In many ways Kaleen has an excuse for being as he is. Some of his terrible behaviour is ingrained in his culture. What is your excuse? You had a strong urge to join him? Why? Does your sister know? After what she went through in Camp *K'Taak*, it would destroy her to find out that you had gone over to Kaleen's side."

"Why would she even need to know? I could simply disappear while we were here."

"If you did that, Connors, listen to me. Be sure that I would find her on Earth and inform her of what you have done." Connors looked at him.

"I believe you would too," he said.

"Believe me. I would."

"Well, I wasn't being serious, you know."

Marayshan suddenly grasped Connors' hands and the human heard the Sikaran's voice in his mind. Connors was completely thrown by the telepathy.

"Connors, you do not understand Gloshan ways. You cannot relate to Kaleen as you would to another Human! You have no idea of the extent of his depravity. Didn't Eva tell you the things that went on in Camp *K'Taak*?"

"I thought it was a part of her illness. Everyone did. No one believed her. We thought that she was living out a fantasy."

"Eva was *not* imagining anything. Let me show you my memories." Connors gazed in horror at the telepathic scenes of what had happened in the Gloshan camps; he wanted to be sick.

"I had no idea, Marayshan," he said quietly, sounding defeated. "Now I am aware of what happened. I will tell Eva that I believe her, at last, if I ever get back to her. I will tell her how you showed me the truth of it."

Marayshan took a small piece of crystal from his pocket and warmed it in his hands.

"Watch this. It helps me to relax if I have had a difficult day. Taking care of Dayton has made me very tired."

The crystal began to glow.

"I am not surprised you're tired. You never look after yourself. You're always helping someone. You should spend more time relaxing. It seems that a lot of people are relying on you. What's it like being a do-gooder and such a positive person?" Connors said with no little sarcasm.

"You should try it and see."

"I shouldn't think I would be much good at it," Connors replied. "Does that gadget do anything else other than glow?"

"It will play music too, listen." After a moment, soft music emanated from it and the light grew brighter and began to pulse different colours.

"That is relaxing," Connors said, leaning back. "Do you mind if I share it for a while? How is it powered, by the way?"

"With good works and positive thinking," said Marayshan pointedly. "As I say, you should try it some time."

Connors smiled. "Could I hold it for a while?"

Marayshan handed the crystal to him. It stopped playing music as the lights faded.

"Oh, what's happened to it?" Connors asked.

"It does not like you."

Connors laughed and handed it back.

After a moment, it began to glow again in Marayshan's hands. "You see?"

"Where's the secret on-off switch?"

"There is no secret switch."

"There must be."

"Please yourself, but there isn't. Now would you mind being quiet and letting me relax."

"All right, I'll keep quiet," said Connors, looking sideways at him.

"Do you really have to lean against me?" Marayshan said then.

"No, but it is a good way to keep warm, don't you think?"

"Try putting on your jacket!" Marayshan replied with some irritation.

"Look, I was only trying to be companionable. You have realized that I am gay, haven't you." Connors replied.

"Yes of course I have. Are all human spies gay?"

"Probably not, how did you guess that I am? No one else has."

"I am a very perceptive do-gooder. I did not ask you to stop leaning against me because of that. I am tired, that is all. I need some space." He stretched, trying to find a comfortable position for himself.

"How many human spies have you met?"

"Two, so far, you and one other, he called himself John Smith."

"John Smith is one of those names that human spies call themselves when they don't want to tell you their real name. I know the spy you mean."

"I thought you might. He had a name for me also. He would call me '*Marzipan*'. I am not sure why."

"He must have thought you were rather delicious. Were you and he very close?"

"We were not even remotely close. Why do you ask?"

"No reason. I suppose that you're completely heterosexual. Are you?"

"Completely," Marayshan replied.

"Pity," Connors murmured.

"Var, not you as well. John Smith fell in love with me," Marayshan said, closing his eyes.

"It's all right. I don't find you *that* attractive."

Marayshan smiled at him, but did not reply.

"You shouldn't be such a kind, friendly soul, should you? Then you wouldn't be so popular with everyone," Connors replied, still shivering and rubbing his hands together.

"If you are really that cold, you can lean against me again to keep warm, if you wish." Marayshan put an arm around his shoulders and Connors looked sideways at him and said, "Thank you. That will help to keep me warm."

Marayshan looked sideways at him and said, "I am sure that it will."

"By the way, Marayshan, John Smith wrote a book of memoirs of the time he spent with Sikarans after he had been captured by them. The title of the book is '*Marzipan*'. I wouldn't read it if I were you. Do you want to know John Smith's real name? It is Nigel. Nigel Westerby-Smythe. He comes from quite an influential family on Earth."

"Let me tell you something. He was truly strange, even for a human." Connors laughed and Marayshan continued. "I was in charge of him while he was with us. None of us knew he was human at ze time, of course. We only knew that he was from one of the planets allied to *Interspace*."

"Well, his memoirs are definitely off the wall, that's for sure. You say he fell in love with you?"

"Yes. When the time came for him to leave us and return to Interspace, he flung himself at me and would not let me go. He was crying also, very pathetically. I was speechless. I did not know what to do. I began to feel very sorry for him. I still do."

"Well don't. For goodness sake, don't! If you ever read what he has written about you in his memoirs, you certainly wouldn't feel sorry for him ever again."

"What could he have written that was so bad?"

Connors looked sideways at him, laughed and shook his head. "You don't want to know, believe me. If it were any other Sikaran he wrote the book about, I'd say fair enough, who cares? But it's about *you* and that makes it so much worse. Next time I meet Mr Westerby-Smythe, I will set him right on quite a few things. Come to think of it, he has made a fortune from the sales of '*Marzipan*'. I think that you and your *Isithan* ought to get a percentage of the proceeds. I am going to contact Nigel and tell him so."

"Thank you, and tell him from me that '*Marzipan*' sends his good wishes and hopes that John Smith has finally found something he enjoys eating. He will know what I mean."

"I will tell him of course. You know, you shouldn't let yourself be taken for granted by the ship's crew the way you do. They're starting to take advantage of your good nature. If I see anyone doing that from now on, I am going to have serious words with them. They have no right to do that, no right at all."

"I enjoy helping people, Commander. I have no objection to helping them."

"Fair enough, but humans are not like Sikarans, some will go over the top. They won't know when to draw the line. You are too nice, that's your problem."

"Thank you for your concern. I will remember what you have said. There are those among the crew who help me in return, though. To thank me, you know, so it is not all in one direction."

"Good. I am glad to hear it," Connors replied.

Nava, Avernyi and Elaan came to sit with them shortly after, and Connors, feeling that he was intruding on the four friends, moved away.

Later back safely on the *McBride*, Heinrich and Chiret became an item. Time went by and Commander Connors contacted Nigel Westerby-Smythe who, believe it or not, turned up aboard the *McBride* several months later. Guess who he wanted to see? His beloved *Marzipan* of course; I felt real sorry for Marayshan, knowing how he had been immortalized in the unpleasantly off-colour memoirs of Westerby-Smythe.

I was there when Nigel came aboard. I hoped he had a good, long apology prepared for Marayshan. Make it good and make it long, I thought. By now we knew everything about Marayshan; that he was an ex-Captain from the Sikaran Space Fleet, a military hero and a Shield Lord of the *Isithan*, and that on a personal level he had a great deal of integrity. He had been cited and decorated with more medals than I knew existed in the galaxy. He was also a really nice guy. He did not need someone like Westerby-Smythe writing all those crazy things about him.

Nigel Westerby-Smythe arrived aboard the *McBride* dressed immaculately in women's clothes and shoes; a beautiful dress and matching jacket, trimmed with lace, and in shades of green and silver. His hair was long, blonde, and delicately curled. It suited him well to be a woman, the top spy of Interspace. He got a wolf-whistle from one of the other security men in the room and I could understand why, he looked stunning. Captain Grey already knew him as they used to go to the same boarding school together back on Earth. Grey was three years his senior.

We were all there to welcome him: Captain Grey, Lieutenant Commander Morgan, Commanders McKye, Yakusa, Captain Marayshan and his two friends, Nava and Avernyi.

"Good morning, Westerby-Smythe. Welcome aboard my ship the I.G.S. *McBride*."

"Alvaston-Grey, good to see you again, you haven't changed a bit, my love, since I last saw you."

"Neither have you, old chap; by the way, I don't use my double-barrelled surname out here in space, only when I am back on Earth and on my Estate," Captain Grey replied then introduced the rest of us. I could see that he was putting off the moment that he would have to re-introduce Nigel to Marayshan for as long as he could and I didn't blame him. At last, the moment arrived.

"Nigel Westerby-Smythe, this is Captain Marayshan, *Shield Lord* of the *Isithan*. I believe that you two have met before."

"Met? Oh my love! This wonderful man kept me alive when I would have faded away through utter despair! I sank into a most terrible depression while I was a prisoner in the Sikaran Empire. Oh *Marzipan*, *Marzipan*, what can I say? What can I say? There are no words to express how I feel."

"John Smith, you have changed somewhat since last I saw you. *Kirathie*, you look extremely beautiful today," Marayshan replied.

"Do you like my outfit?" Nigel asked.

"Yes, it is lovely and makes you look very feminine. I see you have decided to be a woman now."

"Yes, I do tend to dress like a woman these days. I thought you would be shocked."

"Why? You have always believed yourself to be a woman deep down inside, haven't you?"

"Well yes, I have, but how did you know?" said Number One Spy in the Charts, genuinely taken aback.

"I am sure you told me when you were with us."

"Well, so I did, I had forgotten. I hope you won't hold it against me, or perhaps I hope that you *will*. Who knows, my love?" Nigel simpered magnificently.

"I am not your love, John Smith. You gave me a huge amount of trouble when you were in the Sikaran Empire, or don't you remember?"

"Surely that is best forgotten," Nigel replied. "May we continue our conversation in private? I have so much to tell you."

"If you wish, *kirathie*," Marayshan replied smiling now.

"It is such a relief not to be enemies any more, don't you think?"

"I am not sure, where you are concerned, John Smith," Marayshan replied.

Marayshan was more patient than I would have been under the circumstances. I took off my hat to him.

"Oh. You are not being serious are you, my heart's delight?"

"Are you still a spy for *Interspace*, John Smith?"

"Oh yes, absolutely. I like to keep my hand in, you know. Oh I wish, I wish, I wish, things had been different, you handsome hunk of manhood."

"Oh for heaven's sake, will you shut up, Westerby-Smythe," said Captain Grey.

"The same old tedious Alvaston-Grey, always trying to spoil my bit of fun, so upright and proper, you don't change, do you?" Nigel retaliated spitefully. "You know, I never thought, never dreamt that I would see you again, not in my wildest dreams did I think I would see you again, Marzipan!"

"Neither did I think I would see you again, John Smith, but unfortunately here we are."

"You went to a lot of trouble to look after me, didn't you? And you got all my secrets out of me. Still, that wasn't difficult. Your telepathy is quite remarkable, quite, quite remarkable."

"Marayshan, you told us that Sikarans did not use telepathy on prisoners of war without their permission," said Alice Morgan sounding concerned.

"I gave my permission, my love," said Westerby-Smythe. "I couldn't bring myself to think of the alternative: the endless interrogations. I am a dreadful coward, you know. But I asked if Marayshan could be the one to take my secrets from me. He was the only one of the interrogation team I trusted enough."

"Well, I can understand that all right," Alice replied smiling at him.

"It was a long process, Alice. I had to be very careful that I would not harm his mind. We had no desire to harm him, only to obtain his secrets and return him to *Interspace*."

Nigel smiled at Marayshan, "I have a lot to be grateful to you for. Sorry about the memoirs, truly, love. I suppose by now you have heard about the things I wrote about you."

"I have heard, yes, *kirathie*," Marayshan replied.

"It was very bad of me, I know, but I have arranged to donate a substantial sum of credits to your *Isithan*."

"Thank you, John Smith," Marayshan replied.

"Listen, my love, I have a favour to ask. While I was in the Sikaran Empire, I grew so intrigued by your telepathy, that I would greatly appreciate it if we could link minds again while I am aboard. Seriously, will you consider it? I find it all so fascinating."

"I will consider it. Let us discuss it later, shall we?" Marayshan replied.

"Of course," Nigel replied, "whatever you say, Shield Lord, whatever you say. I am your humble servant."

"No, you are not, John Smith. You were the most infuriating *Interspace* prisoner I have ever encountered," Marayshan replied.

"It was not my fault I became so ill now, was it, love? I couldn't help myself. It just came over me, that terrible depression because I never thought that I would see my beloved Earth again. Can you understand that? If it had been the other way around, wouldn't you have felt bad if you thought your number was up and you were never going to see the lights of home again?"

"Yes, but perhaps not that bad," Marayshan replied. "You became seriously ill."

"It was a difficult time in my life; the horror of being captured brought everything to a head. I was young and terrified. It was something of a turning point for me. After all, you know the propaganda against your people and the Gloshans were very intense at that time back on Earth. I had no way of knowing that Sikarans were such honourable, decent people. *Marzipan*, I was terrified out of my wits, can't you understand that?"

"I did realize at the time, John Smith. That is why I took such care of you. I am a trained nurse, a senior nurse. I do not think you realized because I was also one of the interrogation team." There was a pause.

"Laurie, I believe that I should transmit an *Interspace*-wide public apology to the Shield Lord about my memoirs. It could go out on the tele-viewing networks so that everyone has the chance to see it. What do you think?"

"An excellent idea, Nigel, I am all in favour of that," Captain Grey replied.

"Me too, that sounds like a great idea," Alice said.

"Nigel, I have arranged for those of us here to have lunch together in your honour. After all you are the best spy in *Interspace*," said Grey.

"I am flattered, Laurie, thank you. I almost forgot I have brought two gifts for you, Shield Lord. Here, this book contains my real memoirs. This is just for you to read, no-one else. I feel I owe you that much and this is something special from my Estate on Earth. I happened to hear that most Sikarans appreciate crystal," he smiled at Captain Grey before he handed the gift to Marayshan who opened it and gasped.

"John Smith! But this is too much. It must be very valuable."
"Extremely valuable," Nigel replied. "In fact, it is worth a small fortune. If you are ever short of money, then do sell it. I have insured it for you."

Marayshan nodded, "It is very good of you, John Smith, but I have nothing to give you in return."
"You have already given me my life and my sanity, what more is there? You allowed me to return and see the lights of home and live to fight another day. To fight for my beloved Earth, and now *you* are fighting for my world too. There is no greater joy, no better gift you can give me."
Marayshan took Nigel's hand, then bowed over and kissed it. "You honour me with your words," he said.

For once Nigel Westerby-Smythe was silent and, for most of the meal after, he was pensive, speaking quietly to Alice Morgan seated on his left. On his right sat Marayshan, who after a while turned to him and said, "John Smith, I am prepared to use my telepathy with you again."
The Number One Spy turned and held his gaze for a long moment,
"Thank you, it will be like old times again," he finally replied.
"Do not tell me you have missed being a prisoner in the Sikaran Empire, John Smith."
"No, not that, just you," He spoke very quietly, but as I sat opposite, I heard the words.

Marayshan sighed and continued with his meal. I knew he really did feel sorry for Number One Spy, deeply sorry. He put a companionable arm around Nigel's shoulders. I looked at Marayshan from across the table. I could tell from his expression that he was going to befriend Nigel, despite all that rubbish that Number One Spy had written about him. But Marayshan is like that; a really nice guy. Lonely people and people with issues gravitate towards him in a big way, and Nigel had problems I guess.

That's why I love Marayshan, just the way all the men in his *Isithan* group do. He is a really caring guy; popular with the ladies too. I guess he would be he *just* would be. He's a really charismatic guy. Since he worked six months as a stand-in Captain for us while Captain Grey was convalescing, Marayshan's popularity has soared beyond anything I can describe.

The best way I can put it is that he has become a celebrity on board the *McBride*. The younger crew hero-worship him and the older crew respect him, and the ladies fall over each other just trying to get a date with him. Believe me, his friend, Avernyi, sells them a fifty credit ticket for one date. He never eats alone in the canteen without some female or other being on hand, looking her best, fluttering her eyelashes at him, just like Number One Spy there. But Number One Spy has genuine issues, I guess. He's dedicated his life to helping Earth to win the space war. He's given up a lot to do what he does. I guess he's a mighty lonely guy and Marayshan radiates warmth like a five-bar electric heater and we all sit around him basking in it.

I've decided to leave the ship and go with Marayshan to Naiobi. Dave Sanderson and Pete Walsh have too, because we know a good thing when we see it. We've been accepted as Peace Officers so we will continue to work with the Sikaran soldiers, which is how we want it. We've made good friends with Marayshan's *Isithan* group and we don't want to lose touch with any of them, because we've lost too many friends already in the space war. Nothing's going to change our minds: we are going to stick to these guys like adhesive.

Chapter Three: One of the Good Guys

When Joe Marsh had finished recounting all this to Captain Maitland, the next thing Joe did was to give Maitland an envelope that included the personal account Gloria Kincade had written about her experiences with Marayshan. Gloria had given her account to Captain Lawrence Grey, because she wanted to show Grey clearly how much she had valued Marayshan's telepathic assistance and to explain exactly how he had helped her. Gloria wanted only a few people to know the details, the important people, so that they would realize how much they could trust Marayshan and to what extent he might be able to help other humans with problems.

Alice Morgan signed the letter too. Gloria asked for a copy to be given to Dr. Grafton and gave her permission for it to be circulated to anyone in a position of authority on Naiobi who might know any humans who could benefit from his help. The colony psychiatrist Dr. Ryland had received a copy from Dr. Grafton the ship's physician. Joe knew about it because, being her friends, Gloria had included Joe and Alice Morgan in producing her account and had given him a copy to keep. Now Joe felt that he should show Maitland his copy.

"It makes interesting reading, sir. It's real personal about things that happened between Gloria and Marayshan, but I think it needs to be that personal." He said. "I think Marayshan's a special guy. You can trust him to do the best for your daughter if he does try to find her a husband."

"Thank you, Joe," Maitland said, "it's very much appreciated." He then went into his inner office and began to read the formal letter. It began:

To Whom It May Concern.
'This is my personal account concerning the Sikaran Captain Marayshan of the *Levthiryin* Clan, also Shield Lord of the *Isithan* from Computer Engineer (1st Class), Gloria Kincade, of the *Interspace* Grain Ship *McBride,* in recognition of the help given to her by the aforesaid Marayshan, signed and witnessed by Third Officer Alice Morgan, Lieutenant Joe Marsh, Captain Lawrence Grey and Dr. Miles Grafton on the third day of August, Galactic Year _____. This is a very personal account and I'm not apologizing for it, because I want other humans to know the true level at which I was helped by the Sikaran Captain Marayshan,

because I owe him so much that I can't begin to repay him, not if I had two lifetimes to do it. I have taken parts of the account directly from my personal log and have not altered anything.

The arrival of the *Isithan* group of Sikaran soldiers on the starship *McBride* changed my life. A lot of other humans aboard can say that too. There are three particular soldiers who are great friends, and their names are Avernyi, Nava and Marayshan. I have to write about them because I think they're great fun to know. Nava is the life and soul of any party. He is great to be with, loves sports of all kinds, and I am not sure where his brains are, but they don't seem to be in his head. If you believe what Charlene says, he's really wild, but she just keeps going back for more. I think she's addicted to him. He's full of laughs just like Marayshan, and Avernyi's the fairly serious one.

Mind you, there's another side to Marayshan which he hides well, and which I can write about after several weeks of knowing him. A serious side to him, which makes him seem more like Deva when he's in a one to one with yours truly. He is not, in any way, the whacky guy he likes people to think he is. He just enjoys making people laugh, but actually he is subtle and restrained in his relationships. Nava, on the other hand, is totally off the wall, tripped out on human women. He can't seem to get enough of us. Nava isn't my type, so I have steered clear of making love with him. Our security guys are seriously impressed by Nava's stamina and determination. Like all the Sikarans in the group, he is a really attractive guy.

Third Officer, Alice Morgan, lives next door to me aboard ship, and we often gossip together. I like Alice. Alice tells me about how she and Harith are starting to become involved and I am really worried for her, because Harith is the one Sikaran I'd be concerned about. He has a reputation already for being too rough with one woman aboard and I am scared for Alice, because Harith frightens me. There's an angry look in his eyes sometimes that's really not nice.

I'm scared for Alice, because I used to know a guy like Harith back on Earth. He was an Earth Special Forces soldier named Peter Grayson, and I made a big mistake getting involved with him. It was the worst mistake of my life. I have told Alice all about him and warned her to be careful with Harith. Peter was a real angry guy deep down inside like Harith, and he used to take it out on me while we were making love and he would hurt me a lot sometimes. Afterwards, he was always sorry, but it began to get me down. Then things took a turn for the worst, when Peter arrived home stressed out from a space battle against Gloshan ground troops. That was a night I will never forget and the next day I walked out of his life, went to my parents' home to recover and took a job aboard the I.G.S. *McBride* to try and build a new life for myself.

"Alice, please don't go with Harith. I've seen that look in his eyes," I said. But Alice assured me that Marayshan had asked Harith to be good to her and Harith was his friend and listened to him.

"Do you really think that will stop Harith?" I said in disbelief. "Alice, he's too tough for you."

Alice did not reply to that one, but then she said, "Gloria, honey, I've gone and fallen in love with him."

I heard the clanging of a bell in my mind that sounded some terrible doom. "Oh God, no," I thought, "not Alice too."

"He's all right, Gloria, Harith's okay, really," Alice said in reply.

The next night, I picked up a nice guy in the bar. It was late and he came back to my room and made love to me. He left with a shrug and a smile, but without as much as a word. I was devastated. I liked the guy and I really wanted him to stay the night. I started crying and I couldn't stop.

Alice heard me and came round to see if there was anything she could do to help and made me some coffee and asked me if I minded if she had a word with Marayshan about me. I really didn't know why, and then she called Dr. Grafton. He sat and talked to me for a long time and gave me something to calm me down.

I told him about the flashbacks I kept having about the night before I walked out on Peter Grayson back on Earth: that awful night when he used me so badly. He just wouldn't stop. I pleaded with him. I said I couldn't take anymore, but nothing would stop him. He was relentless and I could not get away from him. He was too strong and so I just had to take it and I couldn't stop crying. He kept telling me to shut up and put up with it, that there were worse things in the galaxy than what was happening to me, but right then I could not think of many.

"He wouldn't stop," I said to Grafton. "He just wouldn't stop."

I was the last one in the bar again a few nights later, feeling wretched and nursing the same drink for an hour. That was how I first got to know the attractive Sikaran soldier named Marayshan. He was a real handsome hunk. I could tell he was looking in my direction and I thought he was interested. I had seen him there before and, by all accounts, he was a nice guy. Alice really liked him and that was enough for me. I looked at him and smiled invitingly and held up my glass. He held up his glass in return and nodded to me.

"Why don't you come over and join me?" I said. "My name's Gloria, Gloria Kincade, computer engineer 1st class, complete no hoper, all time loser, and total pushover where attractive soldier guys are concerned. Come over here, attractive soldier guy. Am I making any sense to you?" I babbled on.

He came over and sat with me.

"Hello, *kirathie*," he said. "My name is Marayshan. You are on your own and I am on my own, so maybe we can be on our own togezer."

"Good line," I said, "yeah, good line. I like that." I played with his hands and stroked his arms and kissed him and rubbed my face up against his shoulder. Is this guy getting the message? I thought.

"Geeze, you are such an attractive guy, how's about coming back to my room and having some fun? But, you can only come to my room if you promise, you solemnly promise, that you are gonna stay the night with me. If you're a 'love 'em and leave 'em' kind of guy, then I'm out, that ain't me. No sir. You gotta stay the night in exchange for some fun. Get my drift? That's all I ask." I waved my drink around.

"Listen. I usually stay the night and I always come back a second time," he said quite seriously, which surprised me, considering his usual amusing persona.

"Say, you're my kind of guy," I said. "That is what I like to hear. My room's not far away. I'm next door to Alice Morgan."

"Yes, I know," he said. "Alice told me about you."
I hesitated for a moment then said, "Yeah, Alice told you about me? What did she say? Come on, come on, you can tell me."

"Alice said you need someone who can give you a good time and zat you need cheering up."

"Well, that's true enough, that's true enough. So you're gonna give me a good time? Hey, well, I like the sound of that. Come on, let's go." I took his hand and led him to my room. He touched my face then, oh wow, I got inside and threw most of my clothes off. I don't waste time. I had an early start in the morning.

He removed his jacket and shirt and embraced me. Oh wow, he kissed me so tenderly. It was wonderful. Then, he said, "Don't be afraid, *kirathie*."

Surprised I replied, "I'm not afraid. I really like you. Do you think I would be afraid of you just because you're Sikaran? It's the kind of guy you are that counts, not which planet you come from. I guess some of the women aboard are scared of you and your friends, but you see, after the human boyfriend I had back on Earth, anyone, just anyone, has got to be an improvement. Believe me."

He rested his hand on my chest then, and concentrated, and I felt warm and wonderful all over and really relaxed.

"Oh, what are you doing?" I murmured, "Whatever it is, please don't stop." I just lay there in his arms feeling wonderful. I began to sense something in my mind. I began to feel him in my mind. It was an odd sensation and unsettling.

"Are you telepathic?" I asked.

"Yes, *kirathie*, but I am only using a surface link, not a deep link. I am telepathic through touch and the closer we become the better it will be for you."

"Well go for it!" I said. "Let's get really close." And then he said something that made me laugh. "Hey! Close your eyes. Lie back and enjoy it!" It sounded like a command.

So I did close my eyes and it was amazing. I can't describe it. I just became incoherent, sighing, and filling up with pleasure. The guy was really being good to me. I would have to tell all the other women who came to Alice's gossip sessions. Well, nothing very energetic happened. It was very low key and relaxed, but we were together for maybe an hour. I lost track of the time. The strangeness of the telepathic contact and the prolonged intimacy made me feel faint.

At the end he said, "I will stay with you tonight."

I slept with his arms around me. I couldn't believe he really stayed the night.

See this guy, I said to myself. This guy was my enemy two years ago, and this guy is staying the night with me. Each time I awoke, he was still there and kissed my hand. I was bowled over by him. Whatever he asked of me, from now on, I would gladly give, I was so pathetically grateful that he had stayed with me. No one was forcing me to do this. This was me making the decision to go on, and to see him again. At first I never talked much to him, knowing what soldiers were like; they never seemed to want to talk more than they had to, and I did not want to put him off coming to see me.

"You can speak to me, you know," he said, the third time he visited me. "You will not put me off. I told you ze first time we met, I usually come back for more and I very much enjoy visiting you."

He embraced me then and it felt good. For a few hours, he drove away the memory of that last awful night I spent with Peter Grayson back on Earth. The flashbacks were still happening, and if anything they were getting worse.
"Are you sure I can speak to you?" I replied. "Soldiers don't usually appreciate much conversation in my experience."

"I am different, I like to talk," he said and I smiled at him.
"You certainly are different in private to the way you play the fool with Nava and Avernyi. Mind you, you do keep everyone entertained. That is really appreciated, you know. You seem to be able to cheer up a lot of unhappy people. A lot of people out there love you."

He thanked me for telling him.
"Do you really want to do anything tonight?" I asked.
"You don't feel like it then."
"No, not really, it's been a long day. I'm sorry, but stay and talk, won't you?"
"Of course," he said and kissed me while we talked.
"You don't get fed up of kissing me, do you," I asked. "And it's not just because Alice asked you to cheer me up now, is it?"
"No, not just because of that, I think you are beautiful in many ways."

It was a really nice thing for him to say, considering I was not really beautiful. I wasn't bad, but not an out and out stunner like Charlene, Nava's daffy bit of fluff. The sort of woman I thought Marayshan would have preferred. Charlene was another woman who really liked going out with soldiers. I stopped talking because he made me feel so good again with that surface link telepathy and I would never get tired of that, I can tell you.

Two weeks later, I was injured in an attack from Gloshan warships in the vicinity, and ended up in sickbay where

Marayshan came to visit me. I wasn't expecting a visit, but I got one, which surprised me. I always thought that, despite everything, he was just using me like Peter Grayson used to do. But now, I realized he liked me and valued me.

"Hurry up and get better, *kirathie*," he said.

"You've got other women you can go with," I said, not reproachfully, but as a matter of fact.

"That has nothing to do with it. I like you and I enjoy being with you," he said.

I smiled and he kissed me.

"Hurry up and get well, *kirathie*," he said and left the sickbay.

I cried when he left, as he had been so nice to me and, when I finally returned to my quarters six days later, he was waiting by the door for me. He kissed my hand and led me inside.

"I have looked forward to seeing you again," he said and embraced me for a long time.

"I've missed you too," I said, beginning to cry. "I've really missed you too." I longed for him to make love to me again and told him so. He was reluctant because of the battle injuries I had sustained and so would not do anything except use his telepathy with me. That night I felt him closer to me than I had felt him before. He seemed to be using the telepathy more and entering my mind much more deeply and I clung to him and said, "Don't please, it's too much. I can't take it." He withdrew quickly and I leaned on him.

"I can't take that. You know you can do anything else with me, but I can't take that deep link." He had tried it once before; it was part of Sikaran sexuality.

"*Kirathie*, I'm sorry, I was so happy to see you that I wished to be even closer to you, but because you are human, you do not seem to be able to take a deep link without a lot of preparation. Please forgive me."

I clung to him feeling wretched, and he kissed me.

Suddenly I plummeted into the midst of an intense flashback, the worst I had ever had, and the viciousness in Peter's face from that night came starkly to me. I cried out and pleaded with him to stop. I clutched at Marayshan's arms, consumed by misery and pain. I became confused because of the flashback and thought that Marayshan was making love to me. He wasn't, but I cried out because suddenly I transposed him for Peter and it became Marayshan treating me so badly and, just like Peter, he would not stop. I could not control the intense feelings I was experiencing from the flashback.

Marayshan looked extremely alarmed, and put his hands on my chest and forehead. He must have guessed what was happening to me from his telepathy.

I cried and cried, especially as I thought that this outburst of mine would put Marayshan off coming near me ever again. I thought he would leave me then, as there was no more fun to be had. Waves and waves of self-pity washed over me. I suppose I did not know him well enough. So, I assumed that being a man, he would very quickly retreat from my emotional collapse, but he did not and that surprised me a lot at the time.

"*Kirathie*, don't, it is all right," he said, embracing me with such tenderness that I almost could not bear it. He began to sing softly to me, a Sikaran song. It sounded beautiful, and he rested his hands on my forehead and chest. Suddenly I saw him clearly, beside me in my mind, on that terrible night. Suddenly, when things were at their worst, he was comforting me. I relived the scenes over and over and each time he stayed with me through his telepathy, until I began to feel as though I could cope and the misery slowly drained away. After that, the flashbacks stopped for good and I knew it was because of the telepathic help that Marayshan had given me.

A few evenings later I started to think about preparing a meal for him. An announcement came over the intercom from Mr. Mckye, the First Officer, that Captain Grey had been taken ill and that the Sikaran military hero and space fleet Captain Marayshan was about to take over in the interim. I could not believe it. I had to sit down.

Several nights later, he turned up to my invitation for a meal, because I told him about a gift I wanted to give him. He came in dressed in the new Captain's uniform they had given him. He looked extremely smart and I felt completely overawed by him, being that he was now our ship's Captain. I gave him the meal and the gift of the crystal ornament and he said, "It is very beautiful, *kirathie.*" He kissed my hand.

"Listen, Captain," I said. I called him Captain now, trying to be formal. "I want to thank you for everything, but I am all right now, no more flashbacks, so please don't feel you need to continue to see me anymore."

He looked at me and said, "I may come back sometime just because you are such a lovely person. Would you object to that?"

"No, of course I wouldn't object," I said, very flattered. "I wouldn't ever object. Why should I?"

He nodded. "Now that I am an acting Captain again, I have many responsibilities, so I need to go now, but at some point I will return, I promise you."

He bowed and left. He did come back to see me just once more, before he was due to reach the Naiobi colonies to wish me well in my future life. I told him about my new boyfriend, Gareth, and about how nice he was and how well we got on. I told him too that we were planning on getting married soon.

He crossed his hands at his chest, and said, "I wish you joy forever," then bowed to me and left. I have never met anyone like him before or since. He was really special. I tell all my friends about him and I always will.

INTERLUDE:.PART 1

Here is the first of a series of articles commissioned by and published in the weekly beta-Naiobi Chronicle. All Sikaran words and names are written in italics. Other words in italics are there for emphasis.

Article 1: The Combined Memoirs of 'John Smith', retired Interspace Spy First Class (real I.D. Nigel Westerby-Smythe) and those of Shield Lord Marayshan, from the time he served aboard the Sikaran Flagship Voran, both as a Commander and later as the Captain.

Month 1: Day 1.
Commander Marayshan's Account:

At last, in two weeks time, I can have some recreation. It has been a long six months patrolling the *Kaloris* border that circumscribes the nine worlds of *Vareysha*, known to *Interspace* as the Sikaran Empire. The space war has been hectic. I really need a break. To top it all, we had some serious trouble with our Chief Engineer Kavril in relation to a crewman: a prospective boyfriend. Give me strength, as if the almost daily battles raging against *Interspace* were not enough, we had to arrest Kavril and try him for a crime that he committed against this crewman. We've all got our problems, but really, this was just a little too much. It need not have happened at all if Kavril had not been so thoughtless and insensitive to his would-be boyfriend. It annoys me because I'm the one who had to pick up the pieces.

I had to act as a *Davracha* for both Kavril and the crewman. To advocate for them, at different times and in different ways, I had to see to their welfare. It isn't my job to do that, I'm a Commander, but I was a qualified welfare worker before I joined the Space Fleet and, as no one else is qualified in the same way aboard ship, I help out as a welfare worker whenever I have the time. Mind you, I do prefer to be a welfare worker rather than a soldier. A lot of the crew appreciate my welfare work, that's why I do it. The Low Clan people I help pay me something when they can, but if I help the High Clans or the Royals I always get my full fee up front. Captain Javrayin maks sure that happens.

I am looking forward to my five days leave so that I can spend more quality time with my wonderful girlfriend, Natira, who is one of the computer technicians aboard ship. Our relationship would be so marvellous if only we had more time to spend together. As it is, we snatch precious moments here and there, sometimes over a quick meal, and then she lets me enter her mind and swim around in it for as long as I like or have the time for and she never complains. It just feels so good. She allows me a lot of liberties, Natira does, probably too many, but do you see me complaining? If we both survives the space war, we may even settle down together and have a family back in the Arakiarth Valley, our relationship is developing that well.

Mind you, there are one or two other crew women that I see from time to time, just to, well, get a different perspective on things. The problem is that they are very welcoming in different ways and it is not as though I really love Natira, because I don't, and she doesn't really love me.

I suppose we are all making the most of things, because we are on this starship, a long way from home, so what else can we do? We have to have some fun some time.

- I am determined to have my five days alone with Natira.
- I will ignore everything that Captain Javrayin said.
- I will ignore all the High Priority Alerts calling Senior Officers to the Bridge.
- I will ignore all the people who come to my door asking me for help: just because I am a *Davracha*.
- I will ignore everyone.
- Everyone except Natira.
- Well, that is the theory, anyway.

John Smith's Memoirs:

I was captured by Gloshans one night in a bar. They became ecstatic when they realized they had caught such a prize: *the* top *Interspace* spy, John Smith. Me. Sikaran officials were there, too, in the bar and they agreed with the Gloshans on a programme of interrogation for me. The Gloshans could have me for two weeks to see what they could get out of me, softening me up, I suppose, and then the Sikarans would take over. Oh joy. Well fancy that.

Just your luck, Lucinda dear, now what are you going to do? That was my name for myself, by the way, Lucinda, when I was wishing that I was a woman. I often did that, fantasizing I was a woman, and that some wonderful tall, athletic handsome male would come along and sweep me off my feet. Yes, you *have* realized, haven't you? I am a transsexual male, and hugely effeminate. Oh hugely so.

Now what do you think four hulking great brutes of Gloshan guards were going to do with someone like *me* in their off duty times? I suspected from other reports that I would have to cope with a lot of rough handling from these four gentlemen. But that the Sikarans, with a reputation for being expert interrogators, always got what information they wanted from *Interspace* prisoners.

So I would have to cope with two weeks of Gloshan hospitality before the Sikarans took over. Oh joy. I heard the Sikarans warn them before they left, they warned the Gloshans to keep me alive, because of my status in *Interspace.* I was far too valuable.

Day 12:
Commander Marayshan's Account:
Oh Natira, I can't take my mind off you. *Today,* my five days leave begins. I am going to spend *all* of it in my quarters with you, just the two of us. I've had some really good news. I am about to be promoted to First Officer of this Flagship. As Commander Astivan has accepted a Captaincy, and Commander Lierschvaan is content to remain as Executive Officer responsible for ship's discipline. Well, let's face it it's what he's *really* good at.

Day 14:
John Smith's Memoirs:
It was two weeks that I will never want to repeat: the Sikarans came to collect me on the fourteenth day and they had to carry me out of the stockade. I was too far gone, but I had told the Gloshans nothing despite everything they had done to me. Now I expected worse treatment at the hand of Sikarans aboard the Sikaran Flagship *Voran,* the most prized starship in the Sikaran Space Fleet. Once aboard the starship, I was placed in a large room with low lighting and left to rest for a while.

Commander Marayshan's Account:
No! I cannot believe it! All leave for Senior Officers has been cancelled, and I have only had *two* days alone with Natira! It is all because of an *Interspace* spy named John Smith who was captured two weeks ago and is being brought on board for interrogation. *He* is to blame for my loss of leave.

This afternoon I have discovered from Captain Javrayin that I am to be on the interrogation team. There are to be four of us on the team, Astivan, Evroshette, Lierschvaan and myself. John Smith is going to talk all right. With Lierschvaan on the team, I don't think he will remain silent for long, although the very rude report from the Gloshans says that John Smith is incredibly stubborn. I don't understand why Gloshans have to write their reports so rudely about *Interspace* prisoners. The reports are badly written and they're full of swear words and graffiti. They're so bad that we always ask the computer to improve them before we log them into our database.

Oh Natira. We were having such a good time in my quarters by ourselves. We talked and talked and laughed and laughed and sang together and then we merged together and became one and I wanted it to last forever, but you got a bit uncomfortable after an hour and a half. So, like a gentleman, I withdrew as I would not dream of distressing you, although I do have the feeling that you should have said something sooner. But you kept quiet for my sake because you knew that I was enjoying myself so much.

MEMO. Must make a note to talk to Natira about this next time I see her. I can't have her putting up with merging for longer than an hour if it makes her feel bad even though I had such a good time. Nava and Avernyi have the same problems with their girlfriends. I supposed they would. All the men who are a bit tougher and more athletic than average seem to merge longer than the norm. It's just one of those things that women make a fuss about: and that we athletic men have to put up with them making a fuss about. I must ask Count Viathol about his experiences of this kind of thing.
I have lost three days of my leave: that is outrageous.
John Smith, you have a lot to answer for.

On designated civic holidays, I always wear my *Davracha*'s outfit, which is a sleeveless tunic, designed to be worn as an outer garment, on top of my Fleet uniform. It is loose, but held in at the waist by a buckle-clasp that snaps together. It is very conspicuous because it is so visible, brightly coloured and eye-catching. Many of the crew, including Natira, seem to like me wearing it.

A civic holiday on a front line Flagship is not likely to be anywhere near as good as the holidays we have at home, but we all try to have a great time despite the fact that we still have our duties to perform. Things are allowed to slacken off on these special days; even Lierschvaan joins in the singing and joke telling.

Lierschvaan *even* initiated a circle dance on the Bridge last time we had a civic day. Much to Natira's joy, he must be mellowing a lot.

It cheered her because she had become rather low, wishing she were home again. At the end of the dance, we all sang some happy songs and Natira looked revitalized and laughed at everybody's jokes, even Evroshette's.

When she and I were together, it always cheered her up, but there wasn't much time to be together. That was the problem. It was the same for everyone aboard, of course, so we couldn't really complain too much. Somehow it always seemed to be worse for me though. Being a Senior Officer and so busy, my leave times become much more precious and Natira longed for these brief days. I thought we'd come a long way in our relationship these past three months. I could sense it, even though we hadn't actually spent much time together.

Two hours later:

I just had an emergency call from the senior nurse in sickbay. It seemed John Smith was in great need. He had some internal injuries and kept vomiting and the nurse believed he'd been traumatised by the treatment of the Gloshan guards who were holding him.

He is also homosexual and seemingly very feminine in his ways. I will visit him as soon as possible, as there are grave concerns about his mental and physical wellbeing. I'll ask Lieutenant Prince Evroshette to accompany me and do my best to help the prisoner, if I can. I think I will try aromatherapy for him and see how he responds.

John Smith's Memoirs:
I could not stop myself from crying. I expected a group of Sikaran guards to enter at any moment and drag me to an interrogation room.
But *nothing* happened.

Instead, a man and a woman came in and spoke quietly. They brought food and drink, and when the woman had gone the man helped me to wash and then to eat, but I vomited several times. They were nurses of course. I was surprised to be treated with such civility. I could not keep from crying though. What the Gloshan guards did to me I will never speak of to anyone. It is locked deep inside me. The barbaric treatment I endured from them was beyond belief.

After he had gone, I was left alone for what seemed like hours. Each time I heard a noise outside my door, new anguish set in. Finally two ship's officers came in. One of them carried a black briefcase. This is it I said to myself, they have given me time to rest, now they are going to start.

I looked with terror at the black briefcase and back to the officers. I began to cry again and plead with them not to hurt me as I spoke Sikaran and Gloshan with ease. I am a very skilled linguist.

They looked at each other then one of them began to take off my shirt for me. Oh God, I thought, they're going to whip me. The Gloshans had done that several times already with an electronic whip and I could not take anymore.

I shut my eyes tightly as the other officer began to open the black briefcase. I could not stop trembling and crying, I was in such a state. The man beside me said something, which I thought I had imagined. He said, "It's all right, *kirathie*, we mean you no harm." '*Kirathie*' is a Sikaran term of endearment, used by Sikaran men for women, and so I realized the Gloshans had told them that I was homosexual.

The Sikaran officer beside me started to massage my back. My eyes shot open in amazement and I looked at the contents of the black briefcase in disbelief. It was full of bottles of oils, and oil burners were filling the whole room with a most wonderful aromatic fragrance. It was heavenly. I suspected that I had really died and was in Sikaran heaven.
"Oh how marvellous," I murmured. "This is truly marvellous."

Once he had stopped massaging my back, he helped me to sit up and as I leaned against him, he fed me very slowly. This time I managed to keep the food down. I watched him. He was incredibly handsome, as most Sikaran men seemed to be. Just a wonderful hunk of manhood, and he was helping me, sitting so close to me. Even in my present state, I could appreciate his closeness. Exhaustion made me go limp then, and I sagged and let my head fall on his shoulder and it felt so good. He let me rest there for a long time, peacefully, supporting me with his arm around my shoulders.

For the first time in days, I slept. He must have stayed like that for a long time, so as not to wake me, and when I finally woke up an hour had passed by. The other officer had left and the oil burners were still fragrant. I looked at him and smiled. I thought I had forgotten how to smile.

"Thank you," I said. "You don't know how much I appreciated the sleep and the food. But is there anything else in the way of other foods that I could try as this doesn't really seem to agree with me."

"Of course, *kirathie*," he replied. "I will arrange for some other food dishes to be brought to you within three hours. You speak our language extremely well."

"Thank you. I am the only one who does speak your language in *Interspace*, you know. The only one who has ever bothered to learn it." I smiled again.

He took my hand and held it. I had realized it was a Sikaran custom and meaningless, but it felt very comforting at the time.

"You are very vulnerable," he replied, surprising me considerably, "perhaps being a top *Interspace* spy is not the best job for you."

"It is what I am good at," I replied. "It is the best way I can help my people."

He did not reply.

"Will I have some more time to rest, do you know, before they come for me? Can I sleep for a little longer?"

"You will have as much time as you need to rest."

"How many will be interrogating me, do you know?"

"Yes, I know," the officer replied.

"Could you ask them, please? Could you ask them, not to hurt me too much? You see, I am a terrible coward ..." I faltered to a halt covering my face with my hands.

"I do not think you are a coward at all," he said surprisingly. "I just think that you have been traumatized by the Gloshan guards who dealt with you." I leaned my head again on his shoulder and this time I ventured to put my arms around his neck.

"Can I sleep again?" I asked.

"You can sleep until you are completely recovered from the past two weeks," he replied.

"May I know your name?" I asked.

"Marayshan, my name is Marayshan." he replied.

"What rank are you?"

"I am a Commander, shortly to be promoted to First Officer of this Flagship."

"My name is John Smith, but of course you know that, don't you?" I replied.

"When you are recovered, there will be questions for you to answer, John Smith. If you answer them truthfully, it will be better for you. We have several ways of obtaining answers. Three ways involve interrogation techniques. There is a fourth way that involves your mind being probed."

"That sounds terrible, absolutely frightful," I said shakily, clinging to him now.

"Actually it is not terrible. It is the best way, the easiest way of the four alternatives. Your mind is contacted by telepathy and your secrets are taken from you. It is not quick, but it is not as bad as the other ways. It would be easier for us if we used telepathy with all our prisoners, but our ethics dictate that with non-telepaths we need to obtain their permission first to contact their minds, and none have yet given their consent."

"Wouldn't there be an element of danger in it for the non-telepath?" I asked.

"The person who looked into your thoughts would have to be extremely careful with your mind. You would have to trust them a great deal. Yes, there would be an element of danger, but I think for you, the alternatives are worse."

"I never realized that Sikarans were telepathic," I replied. "Can you sense any of my thoughts now?"

"No, it would be unethical, but I can sense your feelings clearly though. I cannot stop that, because you are so close to me."

"Then you have realized just how scared I am, and now you'll tell my interrogators." I cried again. He did not reply.

After a few moments he said, "While you rest, think about what I have said. Think carefully about it. Think about the telepathy, think seriously. It might be the best way for you. The alternatives may be too difficult. You see, one way or other, the information you carry and the truth will be required from you."

"You seriously want me to agree to allow an alien to crawl around inside my mind? How can you ask me such a thing?"

He sighed. "It's something for you to think about, that's all. I am only trying to help. I will leave you to sleep now."

"Can't you stay a little longer, please?" I asked.

"I should not. I am beginning to like you."

"Well, what does that matter? Weren't you sent to help me? I like *you*. Why shouldn't you like me? It doesn't change the situation."

"Yes, I came to help you, but not because I had been sent, but because you were traumatized and needed more help than others could give, but I am also on the interrogation team."

"You, oh God, I can't believe it," I replied, not knowing what to think now.

"John Smith, please think seriously about what I have said about the telepathy. Promise me that you will."

"I promise," I said quietly. "Will you still let me try something different to eat?"

He replied in the affirmative.

I was reluctant to let go of his hands. "I … I thought I had found a friend in this place, in this awful situation."

"I will try to be a friend, John Smith, when I can be. If you were to answer all our questions quickly and truthfully, it would be better for you, for all of us."

"Do you really expect me to do that without a fight?" I whispered as tears streamed down my face, "Will you allow me two or three days perhaps, just three days to recover before it all begins? Please, I am begging you."

"*Kirathie*, there will be no interrogations until you have fully recovered. If it takes three days or thirty days, you will have the time you need. I will arrange it."

"Thank you, thank you, I am truly grateful," I replied, unable to believe my luck. I had to restrain myself from kissing him to thank him, I was so grateful.

"I'll return tomorrow to see you, but some food will be with you in three hours. Sleep well, John Smith."

As soon as he left, I slept for six hours of blissful, uninterrupted sleep. When I awoke, I found that several food bowls had been placed on the table beside me, with different kinds of food in each. I grabbed each quickly and tried them, I was so hungry. Three were marvelous and I ate everything and wiped the bowls clean with wheat cakes.

A computer was in the room and I called to it, asking what I was permitted in this room. I asked for music and, to my incredulity, soft harp music stirred around the room. I sank back satisfied and drowsy again. The oil burners had been refilled and were emitting their fragrant scents and I thought of the Commander who had helped me.

Marayshan: his name sounded a little like 'Marzipan' in my exhausted state, and I began to fantasize about him. My story included his telepathy, his arms holding me and my head on his shoulder. The next day I really did call him 'Marzipan' much to my embarrassment, but he did not know the meaning of the Earth word and so ignored it.

Commander Marayshan's Account:
Lierschvaan is very keen to start the interrogations as soon as possible. He tells me he has thought up some new techniques. I am getting a bit worried about Lierschvaan. He is so enthusiastic that he's going to visit John Smith tomorrow and go into great detail about what the interrogations will be like, in the hope that John Smith will get frightened into talking quickly. We usually let Lierschvaan show prisoners around the Interrogation Suite as he enjoys it so much.

Lierschvaan has just come back from visiting John Smith, and not one word has he spoken to the spy about interrogations. John Smith had only to look at Lierschvaan out of sad, tear-filled eyes and Lierschvaan relented. He ended up holding John Smith's hand and then teaching him to play a Sikaran card game.

Lierschvaan wrung his hands as he said to me, "Marayshan, John Smith is too much like a woman! What are we going to do?"

So appalled was Lierschvaan at the state of John Smith that he took it upon himself to go back to the Gloshan stockade where the spy had been held, and to sort out the guards who had traumatized him. Lierschvaan took Lieutenant Devthanyi with him and an electronic whip. I believe that he was going to teach them a lesson in how to be more hospitable guards in the future.

MEMO. I must make a note to tell Devthanyi not to let Lierschvaan spend so much time on his own in the Interrogation Suite or the ship's cells watching those movies. I must rearrange duty rotas so that Deva and Lee are always on duty together down there. I must speak to Lee on his own about all this. He is becoming much too focused on being in charge of ship's discipline again. This really is not good for him. I will have to give him a distraction. I'll put together a programme lasting twenty weeks. What shall I suggest? I have it! He can spend time with John Smith every day, say, three hours a day. That should distract him. They can have lunch together and play cards. Seems like John Smith loves to gossip. Had I been confident that Lee would not be pelted with bread rolls, I would have sent him to the *Dungeon Fleet Bar* to spend some time drinking with the Fleet men. Officers don't often go down there to have a drink. I really enjoy going there myself and I never seem to get pelted with anything. Probably because I'm a welfare worker as well as a Senior Officer and so they treat me with more respect. But as Lee is the ship's Senior Discipline Officer, I am not sure how he would be welcomed by the ordinary crew in their off duty times.

John Smith's Memoirs:

Marayshan seemed to be able to take me in his stride, which is more than I can say about many people back on Earth. He has been doing a great deal of nodding and smiling. That is, he humours me with ease. I am not the only one he humours actually, no, not the only one. I have observed him amongst his fellow Sikarans, and I can see that he has an amazing capacity for understanding people and putting them at their ease, even aliens like me. He is remarkably skilled.

Commander Lierschvaan worships him. Actually most of the ship's officers and crew seem to be smitten by Marayshan in one way or another. They hold him in quite high esteem. I suppose it could be something to do with the fact that he is in the *Isithan*. But as yet, I am not sure what being in the *Isithan* really means exactly or just what this organization called the *Isithan* is all about.

There are others aboard who are in the *Isithan* and they don't seem to be treated with respect in the same way. It must be force of his personality. Charisma I believe it is called. For me it's well, attraction in a big way of course, due to the fact that I am transsexual and he is out and out gorgeous, but that isn't the case for most of the Sikarans, just Natira and one other woman I have noticed, who looks at him very discretely in quite an interested way.

As I grew stronger and less traumatized, each day he came to see me with a list of questions which he marked off as I answered them and he recorded my answers. There was no rhyme or reason to the questions. They seemed arbitrary and rather odd. No pattern could I perceive to them. He taught me to play Sikaran card games and I taught him human ones, with an Earth pack of cards that I had made, using the computer. I wrote my thoughts into the computer endlessly. It gave me a purpose.

My first mission as an *Interspace* spy:
During this time that I was a prisoner with the Sikarans, I built up an account for myself of my first mission as an *Interspace* spy when I was sixteen years old. I am now twenty-one and have been on no less than sixty *Interspace* missions and survived them all without being captured. There are not many people in *Interspace* who can better me in the study of alien languages. If I say so myself: I am an expert and proud of it. At the age of sixteen, I had obtained two university degrees, one in linguistics and the other in computer science and obtained a great deal of kudos. That was when my career with the Interspace Spy Service began. Shortly after Interspace Intelligence approached me and I was asked to spend six months on an Observation mission at Far-station *Dria* on the *Kaloris* borders, used by our enemies in the space war. At the time our enemies were the Gloshans and Sikarans. I was to utilize as many disguises as I wanted in order to maintain my anonymity, as I did have a theatrical flair. I was such a good actor, you have no idea.

There was a very timid and frightened *Interspace* contact on Far-station *Dria*, a *Lasoan* trader named Evod, whom I would link up with and he would find me lodgings. He apparently would never contact Spy Command unless absolutely necessary and give them a minimum of information. He was rather useless but better than nothing. *Interspace* transmitted my details and photograph to him before I arrived. My mission was to perfect my command of the Gloshan and Sikaran languages and to learn as much as I could about anything to do with the Gloshans and Sikarans: their culture, their ways of thinking, and their behaviour as up until then, we humans knew next to nothing about Gloshans or Sikarans.

I found it an exhilarating yet terrifying prospect: that I was to be the first to attempt something like this. My code name was to be 'John Smith' for all covert communications with *Interspace*, but I would have preferred the name 'Lucinda' and requested it to be changed. However, *Interspace* Spy Command would not agree under any circumstances, so 'John Smith' it was. Still, I dreamed of one day being called Lucinda by a wonderful, handsome man I had yet to meet. My favourite disguize was pretending to be an alien woman, any woman actually. I just loved dressing up as a woman, and used my passion to good effect as no one suspected that I was really a man, or so I assumed.

This Observation mission was not as easy as I thought it would be at the start, not where the Sikarans were concerned. The Gloshans however were an 'in your face' type of people. The men were overbearing, loud and arrogant and the women, always made attempts to be tough with their men, as I gathered that that was the way that Gloshan men seemed to like it. The women would often hit the men, not hard, but nevertheless, they would hit them, and the men would laugh, enjoying the attention. If the woman misjudged the blow and it was too gentle, the Gloshan man would laugh at her and deride her. But if it was too hard, then the man would become incensed and respond with significant force. They were very violent men. I was baffled by Gloshan culture if indeed they had any culture. Each night before I slept, I would record my thoughts and send them through to Interspace Spy Central.

The Sikarans on the other hand were much more like us humans in their general behaviour. The soldiers enjoyed playing cards, telling jokes and dancing. The Gloshan men found it difficult to understand Sikaran humour, and I noticed that they were also afraid of the Sikaran men, and would often defer to them if they were around. The Gloshan women, however, seemed braver in this respect. They would go up to the Sikaran soldiers and embrace them with real enthusiasm, which made some of the Gloshan soldiers seethe with jealousy and which seemed to amuse the Sikaran soldiers in a quiet way.

I did not blame the Gloshan women for doing that actually, as most Sikaran men were remarkably handsome, and they did not appear to be outwardly violent or aggressive the way the Gloshans were. I would have tried to chat up the Sikaran soldiers myself if I had had enough nerve, as I found them amazingly attractive. Oh hugely so, but they were the enemy after all, so I tried to restrain myself.

The Sikaran soldiers would start dancing at the smallest excuse, and it was mostly like Earth Cossack Russian dancing. But they also did circle and line dancing, in which they involved the Gloshan soldiers, which amused the Gloshans greatly and they seemed to enjoy the social interaction, laughing and clapping their hands to the music.

Although I could not fathom out Gloshan 'culture', if that is the word, the Sikarans seemed to understand some of it, and were even able to use Gloshan gestures at times which thoroughly impressed the Gloshans. I think they were easily impressed.

The Gloshan soldiers did not seem to be well educated, whereas it was obvious to me that the Sikaran soldiers were extremely knowledgeable and able to read complex literature while the Gloshan soldiers struggled to read even the simplest newspapers. It was rather sad really. Sometimes the Sikarans would take pity on them and either read the news aloud to them or attempt to teach them to read *Gloshanese*, which the Sikaran soldiers seemed well able to do themselves.

I called myself '*Lucaja*', a Lasoan name, as near to the human name 'Lucinda' as I dared. After a month in that awful Far-station, I began to feel truly isolated, and I started crying for no reason as I walked each night back to my lonely rooms. I realized that if this got too much worse I would have to return home to Earth, but things soon started to change for the better as I acquired two companions. They were not boyfriends exactly, just friends I believe, although they both danced with me and bought me drinks. They were two Sikaran soldiers. I knew now that I had to be terribly careful not to give anything away to them about who I really was, but I was desperate for some company.

One of the two men appeared to be as good as I was in the linguistics department, the one whose name was Navaronschyia. He had a good friend by the name of Avernyi who, as the days went by, became more interested in me and began to ask me to dance with him a lot. I could not refuse of course. It would have looked out of place if I had, as all the women in the bar always danced with every man who asked. Avernyi was always pleasant, polite and extremely kind. I found out that he and his friend belonged to a Sikaran organisation called the *Isithan*, but I never found out what it was. I thought they thought I was a woman, being as I was disguised as a Lasoan woman, and so I had to play it very carefully indeed.

Avernyi began to sit with me regularly at my table and his friend Navaronschyia would sometimes join us. Avernyi would buy me drinks and a meal too and tell me jokes and make me laugh. It surprised me that I could really understand Sikaran jokes. They seemed to be so similar to human ones. Both of them held my hand, at different times and sometimes together, sitting on either side of me in the bar. Now from my observations of Sikaran soldiers, this seemed to be one of their customs to hold hands with each other and with everyone else, even the Gloshan men, who found this very strange and highly amusing when it happened. So I could not tell from this, as to whether they really fancied me or whether this was just something they did as part of their tradition.

Avernyi spent a long time holding my hand in the bar in the evenings. I did begin to wonder at the reason behind it and would sometimes look him directly in the face trying to gauge his feelings, but he would never drop his guard, would never show me any emotion, except that of an amiable companion. He would smile when I looked at him like that, and I would smile in return. I was very grateful for the contact I can tell you. It dispelled my loneliness and sense of isolation like nothing else had done up until then. I did not cry anymore on my way back to my rooms in the night.

After a month of this companionship, I dared to do something that I should not ever have done, not ever. I dared to invite them both to my rooms. It was a really idiotic thing to do, but you have to understand how much I valued their friendship by then, despite the fact that they represented the enemy, and were bound to hand me in if they discovered that I was an *Interspace* spy. I longed to share my rooms, my ideas, my poetry and the songs that I composed with them and I longed too to tell them that I was as I am, a transsexual man, who had always felt as though he was a woman, locked inside the body of a man. I longed to know their opinions concerning homosexual men. I thought that I could bring up the subject very casually, saying that I had noticed a man the day before in the market, whom I thought was a homosexual. I thought that I could ask them how homosexual men were treated in Sikaran culture, just casually, you understand.

I bought two bottles of *iskari* for us to share and lots of food, and set out trays of snacks just as the maid and butler had done whenever visitors called at our estate. They arrived and bowed to me politely and I indicated that they should sit down and gave them drinks. I went into the kitchen to bring out the trays, when Navaronschyia called in to me and said, "*Kirathie*, don't you ever get tired of wearing women's clothes? Don't you ever just want to relax in men's clothing, considering that you are a man?"

I can tell you I nearly dropped the tray I was carrying. I cleared my throat and came back in and put the tray down in front of them. I sat for a while, and then said, "I thought I did a very good impression of being a woman, and no one else had guessed that I'm a man. How long have you two known that I'm not a woman?"

"From the first time we met you, *kirathie*," Avernyi replied.

"Then, if you know that I'm a man, why do you call me *kirathie*?" I asked. *Kirathie* was the term of endearment that Sikaran men used with all women.

"Because we've realized that you're not just a *Lasoan* man pretending to be a woman, as an actor might. But you're a man who very much wishes that he was truly a woman. Am I right? We think that you are a very young man; too young to be in a Far-station like this on his own. Perhaps you are not even a *Lasoan*, but from some other culture and place in the galaxy."

"Of course I'm *Lasoan*," I replied, trying not to look either of them directly in the face, because I knew that if I did I would give myself away completely. My God they were smart, these Sikaran men, just a little too smart.

"Before this conversation gets too silly," I said, trying to make light of it, "can I ask you a question, Avernyi, why do you keep holding my hand for so long in the bar in the evenings? I know that it's one of your customs, but this does seem to be more than the usual."

Avernyi smiled then said, "It is for two reasons, *kirathie*. Firstly, to make the Gloshan soldiers who use the bar think that you and I are romantically involved, so that they will leave you alone, and secondly, because I sense that you have been enjoying it and would not wish it to stop."

"Yes, I have been enjoying it, very much. You see I have been very lonely." My voice trailed off.

I should never have said these words.

"There are many other *Lasoans* on this Far-station, *kirathie*, why have you been so lonely?" Navaronschyia asked amiably, but there was an undercurrent of something unspoken in his voice. At that moment, I imagined a Sikaran hand laser being raised and pointed at me, and I could see myself disintegrating into a million pieces. I shut my eyes to try and calm myself, anxiety hitting me in waves. I picked up something to eat, to delay the dreadful moment when I would have to answer, and the moment when they would know that I was an *Interspace* spy and either kill me themselves or take me to a dark, miserable cell somewhere.

Avernyi spoke then, "John Smith, listen to me," he said.

He even knew my code name. I was devastated.

"John Smith, we have known all along that you are an *Interspace* spy. We have been sent by Sikaran Intelligence to keep an eye on you, and to make sure that nothing happens to you, as you are so young. You see, we intercepted the communication from your Spy Central to the *Lasoan* trader Evod here, and realized that you are ludicrously young to be sent on such a dangerous mission into enemy territory, so we decided to come here for six months to look after you. We realized that your mission was simply one of observation and so of no threat or consequence to us."

I sat and stared at them both for a long moment then finally found my voice.

"That is right, Avernyi," I said. "I am just here to perfect my spoken language skills in *Gloshanese* and *Sikaran*, and to try to find out a little about your people and also about Gloshans."

"Your command of our language is truly remarkable," said Navaronschyia. I tried to smile to thank him, but I felt quite ill, terror causing my stomach to knot up.

"What are you going to do with me now?" I asked quietly.

"There is nothing to be done. You have four more months of your mission to serve, and we will remain with you and keep you safe and be companions to you until we find a safe passage for you back to your *Interspace*. We have sensed that you are indeed very lonely. We are sad for you." His words surprised me.

"But, I am your enemy, Navaronschyia," I replied.

"Yes you are our enemy, John Smith," he replied. "But you are not in a position to do us any harm, not here and now. You, yourself, are vulnerable, so we see no reason to make you our prisoner. The Gloshans, on the other hand, if they knew about you, would take you to one of their stockades from which you might never return. It might also prove to be extremely unpleasant for you; Gloshans are not renowned for their compassion towards enemy prisoners. We however are different to Gloshans."

"John Smith, tell me, why did you invite us here tonight?" Avernyi asked.

"I wanted to talk to you, for hours and hours and hours, without being interrupted by the noise in the bar. I wanted to read you some poetry that I have written and to sing you some songs that I have composed."

"I like poetry," said Navaronschyia.

"So do I," Avernyi replied, "why don't you read us your poems and we will give you our opinion of them?"

"Seriously," I said, "You would really like to hear my poetry?"

"Well, it just has to be an improvement on Gloshan poetry," said Navaronschyia, which made me laugh.

"By the way, which *Interspace* world is your home planet, John Smith?" Avernyi asked.

"I would rather not say, if you don't mind, Avernyi," I replied.

"I don't mind," Avernyi replied, surprising me again.

This time he smiled at me. The thought suddenly came to me that they were both playing some dreadful sinister game with me for their own amusement. That must be it, I said to myself. I could have wept buckets. These two aren't really my friends at all, they are just playing with me and they're going to do something nameless and terrible to me, and I have invited them into my rooms, and how will I ever get rid of them? How? It was impossible. They were pleasant now, but the moment their mood changed, I would be in for it. I could never defend myself against them. Not in a million years. I had a vivid imagination, which was now running riot. Navaronschyia interrupted my agonized thoughts.

"Lucaja, you're not eating, why is that? These are delicious."

I took something quickly and ate it, hoping to keep them happy for as long as I possibly could.

"Yes, they are good." I said.

"Tell us about your *Interspace* spy commander. Is he crazy or something?" Avernyi said.

"What makes you say that, Avernyi?" I replied casually.

"Oh, I am just interested in trying to understand why your spy commander should send someone so young on his own to a dangerous place like this?"

"Well, I suppose, it's because I'm very intelligent. He offered me this mission because of my linguistic skills and I took it because I thought that I could do it. I suppose it was a bit risky after all."

"He should never have offered you this mission in the first place!" Navaronschyia exclaimed, "It would be unbelievably dangerous for a combat-trained, experienced soldier. Are you combat-trained? Are you an experienced soldier?" he asked emphatically.

I shook my head on both counts.

"John Smith, I don't think that your spy commander likes you, or he would never have sent you here."

"Well, it's true enough that he doesn't like me. Actually I think that he is just like my father. He dislikes me because of my feminine attributes, but he seems to value my skills as a linguist very highly you know, at least I think that he does." I faltered to a halt.

"He should have sent an older, more experienced man with you to protect you." Navaronschyia replied.

Avernyi added, "You know, we intercepted several communications that your spy commander made about you to his colleagues in your Spy Central. We believe that he sent you here to *Dria* because he did not want you ever to return to *Interspace*."

I looked at him in silence, shocked by the revelation. Tears came to my eyes as I realized the truth of what he said. I wiped them away hastily.

"What's wrong, Lucaja?" Navaronschyia asked.

"Nothing really, it is just that my life hasn't been at all easy because. I feel so different inside. I feel so, well, feminine. I thought that by dedicating myself to this career, I could help my world in the space war, and if I was as successful as I have been in my two university degrees, then even more people would accept me for what I am and admire me." I burst into tears.

Avernyi held my hand again and put a fatherly arm around my shoulders of which I was pathetically grateful.

"Thank you," I whispered.

Avernyi sighed, then said, "It is a pity that you were not born a Sikaran, Lucaja. You would have been treated in a much better way and would have had a much happier life."

"Do you really think so, Avernyi?" I replied.

"Yes, I really think so," he said sounding very concerned.

I realized then that they were genuine in their desire to help me and that this was all they were offering: help and companionship until the end of my mission. There was no hidden agenda, no terrible, nameless threat from them.

"Lucaja, you haven't read us your poems yet," Navaronschyia said. "I would really like to hear them."

"You're very kind," I said, "both of you. I should have thanked you for your kindness to me long before now. I'm sorry that I have been remiss in doing that."

Avernyi smiled and said, "We will surprise your spy commander greatly, when you return from your mission alive and well."

I nodded and smiled in return.

"You wouldn't like to come back to my planet and visit my estate, would you?" I said, then added, "I'm only joking."

They both laughed at the ludicrousness of the suggestion and I joined in.

"*Yes*, I can see it now," I said theatrically. "John Smith returns to Planet X with two Sikaran soldiers as his minders, one on each arm. The thought appeals to me immensely. It really does, Avernyi! It really does!"

"It would be an amazing event if it were to happen, Lucaja," said Navaronschyia, "considering that Avernyi and I are in the Sikaran Special Forces."

This pronouncement made us laugh even more and, by the end of the evening, I felt so much better. All my misery had disappeared completely. I had two of the most attractive men in the universe as my minders and my friends. What more could I ask out of life? I had it all. I just had it all.

Back on the Flagship *Voran*:

Now you have no idea how delighted I was when who should come to visit me yesterday, but Avernyi and Navaronschyia. I just could not believe it. They were officers aboard the Flagship *Voran*. I flung myself at each of them and did not think I would ever let go. They did not seem to mind and embraced me in return.

"John Smith! Lucaja! Why do you get yourself into so many difficult situations?" said Navaronschyia. "Surely there are easier ways on your planet for you to make a living. We warned you to stay away from the Gloshans, didn't we?"

They had come to visit me four days after I was brought from the Gloshan stockade, and I was still in a terrible state.

"We couldn't believe it when we heard that you were aboard, Lucaja. How long has it been since we last met?" asked Avernyi.

"We last met when I was sixteen and now I am twenty-one, so it was nearly half a Galactic year ago when we last were together."

"You look really awful, Lucaja," said Navaronschyia. "What did the Gloshans do to you?"

"What didn't they do to me?" I replied miserably.

Navaronschyia apologized that he had to leave then, but Avernyi stayed. He sat with me for a long time and gradually, very gradually I confided in him everything that had happened in the Gloshan stockade. I never thought that I would talk about it to anyone, but now Avernyi was with me I told him everything and got it all out of my system.

Month 5: Day 167.
Commander Marayshan's Account:
After twenty-one weeks—Sikaran weeks have ten days in them unlike *Interspace* weeks that have only seven, I called an urgent meeting of the interrogation team.

"There is something that you should all know," I began. "I have been testing John Smith with all kinds of tests, asking him endless questions, really getting to know him. He's an extremely intelligent and very brave person. He's also incredibly vulnerable. I have tested him using the '*Sholathyir Index*' and he has come out in Band Two on a par with Captain Javrayin."

"Band Two? Yu're not serious, Marayshan," said Astivan. "If he is like Captain Javrayin, then he is extremely vulnerable, and ethically there is no way we can interrogate him."

Lierschvaan agreed. "There *is* no way we can interrogate him. The look in his eyes has haunted me since I first saw him on the second day of his arrival. He is too much like a woman. I have no idea how we are going to get any information out of him. It's such a terrible dilemma."

"Well, all is not lost, friends," said Marayshan. "I thought you would like to know that with the help of Avernyi, I have finally succeeded in persuading John Smith to have a telepathic mind probe and he has agreed as long as it's me who is doing the probing."

"Who better to do it than a *Davracha*," said Evroshette.

"John Smith will go down in history as the first non-telepathic prisoner to agree to this. He must be extremely brave," said Astivan.

"John Smith has lost some of his fear of Marayshan, I think, because he's developed some feelings for our friend here." Lierschvaan said, looking at Marayshan.

Marayshan nodded, "Well, at least it means that he now trusts me, Lee, and that will help a lot in establishing the link. I had realized that he does have some womanly feelings for me, yes."

"*Some*," said Evroshette, "if he were Sikaran, you would be obliged to accept him as a male partner. You know you could still do that, I suppose, even though he isn't Sikaran. Your girlfriend Natira has no objection, she told me so. His feelings for you are almost tangible! As it is, well, I am not sure that you could justify taking a top *Interspace* spy as a partner, being our enemy and everything. Anyway, it probably isn't a tradition where John Smith comes from, but who knows? Marayshan, why don't you let him move into your quarters while you're developing the telepathic link with him? It would show that you were honouring his bravery immensely by allowing him such a privilege."

"Evroshette, I am *leading* this interrogation team! Don't you think it might put me in a bit of a difficult position?" Marayshan said, sounding exasperated.

"We wouldn't object, and neither would Natira. While John Smith is with us, it might do him a lot of good to share your quarters, Marayshan." Lierschvaan said.

"I agree," said Astivan.

"Me too," said Evroshette. "I have grown to like John Smith very much and feel that he deserves some happiness. Marayshan, come on, treat him as though he were one of our people, give him something special to remember. We all think you should, because we are all feeling sorry for him."

"All right, if you put it like that, Evroshette, then he can stay with me for the rest of his time here and I'll pretend that he's Sikaran. Will that satisfy you all?" Marayshan replied.

"Absolutely," said Astivan. "John Smith is deeply enamoured of you and very lonely. It is sad to see."

I sighed. So much for the Interrogation Team's iron determination, so much for Lierschvaan's steely reserve; I would get all John Smith's information, of course, through the mind link, but in return I would honour him by letting him share my quarters with me. Well, I suppose, thinking about it, it would be the best thing for him on a personal level. It would certainly make him happy.

John Smith's Memoirs:

At last, after twenty-one weeks of rest and recuperation, I agreed to allow the Sikarans to use their telepathy on me, but on the proviso that it was Marayshan who contacted my mind, and only he; my handsome hunk of manhood. I wished he had not had a girlfriend aboard. Natira was her name and, in my fantasies, I became deeply jealous of her. In reality, she was a lovely, kind, considerate woman who would always talk to me and I grew to enjoy her company, putting aside my jealousy. We often gossiped just like sisters.

The day Marayshan came to me and asked me to share his quarters with him was the best day of my life. Why, because, up until then, I had been rather wretched in one way or another at a personal level. I took his hand as he led me into his quarters and I shut my eyes and made a wish. He explained that he had invited me to share his quarters because we needed privacy to develop the telepathic link. He also said he wished to honour my courage in choosing the telepathic mind probe, so his rooms became mine until such time as they would return me to *Interspace*. No, they were *not* going to execute me, but return me to my home and I was pathetically grateful. I realized then that it was only Gloshans who executed *Interspace* spies.

Marayshan, of course, had never made any amorous advances towards me. This was all in my mind. Of course, it was all in my mind. At the start of the telepathic contact with him, suddenly *he* was all in my mind: amazingly masculine, but curiously gentle. When I first felt the presence of him inside me I all but fainted in his arms. He withdrew, looking astonished. I didn't blame him really. I didn't think he appreciated how deeply I saw myself as a woman locked inside a man's body; I am hugely feminine, believe me.

The next time he tried to communicate using the telepathy, I was ready for him with open arms and … well I was very welcoming to him. Actually, I welcomed him in every way I could possibly think of. Why did I do that? Well, I reasoned that as he was taking all my secrets, I might as well get something out of it in return. Why couldn't I get something that I enjoyed? I could tell that he found me most, well, perplexing. But I could not help myself. He was just so gorgeous. Enemy or not, I *really* did *not* care. Whilst I was languishing in his arms, he was retrieving all the information I had; every last scrap of it. He thanked me each time he finished with me. Well, Sikarans are very polite, I will give them that much, even when they are stripping all your secrets from you.

In my mind, he saw my yearning for him. Of course he would, how could I hide it, and then he did something I never expected him to do. He took pity on me. He gave me a gift. He kissed me telepathically, not physically. This happened several times and it was all in my mind. It was an amazing experience and just too wonderful for words. He gave me another gift before I left: a small piece of crystal on a chain.

"This is something special to remember me by," he said.

Those were his words. I never lost the piece of crystal and I never forgot him. Each time I held the crystal and closed my eyes, I saw his face and it was as though he smiled at me. It sustained me through some low times in years to come.

Shortly after he had retrieved all my secrets, I had the misfortune to witness a very strange event on the Bridge. And very tragic, too, as it turned out, after I understood what had happened. There was a battle going on, the Flagship *Voran* was under attack from *Interspace* allies. It was not as fierce as it might have been, but still it was not easy for the Sikaran crew. I sat in my usual place now, accustomed to being on the Bridge with Marayshan when he was on duty.

Suddenly during a quiet moment, Marayshan gasped, and stared in front of him, calling out, 'Natira, Natira!' in anguished tones. Now Natira was nowhere on the Bridge, and I wondered what on earth was the matter with Marayshan.

Lierschvaan, nearest to him, went and put his arms around him and held him tightly.

"Lee, Natira is gone," Marayshan said in a tearful voice. "Natira is gone. I saw her just now. She came to say goodbye."

"I am deeply sorry, Marayshan," Lierschvaan replied quietly.

I shuddered at the supernatural overtones, and soon after it was confirmed that Natira had died from battle injuries in the sickbay. The doctor called up to the Bridge to tell Marayshan.

"Natira is gone, Marayshan," he said. "Natira has faded. Please forgive me, we could not save her for you."

Marayshan leaned on Lierschvaan's shoulder and cried. I had not yet seen him cry and it was the most dreadful moment of my life.

I wished then that I had died instead of Natira. This might seem like an odd thing to think, considering they were the enemy, but I would have died in her place to save Marayshan all the anguish. He looked distraught, trying to come to terms with what had just happened and I could not stand to see him like that. I tried to pretend like I was looking at a computer screen. Lierschvaan was still hugging him, and I could feel tears come to my eyes and trickle down my face. I wiped them away hastily with the back of my hand, trying not to show that I was upset. But my feelings were impossible to hide, and many of the Sikarans on the Bridge seemed to detect my feelings. They turned to gaze at me with questioning looks on their faces.

"I really liked Natira," I said, because I had to say something. "She was a lovely woman and she helped me a lot. She listened to my sadness and became a friend to me. I grieve for her and with Marayshan, whom I am privileged to call my friend, despite the fact that we are supposed to be enemies."

"Thank you for your words," replied Captain Javrayin. "We are disconcerted yet content that you, our enemy, should have such feelings towards our people. It is … unprecedented and requires careful consideration for the future."

"You have treated me with nothing but respect and great kindness. You have allowed me to keep my dignity," I replied. "I have the greatest esteem for your people, Captain Javrayin, and I will tell this to *Interspace* Command when I return home. I am truly, deeply sorry that your people and my people are at war."

The real tragedy was that Sikarans and Humans were at war with each other in the first place, not the passing of Natira although that was bad enough. And now I knew how I was going to spend the rest of my life: I would dedicate it to stopping this damnable space war.

Later that night in Marayshan's quarters, I sat holding his hand as he grieved for Natira. It was my turn to try to comfort him. I did what I could. I hugged him as Lierschvaan had done, and I even kissed him. I felt so bad about it all. Finally, he slept on my shoulder, and I sat as still as I could and let him sleep.

"It was time for me to give something back to you, in return for all the help you have given me," I said when he awoke. Avernyi and Navaronschyia came in later and helped him with their telepathy and afterwards he spent a restful night.

The Captain of the *Interspace* ship who collected me, found me extremely healthy and what passed as happy for me. You see I had my memories. I had lost my espionage secrets to Sikarans and other more personal things to Gloshans, but I had my two gifts from Marayshan.

"Mr. Westerby-Smythe, do you feel able to give me a report on your imprisonment," the Captain said briskly, in a hearty fashion.

"Of course, Captain, but do call me Nigel," I said and began my tale. My opening words were, "*Dear* Captain, I have *been* in Sikaran heaven." I sipped my tea. When he heard me out, the Captain told me that he thought I had been drugged by the Sikarans over a prolonged period of time, but my medical report did not back up this assertion in any way. The Captain was perplexed.

"They must have used some new biochemical substance undetectable to our technology," he said.

So I replied, "Yes, wait, I *remember* now. They gave me a special tonic. They called this tonic '*Marayshan*'. That must be it."

The Captain was satisfied. His theory had been confirmed. So Marayshan went down on record as a new, very effective Sikaran substance, used to interrogate *Interspace* spies, and *impossible* to resist.

Planet Earth: Eighteen years later: John Smith's Memoirs:

Yes, years passed and I found all three of them again aboard the Interspace Grain Ship *McBride*. The Sikarans had signed a treaty with my beloved Earth and were on our side now in the space war and I was overjoyed.

By this time in my life, I was a rather outrageously colourful character and my father was unhappy with me, but at least my mother understood. I could rely on her always to understand and I loved her to distraction. I loved my father too, that was the tragedy because I think *he really disliked me*.

Marayshan and a group of Sikaran soldiers were being transported to the *beta*-Naiobi colonies. I thought I had forgotten all about them until a fellow spy contacted me from the *McBride*, telling me that Marayshan was now a Shield Lord of the *Isithan*, which I now knew to be the Sikaran Special Forces, and he had become quite a celebrity. I learned, too, that his two true friends, Avernyi and Navaronschyia, were also with him and my heart sang. I never thought I would see any of them again.

I realized quite quickly, upon seeing Marayshan again, that I had only really been infatuated with him all those years ago, and that the feelings had evaporated. I felt, too, that he was rather beyond my reach, being a Shield Lord of the *Isithan*. However, my feelings for Avernyi remained as strong as they ever had been and I confided to Marayshan how much I admired and respected and cared for his friend and, of course, he told Avernyi.

In my quarters the next night, I was visited by Avernyi and we had a drink together and sat and talked, just like old times.

"You know, Avernyi," I said, "even though nearly two Galactic years have passed since I last saw you, my heart still sang when I met you and Navaronschyia again, but especially you."

"Do you want to be my partner, Lucaja?" he asked. Then, to my amazement, he continued to say, "It is a Sikaran custom, that if a homosexual man has feelings for another man, then he can become a partner to that man, and that the man is free to marry a woman later if he wishes. There is a woman that I would like to marry at some point, so would you like to be my partner?"

"Of course I would like to be your partner!" I exclaimed, "It would be a dream, come true. When I first got to know you all those years ago, I thought you were the most wonderful man in the universe, not just the galaxy, but the universe. Now I am thirty-nine Earth years old and I still think that you are."

Avernyi smiled and nodded and then kissed my hand.
"We'll have a joining ceremony then, Lucaja," he said, "in a few months time. In the ceremony, we will merge telepathically, so we'll have to practice that a lot beforehand, because you're not Sikaran. I'll have to be careful with your mind."

"I'll practice absolutely anything with you, Avernyi," I replied, in my usual outrageous fashion. "May I contact my parents and let them know about the ceremony?"

"Of course, and I hope they will be there."

"Well, I am sure that my mother will attend the ceremony, but my father is another matter. He was an Admiral you know, in the Earth navy, he is now semi-retired. The rank of Admiral is equivalent to your rank of High Commander. He is very upright and proper, rather like you, actually, Avernyi. You know you remind me a lot of my father."

"When we reach Earth, I would very much like to meet your parents," he said.

"Yes of course, and Navaronschyia and Marayshan must meet them too, if Marayshan has the time."

"I think that he will make the time," Avernyi replied, "as he and I are *Dartha Ishalanyi*. We have been friends for a very long time."

I did not delay in contacting my parents via a computer link from the *McBride*.
"Mother, Father! Good day to you!" I said.
"Is anything wrong, Nigel, dear?" said my mother.
"No, mother, dear," I replied. "Everything is right, at last, in my life. I have acquired a partner, a Sikaran partner, and his name is Avernyi, and I am bursting with pride. He is truly wonderful."
"Avernyi? You used to know a Sikaran soldier by that name years ago, didn't you, dear?" mother said.
"Yes, I did. He is the one who protected me on my first mission. Yes, it is the same Avernyi, mother. He would very much like to meet you both when we reach Earth."
"Oh, how exciting, dear!" mother replied.
"Hrrumph!" said my father. "Sikaran, you say; not the done thing, surely."
"I beg your pardon, father." I said.
"That is the last thing I expected, Nigel," said father, "the last thing. A Sikaran boyfriend! I cannot believe it."
"Well believe it, father," I said. "Because it's true, and we're to be married in a Sikaran joining ceremony, a telepathic ceremony."
"No Sikaran is going to scramble my son's brains with telepathy!" said my father.
"Father, Avernyi is the nicest man in the universe. He would not dream of scrambling anything of mine, especially not my brains. I assure you, he is the most considerate man in the universe."
"Do not talk rot, Nigel," said father. "I did not bring you up to talk rot!"
"You did not bring me up at all, dear father. You were in the navy, don't you remember, being an Admiral or something of the sort?"
"Hrrumph!" said my father.

"Do you remember how you used to come home on leave and find me all dressed up as a young lady? I did love it when you treated me so charmingly, dear father."

"What else could I do?" said father, desparingly. "You were impossible, Nigel, utterly impossible!"

"I am sorry, father," I replied. "I do love you, you know. I love you terribly."

"I know, Nigel and, although you might not believe me, I love you too."

"Really, father, do you really mean that?" I replied.

"Yes, I really mean that," father replied. "That is why I am very unhappy that an alien soldier who was our enemy not so very long ago, is going to get inside your mind and do unspeakable things to you."

"We are just going to practice telepathy father. We are going to do telepathic exercises together, that's all."

"Nigel, I want you to promise me something. Please, do not start any of this telepathic practicing until you are here at home with your mother and I. I want you here Nigel, with us, so we can keep an eye on you to make sure nothing untoward happens."

"All right, father, I promise you," I replied. "By the way, I think you are going to like Avernyi. I love him hugely."

"You love everybody, dear," said mother blandly.

"I know, mother, but this time, this time it's so different, it really is."

"We shall see, dear, we shall see," said mother. "Now look after yourself until you get back to Earth. Goodbye dear."

"Goodbye, mother, father," I said.

"Hrrumph," was all I got from my father.

End of Article 1.

Chapter Four: The trumpet sounds the Final Offensive.

Just before they reached Earth, at the end of the ten month voyage half way across the galaxy, many of the *McBride*'s crew had asked Captain Grey if he could arrange for them to say farewell to the Sikaran soldiers formally. So, the captain put together a ceremony in which he presented them with all the medals they had earned on the ground missions they had been on with the security team. Several people requested to say a few words and many others wrote letters to the Sikarans, thanking them for all their help.

Alice had gathered together over a hundred letters and placed them in an attaché case, which Captain Grey had bought as a leaving present for Marayshan and on which were engraved the words '*Shield Lord Marayshan, Civic Governor of the Naiobi Colonies*'. This was the new posting that Marayshan had been given, on the recommendation of Captain Grey, Dr. Grafton and Commander McKye. Alice Morgan had bought gifts too for all the other Sikaran soldiers and presented them at the ceremony.

Lance Dayton stood then spoke. So did Marcie Jones, saying,
"All I have to say is this, Marayshan is my hero and I'll always be grateful to him for saving me and my baby."
Commander Baillie then spoke and there was an impromptu few words from Heinrich who took the microphone and said, "I just wanted to say thanks, thanks for your friendship, guys. I'm gonna miss you."
Connors got up then and said, "Deva, I ain't forgot, I still owe you one."

Suddenly all the security team were standing and began a round of applause. The Sikarans looked at each other then Marayshan brought them to attention and saluted the human soldiers who then saluted in return. Then, several other people in the hall picked up. Saunders started to call for a speech from Marayshan.
Marayshan went to the microphone accompanied by a huge round of applause. He had become quite a celebrity aboard the starship.
"How can I speak when I am crying?" he began. "But I will have to stop zis, because I have quite a lot that I wish to say to all of you." It took him a moment, but with Nava's help, he pulled himself together.

"First, I wish to thank you on behalf of my men and I for this wonderful send-off. I do not think any of us will ever forget it. Thank you also for the gifts that we will treasure and for your friendship. And thank you to some of you for your love. I know that Voshan is taking his girlfriend with him. Lucy Price, you have made him very happy. And Alice Morgan, Harith is overjoyed that you will be accompanying him also to Naiobi. We are very pleased too to have some of the security team joining ze Naiobi Police as Peace Officers, so we can continue to work with them. Well, now zat I have said all the fun things, I need to make a more serious speech. Captain Grey knows about zis and he has been contacted by the Sikaran High Council with my authorization to speak on their behalf. Captain Grey has arranged for this speech to be broadcast to all the allies of *Interspace*, to the planets Earth, Ringul and Kalesia and for the message to go out on 'extra-range' to reach the home world of the Gloshan Empire."

There was suddenly complete silence in the hall.

Captain Grey said, "Marayshan, all communications are in place now, so you can go ahead whenever you're ready."

Marayshan nodded and thanked him, and then he put on his reading glasses and took out his speech.

"To all leaders and people of Earth, Ringul and Kalesia, I greet you." he began. "I am Marayshan of the Levthiryin Clan, Shield Lord of the *Isithan*. I have been authorized to speak on behalf of the Sikaran High Council. Half a Galactic year ago, my people acknowledged that we had made a serious error in siding with the Gloshans in the space war and so we changed sides and allied ourselves with *Interspace*. Now we wish to make more positive moves to end this space war once and for all. This message comes in response to a recent atrocity committed by a group of Gloshans led by a Captain named Kaleen, known personally to me. He was the commander of the Gloshan war camp *K'Taak*. I refer now to the capture of the Earth civilian space passenger vessel '*Carlotta*'. I do not need to remind you of the horror of what Kaleen did to the humans aboard as he took great delight in broadcasting film of what he had done to the whole of the galaxy. I presume you are listening to me, Kaleen. I hope that you are, because I have something to say to you. I am certain that you remember me from our time together in Camp *K'Taak* when our people were allies. Kaleen, I have made a solemn pledge that this is the last atrocity you will ever commit, and you know me, Kaleen. You know that I keep my word in everything, so rest assured that I am going to get you for this and it is personal. People of Earth, Ringul and Kalesia: the order has been given to mobilize all Sikaran forces in preparation for the final battle in this space war. All space battle cruisers are moving into position. All military personnel are standing by on High Alert awaiting my order to begin a full-scale attack on the Gloshan Empire. I speak now to the Gloshan Warlord Shtol. The High Council of Sikarus gives you an ultimatum: we require your unconditional surrender to us within three months of today. If you do not surrender, this is what will happen to your home planet of *Gloshos*. We will knock out your planetary defences one by one and then we will target the infrastructure of the planet. We will not harm civilians, however, and will give them sufficient time to evacuate before each area is destroyed. You must surrender. Your entire space fleet must stand down and immobilize all weapons."

"Captain Grey," said Alice Morgan, "a message is being relayed in *Gloshanese* to Captain Marayshan. Our translators can only pick out some of the words however. We're really sorry, sir, we can't give you the whole message." Alice Morgan said.

Marayshan replied, "It is no problem, Alice, I speak *Gloshanese*. Let me hear the transmission." After a few moments it ended.

Marayshan spoke again. "Ah. It is mostly in Gloshan slang. That is why your translators could not understand it. It is mostly swearing actually. I am being told by Warlord Shtol, to go and take my *ichvru* and shove it up my *utchaya*. Perhaps I had better not translate all of that. In a nutshell, the Gloshans are not going to surrender to us."

Some of the other Sikarans winced as they also knew the meanings of the slang words. The security men laughed.

Marayshan continued. "People of Earth, Ringul and Kalesia, I am raising the yellow flag. Since Warlord Shtol has refused to surrender, this has changed things and so today in your hearing, we begin the first stage of our final offensive against the Gloshan Empire. All Sikaran space battle cruisers, you have your orders. Immobilize every Gloshan space vessel you encounter, but do not destroy them. Take them back to the Sikaran Empire and confiscate all weaponry. All Gloshan crews are to be debriefed and re-educated. They will be taught that there are better ways to live than to forever fight a space war. All Sikaran forces, the yellow flag has gone up. The final battle is approaching. May Var be with you: *Elaran, Isithan, Isithan, Kai-ithan. Hai Cheh!*"

Pausing, he then added, "All Sikaran battle cruisers and all military forces on my command: begin the first stage of the final offensive against the Gloshan Empire. *Chyasar, chyasar, chyasar! J'yi ashar. Chyasar, chyasar, chyasar!*" He repeated it in Galactic, "Attack, attack, attack! I repeat, attack, attack, attack!"

He paused again then added, "So now I will address myself to all soldiers of *Gloshos* who knew me in Camp *K'Taak* and who became my friends. Soldiers of *Gloshos*, you who are brave and strong: *now* is the time to show your allegiance to me. Rise up and stand against your Warlord Shtol. Fight with pride alongside the *Isithan*. The final battle is almost upon us. Let us, between us, bring peace to the galaxy and your names will be honoured forever in the halls of your ancestors. We, the *Isithan,* the Soldiers of the Dawn, salute you. Stand up now and be counted. Fight *for* us not against us. The trumpet has sounded for the final battle. May our god Var be with us as we move forward to defeat Warlord Shtol and Captain Kaleen and all who side with them: take courage and stand: do not lose heart because the *Isithan* will never desert you in your time of need and you know we are true to our word. My friends, may Var be with you."

"Captain, all Sikaran forces are responding!" Alice Morgan said urgently. "All Sikaran battle cruisers reporting in to you, Shield Lord; they are saying,
'*Yellow for go, yellow for go, attack protocol, acknowledged, attack protocol, acknowledged; moving into position around the perimeter of Gloshan space and to the Kaloris border lands, and on course to all Gloshan bases.*' Other battle cruisers are saying that they are heading for *Lasos 5* and the other colonies taken over by Gloshans, in order to begin the liberation of the people there. Your Number Three Squadron is reporting in, sir. They have taken up positions on the perimeter of Gloshan space and await further orders."

Marayshan replied, "Number Three Squadron, take out the sector defences for the northern quadrant and wait for Squadrons One, Two and Four to arrive."

"Sir, Squadrons Two and Four have arrived and Squadron One is on its way. All Squadrons now in position at the perimeter," Alice said.

A message came in then on the extra-range channel and Alice said,

"Wait! This message is from a Gloshan space warship captained by Kaleen. They say they have captured an Earth far-space colony of fifty thousand humans and will wipe out everyone and everything unless you withdraw immediately from the Gloshan perimeter. The colony is *Aldebaran* 9."

Marayshan reacted quickly, "Attention all Sikaran battle cruisers in Squadrons One, Two, Three and Four. Withdraw from the perimeter. I repeat. Withdraw from the perimeter. This is an emergency retreat due to a hostage situation. Captain Kaleen has taken the human colony *Aldebaran* 9 and will destroy it unless we retreat. Kaleen, we are standing down, release ze humans from *Aldebaran* 9," Marayshan said.

"Hello Shield Lord Marayshan," said Captain Kaleen, "ah, bright, bright, bright. I think I will kill the humans anyway, just for fun, or perhaps I will keep them and have even more fun with them," said Kaleen. "What do you think?"

"Touch just one of ze humans, Kaleen, and we will destroy your home world from one end to the other. I mean it! We will wipe it off the face of this galaxy and you along with it!" Marayshan responded angrily.

"All right, all right, I wasn't being serious, Marayshan. It is just my little joke. You know what I am like. Don't you remember? I liked my little jokes, especially with the alien prisoners. Oh yes, I did like my little jokes in Camp *K'Taak*, didn't I?"

A cold fury settled on Marayshan as he spoke at length in Sikaran.

"I did not quite understand that, Marayshan. I do not speak Sikaran. What did you say, ah, bright, bright, bright?" said Kaleen, in an insinuating, sickly sweet voice. "I do so like to hear you speak. It makes me feel well very, very good all over. I don't think I ever told you that, no, I don't think I did. I thought I would keep it as a nice little surprise for you. Such a nice little surprise: just you and me on our own, together. Somewhere on a lovely warm beach; you would have your arms around me and *choy i-shu diat-thu jiassu dh-sinitu*." He said the last few words in *Gloshanese* then went back into Galactic.

Alice Morgan looked at the translation of the words on her screen, with a shocked expression on her face and covered her mouth with her hand and the expressions on the faces of Marayshan and his men spoke volumes.

"You know, I recorded your voice, each time you came to speak with me, and I recorded you when you sang around the camp too. I would listen to it, over and over again, and listen to it ever so softly in the still of the night, ever so softly. And then I would go and play my little jokes on the alien prisoners. I thought I could make them laugh, but all they ever did was scream and that was such a shame, you know, such an awful pity."

"Kaleen, I knew something was wrong with you, but I never realized the full extent of your problems. You know, you need help. When I find you, I will take you to ze Central Temple on *Sikarus* and the priests will try to help you. Would you like that, Kaleen? In the meantime, please leave the humans on *Aldebaran* 9 alone. Will you do that for me, just for me, Kaleen?" Marayshan responded.

"As you ask so nicely, ah, bright, bright, bright, Marayshan, I will leave them alone. Did you know that I have a container full of holographic images of you and I look at them often and I touch them ever so softly; I have had a little statue of you made too and I play with it; I hold it and kiss it, and it speaks to me in the silence; I can hear it speaking to me in the silence. No one else can hear it though. I wonder why?"

"What does it say to you, Kaleen?" Marayshan asked, in disbelief looking around at his men.

"It says, 'I love you, Kaleen, and why don't you try to be nicer to people?' But I do try, you know, I do, I really try." He laughed manically. "By the way, I am nowhere near *Aldebaran* 9. That was a little bluff. Sorry, I just wanted to get your attention, Shield Lord. I hope I have not made you too cross with me. Please do not be too cross with me. Although, that would mean you would just have to punish me just a little when next we met, wouldn't it? And I would so like that, you know. I really would," he said, whispering the words.

"Var," Marayshan said furiously, unable to take much more, "Squadrons One, Two, Three and Four, resume your positions around the perimeter and begin taking out the perimeter defences. Do it now!"

"Marayshan, you won't forget, will you? I do hope that we meet again. Oh I do hope so and then you will put your arms around me, won't you?" He laughed strangely.

"Kaleen, *please, please, will you get off this line*," said Marayshan very calmly, "I am in the middle of conducting a very important space battle here. Now listen to me, will you listen, put on some of your favourite music now and go to sleep. It will make you feel better. And leave the humans alone. Will you do that for me? Any human you come across, no matter who, just leave them alone, all right?"

"Of course I will do that for you. You only had to ask, Shield Lord. Your voice is so beautiful. I love it just as I love you. I do hope we meet again soon."

Marayshan could not stop himself from shuddering in disgust and covered his eyes with his hand for a moment then said, "Goodbye, Kaleen. I am sure we will meet again, but I hope we will not."

"Goodbye, Shield Lord, your statue is speaking to me," Kaleen whispered in reply.

There was a stunned silence from everyone in the room including Marayshan who looked from Alice Morgan to Lawrence Grey, who both looked back at him with a mixture of shock and sympathy.

Captain Grey went to stand beside Marayshan and said, "The man sounds like a complete maniac, Marayshan. I shouldn't let him worry you, and he may be beyond anyone's help. Even the priests in your Central Temple may not be able to do anything for him."

Marayshan nodded, "It is possible that nothing will ever help him, Captain Grey, but I believe that miracles can still happen in this galaxy. The problem is that he is incredibly dangerous, even in his present condition."

Marayshan sent out an extra-range message then to Warlord Shtol. "Warlord Shtol, I know that you can hear me, so please don't pretend that you cannot. Tell me, what it will benefit you to lose most of the infrastructure of your home planet *Gloshos?* It will only harm your people, your own people. You will lose all the ancient treasures of your ancestors. Why must this be? Give it up, Shtol. Surrender to me; you cannot out-shoot and out-manoeuvre the entire Sikaran Space Fleet. We are too powerful for you. Give it up."

"A channel has opened from Warlord Shtol," said Alice Morgan, with anxiety in her voice.

Marayshan nodded. "I see I have got your attention, Shtol. Listen to me. You must stand down now. Do not let this happen to your people. I know how they feel about their home world, how deeply they and you care about *Gloshos*. Surrender to us and we will be merciful, Shtol. Once you and I were friends, weren't we?"

"Ah dark dark dark; yes, friends we were once, at least that was my belief, but now, you left us, you deserted us. So, in order to have your friendship back, I suppose I must surrender, and then we can be friends again, I suppose. But I don't think I want to be your friend anymore, so no, I won't surrender. Not even for you, Marayshan, much as I like you."

"Shtol, then at least do one thing for me, for the sake of our old friendship, tell me where Kaleen is hiding. I wish to take him to the Central Temple on Sikarus."

"What will they do with him there? Well, I suppose you can have him, for he is past his usefulness to me. I cannot understand what is wrong with him these days; he used to be my right hand man. Now he dribbles sometimes when he speaks. He is such an embarrassment to me. I cannot stand to have him near me. You will find him at *Chanurgh isath*, patrolling the northern sector of *Kaloris*."

"Then you have deserted your old friend Kaleen too, even as I deserted you."

"Yes, I suppose that is true, if you put it that way. Sorry I can't oblige by surrendering to you, but that's just the way things are here, you know – no one has ever surrendered on *Gloshos*. Not the done thing you know: ah, dark, dark, dark."

"Shtol, I want you to consider it, to think carefully about it, I want you just to try and think for once in your life!" Marayshan shouted, letting his anger get the better of him for the first time. "Shtol, we are much more powerful than you. You cannot win this space war, so let us end it now, and let us have peace for the galaxy. Please. Let us have peace."

"But I think that we can win the space war, Marayshan, I believe that we can defeat you," said Shtol mildly.

"You are deluded if you believe that, Shtol," Marayshan replied.

"We Gloshans have never been defeated."

"You Gloshans have never fought against the Sikaran Empire before."

"True, but we are not afraid. We will not surrender, Marayshan, don't be silly."

"I want you to take time to consider it, Shtol. I will give you another six months to think about it."

"Well, I suppose I could think about it, couldn't I? All right, that's what I will do. Tell me, do you think the people in your Central Temple will be able to stop Kaleen from being an embarrassment to me?"

"I am not sure, Shtol. He has an illness of the mind and it is severe."

"But no one ever needs help with their minds. Don't be silly. Listen, I must share this with you. I have thirty Interspace spies in my dungeons. I am planning the most splendid Grand Execution for them you know. It will be such fun. There will be all kinds of entertainments, the kind of thing that Kaleen really loves."

"Shtol, I have told you about that before. You should not execute prisoners, let alone use them for your entertainment. You are infringing the galactic *Treaty of Naforek* which protects prisoners of space war."

"Oh Marayshan, don't be silly. I really do not care about the *Treaty of Naforek*, you know that. I allowed you to take my prisoners away from my dungeons once before to please you when you were my friend. I allowed you to make that bargain with me, remember? You will not have them this time though, oh no. No, no, no, despite the fact that I would dearly love to make another such bargain with you. This will be the best entertainment programme ever, you will see. And it will take place in thirty days, on the *Time of Planting Seed* and I will broadcast it to the entire galaxy that they may see my *ichvru* brimming over with power and my potency will dazzle all who behold it."

"Shtol, no one in the galaxy wants to see your *ichvru*. This is very wrong. Do not do this please," Marayshan said.

"Now you are boring me, Marayshan," Shtol replied. "So, please, go away. I will speak to you another day when you are in a better mood. I do not like it when you are not nice to me, ah: dark, dark, dark!"

He closed communications.

Marayshan sighed in exasperation then said, "Alice, please put me through to my squadrons. Thank you. Attention, attention, attention, all Sikaran battle cruisers and military forces. The Gloshan Warlord Shtol will not surrender. Approach all Gloshan vessels with extreme caution, attack but try not to destroy them and then impound them and take them back to the Sikaran Empire. I would like Squadrons One, Two and Three, to stay in position on the perimeter. Secure each sector of Gloshan space as you capture it. It will be a long and dangerous task, but it will be worth it. If you can, take Warlord Shtol into custody. Somebody please find the Gloshan Captain Kaleen. He is in a space warship near *Chanurgh isath,* patrolling the northern sector of *Kaloris*. Take him to the Central Temple on *Sikarus* as soon as possible, for all our sakes. He is extremely mentally ill. Ask them to take care of him. Do not, I repeat, do not let him approach any humans you happen to meet on the way. Squadron Four, I have a task for you. Go secretly to *Gloshos* and break into Warlord Shtol's dungeons. You will find thirty *Interspace* spies there. I want you to rescue them if you can and return them to their homes. You have to do this within thirty days or Shtol will prepare a Grand Execution for them to celebrate the *Time of Planting Seed* and you know everything that goes with that. We cannot allow him to do this. The rest of you, continue to keep to agreed protocols. This is your Shield Lord closing communications for the present. Please keep in touch with me and tell me your progress: Var be with you all."

INTERLUDE: <u>PART 2</u>

Here is the second of a series of articles commissioned by and published in the weekly *beta*-Naiobi Chronicle. All Sikaran words are written in italics.

Article 2: Shield Lord Marayshan's thoughts of his time in space with the Sikaran Flagship '*Voran*'.

Now that I have been the Governor of the Naiobi colonies for over a year, I have to say that I am thoroughly enjoying my life on Naiobi amongst the predominantly Human colonists here. Those who tend to settle in these colonies are usually Human, even though there are those from other parts of the galaxy who visit and stay for short periods of time, like the Sulans, Kalesians and Ringulians. They come because like Sikarans and Gloshans. They are very human in appearance and compatible with Humans in many ways and thus wish to interact and socialize with them.

I have noticed that Human people have a great difficulty in accepting aliens who are not human to look at. They become disproportionately afraid. Of course, the reason for this may be that Humans have not had much exposure to other types of peoples as my friends and I have had, being Sikaran and accustomed to space travel.

We do not feel in any way frightened or threatened. For instance, we meet Kilarans, who are bug-eyed creatures with thirty tentacles, four mouths, and two heads. They are friendly creatures and like to make the acquaintance of any people alien to themselves by wrapping a tentacle around them and singing a Kilaran song to them. A few months ago, I tried to introduce a Human friend to the Kilaran ambassador, but things did not work out. My Human friend almost lost his wits through fear. As a result, the Kilaran ambassador now has to restrict his conversation only to Sikarans like myself and my men who are stationed here on Naiobi.

I have had requests from the Human colonists here to describe several things for them. I have been asked to write down some of the events that happened to me when I was in the Sikaran Space Fleet aboard the Flagship *'Voran'*. They have also asked me to detail any incidents I can think of that might highlight the differences between Humans and Sikarans. Our two peoples are quite similar in many ways, even though unlike Humans, our complexions are a violet colour We have ears that look a little different to Humans and our metabolism is based on manganese and not iron. The Human Chief of Police Captain, Geoffrey Maitland, has also requested that I write something about our Sikaran justice system, as so many Sikaran soldiers here work as Peace Officers with the Human Police Force.

As I have said, Sikarans are very similar to Humans to look at, except that we have violet-coloured complexions, and not only that, many of our feelings and emotions overlap with those of Human people. Sikaran ethical and moral dilemmas can usually find a comparison somewhere in Human society.

After speaking with my Sikaran friends, we decided to pinpoint one particular incident that happened aboard the Flagship *'Voran'*, which we felt our Human friends would think was very different from anything they were likely to experience. It might also seem quite alien to their understanding. It will also elucidate something about our criminal justice system. So this is what I have been asked to do by the Humans here and this is what I have done. I will make no apology for it, even though I sense that those Humans who read what I have written will find it difficult, and should not read on if they are not prepared to be unsettled by it.

Let me proceed to my life aboard the Flagship *'Voran'*. You will be relieved to know that whatever I write, from this point on, is included with the permission of those who are named or, if they are deceased, then their nearest relatives, and there is one whom I will speak of by the name of *Kavril*, who has long since faded or 'passed away' as it is termed by Humans.

As you know, Captain Lierschvaan ('Lee' for short) is the military Principal of the private Human school here, so I will write something about how we first met aboard ship. Captain Lierschvaan was a Commander when I first came aboard the *'Voran'* as an Ensign and a three-year conscripted man. Unless we enter the space fleet of our own accord at an earlier age, Sikaran men and women are all required to do three years active service in our Space Fleet when they reach the age of thirty.

Lierschvaan was a career officer, and had joined the merchant space fleet when he was nineteen-years-old. He did a year there and joined the Land Army then for several years and, from there, he was recruited into the main Space Fleet. He is about fifteen years older than me. I was also in the Land Army on a five-year commission and having a talent for it, rose quickly to the rank of Lieutenant, as indeed did Lierschvaan before he went into the main Space Fleet.

As I went up in the ranks of the *Isithan*, that is, the Sikaran Special Forces, I was promoted in parallel by the Land Army. As I became a full Brother of the Sword, I became a Lieutenant Colonel of the Land Army despite not being on active service with them at the time. That is how our military life is organized: once we are in the *Isithan*, we become ranked in the Land Army even if we have not joined up.

About six months after I was conscripted into the Space Fleet, I was made into a full Colonel of the Land Army, and was now ranked the same as Lierschvaan. Even though in the Space Fleet, he was then a Commander and I began ironically as the most junior officer rank, an Ensign. Avernyi and Navaronschvia ('Nava' for short) were also given the honorary ranks of Lieutenant in the Land Army, although they had never joined as Lierschvaan and I had done. Lierschvaan had been recruited for the Space Fleet as an Executive Officer in charge of ship's discipline. This was a post that could only be filled by an officer ranked by the Land Army, so it would have to be someone who had been on active Land Army service or in the *Isithan*. It happened that Lierschvaan was both these things, so there were many similarities in our careers as we progressed. When we left active service in the Space Fleet as Captains, we were also both Generals in the Land Army.

I have to admit that Lierschvaan did sometimes amuse himself on the *'Voran'* at my friend Navaronschyia's expense. He realized, quite early on, that Nava was rather wary of him, and he found out that Nava thought that Lee liked him more than was usual for two men, even though Lee was not like that. So, sometimes Lee played on it.

In those days, Lierschvaan could be rather a difficult character and, being a Commander with responsibility for ship's discipline, he was also extremely powerful. However, over the time we were on the *'Voran'*, I saw him change in some ways; he grew kinder and less inclined to pick on people. Actually, he never did aggravate Nava when I was around, but at other times in small ways, he did get at my friend. However, I think Lee made it up with Nava, because one day when my friend was day dreaming on duty--something he often did, he made a serious error. The section head reported it to Lierschvaan as a disciplinary matter. But when Lierschvaan checked over Nava's work, he said that it was computer error that had caused the disruption, and did not log any punishment for Nava although it would have been a flogging offence for dereliction to duty.

Lierschvaan saved him, which was a very uncharacteristic thing for Lee to do in those days, and Nava thanked him later. In my book, that made up for all past hurts suffered by Nava, but it was not entirely the case with Nava. He took things much more to heart and he never forgot Lierschvaan's pettiness during the first year we were aboard. When we first arrived on the *'Voran'*, I noticed that even the royal officers were a little wary of Lierschvaan. He had a reputation for being the best discipline officer in our Space Fleet and he was extremely good at the job.

When I first met Lierschvaan, we seemed to develop a rapport. I sensed he was not as tough as he would have people believe, and that he would have wished to be comradely with the crew. But there was no way he could be, and I believe the job had brutalized him to some extent. As a three-year conscripted man, I was in an unusual position. I was both in the *Isithan* and the Land Army like Lee, and I felt that this allowed him more freedom to speak with me than with the other recent additions to the crew. I sensed that he needed to talk and to know that his words would not be passed on to the rest of the crew.

I was accustomed to keeping people's confidences as I had worked as a *Davracha*, which was, in some ways, similar to what Humans call a "welfare worker." I was sure Lee sensed that I had been a welfare worker, even before it became public knowledge during the incident with Count Viathol. Lee latched onto me surprisingly quickly. The first few times he came and sat with Avernyi, Nava and I, all he did was have one quick drink with us and go.

At last, he stayed to have a second drink and it was obvious to my friends that he wanted to talk to me on my own and so they left us together. The first thing I asked was not perhaps the most tactful, but still, I asked it.
"How does someone get to be the ship's monster? What's it like being a Discipline Officer, Commander?"
"Why don't you find out," he replied. "I have a vacancy for an assistant discipline officer and no one has applied for the job yet." It did not surprise me that no one had put in for the job.
"Well, I'll think about it, but it may not be my kind of thing, Commander," I said, then smiled at him.
"Then you are a something of a welfare worker, am I right?" he said astutely. I nodded.

"I suspected that was the case when I first met you. You have a kind smile. It says to me that this is a man who is going to be very popular with the crew, so I suppose that there's really no point in you applying to be my assistant."

"Aren't Discipline Officers very popular then, Commander?" I replied in my usual forthright way.

This made Lierschvaan laugh, which surprised many in the officer lounge. I had hardly seen him laugh in the few weeks since I had boarded, and obviously they had hardly seen him laugh for a lot longer than that.

We took up our drinks. "Cheers!" I said, clicking glasses with him, and drank my drink, like him, in one mouthful, then poured a new lot of *iskari*.

Lierschvaan smiled a thin, forced smile as though he had forgotten how to do so.

"You know, I don't usually say 'cheers'. I usually say ….." he whispered a slang word to me that was only used by the lowest of clans and then by the commonest of them.

"Why do you use that word, Commander?" I asked, genuinely surprised. "You don't seem to be common, even though your mother is from Clan Gira."

"I grew up on the streets of Miuskva, Ensign. Remember, I told you I lived in the slums on the East Side? Remember I showed you the quick way to the market down there the other day when we went planet-side before we began the mission?" he replied.

"Yes, I know, but you sound very cultured, sir," I said, "too cultured for words like that."

"No, my mother is Clan Gira but my father is very cultured," he said. "I think he comes from a High Clan."

"You think? You mean you don't know? How is that?" I asked, surprised.

"They married very young, my parents," he replied. 'They fell in love, but my father's clan deserted him because he married into Clan Gira. My mother is very common. I used to get angry a lot because my father was unhappy with his life in the slums, but he never told us, his clan. And, he tried not to show his feelings, but I sensed how he felt inside and it sent me wild when I was a youth. I really hated the High Clans. I still do."

"I can't believe you were wild when you were young," I said, holding his gaze.

"It is true,' he replied. "I got in with one street gang and then another and another, each one worse than the last. I played truant at school and ended up as a gang leader."

I did not reply, but he covered my hands with his and, through touch telepathy, he let me sense that he was telling me the truth.

"*Var,*" I said quietly, and I realized it was the first time he had ever told anyone aboard ship. I could feel his relief and embarrassment mingled, and his anxiety as he wondered how I would take it.

"You had quite a boyhood then, all things considered. You've done well to get where you are today, with all the truanting. How did you manage to get an education?" I asked.

"My father taught me at home, when I refused to attend school," he said. "Mmy father is very learned. He's been writing books for years and now he makes a decent living out of it. My mother is clever too. Despite playing truant, I never missed any school exams. I was always one of the first there. This baffled my teachers and, even more baffling for them, was that I passed all the exams without cheating. Later, I joined the merchant space fleet and then I entered the Land Army then moved to the front line in the space war. I became a career officer and worked hard for my wife and children." I smiled at him. For some reason, he seemed keen to impress me.

"When did you join the *Isithan*, Commander?" I asked.

"That's a story in itself. When I was nineteen-years-old, the *Isithan* heard that I was a successful gang leader and decided that they wanted me. They took me away from Miuskva, initiated me into the *Isithan*, put me in a uniform from the merchant space fleet and booked me onto the first merchant vessel they could find. It was just after the Second Gang Wars on the East Side of Miuskva."

"You took part in the Second Gang Wars?" I said incredulously, and he nodded. I should not have asked which side he had been on, but I did. The answer gave me pause for thought. He did not speak the name of the gang, but traced out three letters of the alphabet on the table, checking first that we were not overlooked. He traced the three letters that I did not want to see: *Ja – Vo – Ra*, the name of the most notorious street gang in Miuskva. The letters stood for *Javissa Vothara Rasirra* (which translated into Galactic, means: "Those who have no fear of God," or "Fearless and Godless". There are other translations, but I will not include them here).

"What about their famous tattoos?" I asked.
"I have covered them with synthetic skin," he said quietly.

I said no more, but poured out another drink for him and began to deal a hand of cards for both of us.

"No! Don't! I can't!" he whispered, "A Commander should not be seen playing cards with an Ensign, not in here anyway, even if you are much too old to be an Ensign and are ranked in the Land Army as I am. In my quarters, another time.'

"I'm sorry, Commander. I didn't realize," I replied quietly and put the cards to one side.

Lierschvaan did something then that I had not expected him to do. He tried to be discrete, but many eyes caught his next move. He reached and took my hand and held it, willing us to be friends. I let the feeling pass to him that I would be a friend if he wanted me to be and, again, he managed a smile. I decided then to be bold in my usual fashion and, in an open gesture of acknowledgement of friendship, I rested my other hand on his chest.

I thought, hang it. Why should Lierschvaan want to be so discrete, after all? We were roughly the same age. Now, I have to say that this gesture really was noticed, and stunned many to silence, including Lierschvaan. He did not speak again, but after a long moment, he stood, removed my hand carefully from his chest and, in answer to my open gesture, he made one himself. He lifted my hand to his forehead in acceptance of all that friendship can offer. It was not *Darth Ishala,* by any means, but it was one step in that direction. He bowed to me then and left the officer lounge.

I was not alone for long because the 2nd Officer a royal officer, Prince Evroshette, joined me then, and that did surprise me. He began, "I could not help but notice that you have a new friend. I am pleased for Lierschvaan. I believe he needs someone to confide in. Now, I have come for some advice, Ensign. The Captain tells me that you give very good advice on personal matters. My sister is due to join the '*Voran*' shortly as an Ensign. Like you, she is older than average for that rank. But I needed her to be near me, so that I can take care of her. She has of late been quite ill."

"What has been the matter with her, Prince Evroshette?" I asked.

"My sister Valeya was trapped by a man from Galthais. Valeya went to visit an acquaintance exiled there, knowing the risks, but thought she was able to look after herself. It was the poison of a *votharis* that trapped her and held her, until I requested the High Priest of the Central Temple to rescue her from there and take her into a hospital. Now that Valeya is recovered she can be with me, but I am worried about her. She has lost her gaiety and love of life. Only sadness seems to follow her now."

"I am very sorry, Prince. Your sister has been through a lot," I said.

He nodded thoughtfully, then said, "Ensign, will you walk with me to my quarters? It is not easy to talk here."

I got up and went with him.

Once inside his quarters, he surprised me even further by telling me that, like Lierschvaan, he wished to be my friend, but because he was royal, it would have been difficult to take my hand in public, so he did it in the privacy of the cabin. I would never have expected a prince to acknowledge friendship to someone from the Levthiryin Clan, even though he might be feeling it.

"Will you accept my friendship?" he asked astonishingly.

"Yes, of course, Prince. You do me great honour," I replied, bowing over his hand.

"Are you only saying that because I am royal and you do not wish to offend me?" he asked.

"No, actually, when you first sat down at the table tonight, I was thinking that I would like to make a friend of you, but I thought that it would be impossible because of your royal status," I replied.

"It pleases me greatly that you also wish to be my friend," Evroshette smiled, and then continued. "If you wish, you may touch me, to return the gesture. I would have no objection." I placed my hand on his chest, as I had done with Lierschvaan, and held his gaze for a long moment. I had the feeling that he was a royal that I could trust and one that I would like to have as a true friend, *Darth Ishala* in our language.

"I, too, wish for true friendship with you," he replied, sensing my thought. "In time, I am sure that we shall speak the vows of *Darth Ishala*. I would like that very much. Only once before have I had a true friend, but he died in the space war."

Friendship drew us together then and we rested our hands on each other's faces for a moment. Longer than that would not have been proper as we were only beginning a friendship, and then we touched palms. So it was that I made a friend of a prince named Evroshette and an ex-gang leader named Lierschvaan. I also thought that I had made an enemy of an arrogant and extremely irritating Count named Viathol within the first three months of being aboard the '*Voran*'.

There were many dull hours aboard the flagship, despite our attempts at entertaining each other by arguing or telling tall tales. There were also some computer-generated games in the various recreation areas and I used to book myself in as often as I could when I was off duty, and not caught up with someone else's problems. Mind you, I did enjoy a good problem, but I still needed some time for my hobbies and I was able to lose myself in the computer-generated games.

They were fast moving space games and if you could break the record of points awarded, then you could win prizes of one thousand, three thousand or ten thousand sillar, which had been put up by the company who produced the game as a promotional effort. These were greatly coveted sums by those of us from the low clans. I was good at that kind of "shoot down the aliens" game. There had been two such games consoles in Kirai, and Navaronschyia, Avernyi and I had often fought against each other in such competitions when we were boys. I got to be really good at it and often got the highest score, even when we challenged the boys from the next village of Devoya.

Aboard the flagship, I had my eye on the one thousand sillar prizes and was sure that it was in my grasp, so I put my name down for a turn, every night. Each allocated slot lasted thirty minutes, and people would usually watch the game as it progressed. If you started on level 3, you could easily go for the prize, in the half hour that you had, but it was no easy matter. This was a good way of relieving boredom though, and when I played, it seemed to attract a lot of people, from the lowest of crewmen and crewwomen to the officers.

I began to notice that Count Viathol was there often with Prince Evroshette. Lierschvaan would follow. Avernyi and Nava noticed it, too, and commented upon it once or twice, then accepted that in my off-duty hours, those three officers appeared to follow me around. Evroshette and Lierschvaan were new friends, so I could understand that, but why Viathol followed me around was a mystery. I realized why later, of course, but then I was frankly baffled by it.

Forcing me to kneel at his feet and striking me repeatedly, in a way that could have initiated a clan war, did not completely endear me to him when I first arrived on board. He was very childish then, and I think that he wanted to show that he could bully someone who was a full Brother of the Sword, so he took offense at something I said. It was Avernyi who stopped him hitting me, by informing him that I was also a fully licensed *Davracha* as well as an *Isithanyi* (full Brother of the Sword). He was completely incredulous that I should be a *Davracha*, but the thought of such a bogus claim amused him so much that he left me alone.

The night that I won the game, I was coming to the end of my thirty-minute slot, with three minutes to go. I reached level twenty and got the one thousand sillar prizes.

A voice called out from the crowd, "Keep going, Marayshan, I'm on next so you can have my go!"

Another voice came from the game console and said, "Congratulations! Now that you have the one thousand sillar prize, will you continue for the ten thousand sillar reward?"

I pressed the "yes" button, and a hush fell across the room as I began to play again.

What seemed like hundreds of alien vessels flashed up on the screen and I had to shoot them down at breakneck speed. They were coming at me from all angles, but by an incredible stroke of luck, I kept my cool and shot them all. The lights flashed and music sounded and I had won the major prize. I could not believe it. The two tokens came out of the machine and I looked at them wondering if they were genuine. I took them over to Prince Evroshette and showed them to him.

"Do you think that they really are worth anything, Prince?" I asked him.

He took them from me and said, "I shall check whether they are or not. Cousin Viathol, come with me, let us validate these tokens."

They went to a recessed wall computer and Evroshette slotted the tokens into a gap in the wall. I found out later from them that these words came up on the screen, "Not validated: tokens worth nothing." Apparently Evroshette then rapidly scrambled the screen so no one else could see, and Viathol whispered, "Why don't we place money onto the tokens. We could go halves for the major prize, but not bother with the smaller one. Use our gaming accounts. My pass number is five hundred and twenty eight."

Evroshette nodded and whispered, "Say something. Tell them that the console has gone wrong. Keep them busy."

Viathol turned to us and said, "Something appears to be amiss with the computer terminal, but Evroshette will clear the problem in a moment, never fear."

Evroshette deftly moved three thousand sillar rapidly from each of his and Viathol's gaming accounts onto the tokens, and then said, "Ah, at last I have it.

Marayshan, the one thousand sillar token cannot be validated, but the ten thousand sillar token is validated! You have ten thousand sillar! Here! Take it and congratulations!"

"I have won ten thousand sillar!" I said, deliriously taking the token and kissing it.

"Well done. You played with great skill," said Viathol. "Those aliens never had a chance." He and Evroshette smiled at me and then at each other.

"It is well deserved. Do not lose it all at once in a card game," said Evroshette.

"A card game?" I replied. "Prince, this money is going home to the Arakiarth Valley, to my parents. All of it, I have five sisters who could do with some money for their dowries."

"So many sisters,' said Viathol. "It must be intolerable for you when you are at home. I find that one sister is quite enough."

Was Viathol trying to be friendly? Was it possible, I asked myself? They looked at each other, again, in a very conspiratorial way. Viathol's eyes moved to the token. I began to suspect something, something about the token, something that they had done to it.

I bowed to them and excused myself to all there and went to my quarters. Quickly, I called up my bank account and transferred the money from the token into it. I had managed to save one hundred and ninety-three sillar; all I had in the world, apart from my *Isithan* cloak, my clothes and of course, several beautiful dogs on the home farm, who had grown from puppies which I had bought over the years. I've always enjoyed buying puppies and there are many which are carefully bred, but can be had quite cheaply in the Arakiarth valley. Now, there were ten thousand, one hundred and ninety-three sillar in my bank account, but I was suspicious. I asked the computer whether the money had come from the company that had supplied the games machine. After a few moments the word "negative" came up on the screen.

"Where is it from then"' I asked.
"Origin of sources is blocked," came the reply.
I sat up and took notice.
"How many sources?"
"Two," came the reply.
"Why is the origin of the sources blocked?" I continued.
"Because the sources are encrypted bank accounts."
"Encrypted?" I said. "Speculate, who uses encrypted bank accounts?"

"Several groups," came the reply. "Royals, some high clan families, and anyone who possesses wealth that adds up to one million sillar or more. These are the only types of people who can possess encrypted accounts."

I exhaled slowly. I had no idea that you had to have so much money to open an encrypted bank account. Two sources. Viathol and Evroshette. It must be. I had absolutely no idea that they were so wealthy. I tried giving the money back to them, but they would not hear of it and blocked its path, so that it could not be returned to their accounts under any circumstances, although, believe me, I tried.

"You deserve it. You played superbly, with such skill," Evroshette said.

I wanted to hug both of them right there in the middle of the officer lounge, but I could not, being as they were both royal.

Evroshette realized my dilemma, then publicly took my hand and held it, followed by Viathol. Evroshette saw how much I had wanted to give the money back to him and Viathol, so he contacted the gaming company and got the prize money out of them for me. It was amazing what pressure from a royal can do. In the end, I gave some of the money to Navaronschyia and Avernyi, and then sent the rest to my father for my sisters' dowries.

When I first joined, the *Voran* Viathol chose to take exception to something I said and hit me as a consequence. It was a strange scene, happening in the midst of all in the officer lounge. Even the Captain was there. I stood when he had finished and looked directly at Viathol. He stopped laughing abruptly. I really don't think that he realized how much he had offended me. I believe my expression was grim as I turned to leave the room and the dogs of war bayed at my heels. Clan war: seeing my expression, men moved aside to let me pass. There were whispers of "Viathol, come, you must apologize quickly," from his clan compatriots. I could see even my two friends, Nava and Avernyi, looking at me in consternation. They too had read the words, "clan war" starkly in my eyes. It would mean bad news for everyone.

I went to my quarters, washed the blood from my cut lips, and found my licence. I returned to the Officer lounge, to find Viathol looking subdued, picking up the game of cards from where he had left off. I went to him and placed the licence on his cards as he held them. He looked at it.

Evroshette took it and said, "Viathol, this Ensign is a fully licensed *Davracha*. You must pay his clan compensation for hitting him."

"Very well, I shall pay," Viathol replied. He looked as pale as I looked grim. It was unusual for me to look like that.

"I take it that we are not about to go to war," Viathol said, briefly looking at me.

"*Davracha* don't usually start clan wars, Count," I replied. "On the other hand, full members of the *Isithan* do. Which shall I be today, do you think?"

"Be whichever you please! I care not!' Viathol replied petulantly. He sounded so childish that I had a great desire to slap him.

"Which would you like me to be, Count?" I said, folding my arms.

"How can a full *Isithanyi* be a *Davracha* too?" he demanded suddenly. 'It is unheard of! How was I to know? Tell me! How? In all the eons of the *Isithan*, there is not *one* who is a full Brother of the Sword *and* a welfare worker." Viathol was definitely rattled.

"Cousin Viathol," said Prince Mitellen, an ageing royal. "I must point out to you that I believe that clan honour has yet to be fully satisfied. Whenever a clan war is mentioned, in order for it to be fully put aside, the wronged party—in this case the peasant Marayshan, is at liberty to strike you three times, despite the fact that you are going to compensate his clan. He may strike you with as much force as he chooses."

The whole situation was worth it for me just to see the look on Viathol's face. However, I detected a hint of animosity towards Viathol in the old Royal's voice and wondered as to its background. As a *Davracha,* I did not want to be the instrument of anyone's vindictiveness, even though it might be directed at Viathol. So, I put aside my anger and my urge to strike back with any kind of harshness.

Viathol stood up then, saying, "Very well, I have no objection to honour being satisfied. You may strike me now as you please with as much force as you please, and considering that you are *Isithan*, I dare say that I can expect a great deal of force."

He looked at me and I looked at him. There were murmurs all around the room. He had turned very pale. Many of my low clan *Isithan* friends would have done Viathol considerable damage in three strikes and both he and I knew it. But I am not given to unnecessary shows of violence despite the provocation, even though others might be.

Viathol and I continued to look at each other and then I reached and took hold of his arm to steady him and hit him three times, but my hits were not hard because I merely slapped him. To my surprise, he went even paler if that was possible, and became rather tearful. I have to say that that did surprise me.

"He has hardly hurt you, Viathol! What ails you? You are not a coward," exclaimed the old Prince, as amazed by Viathol's reaction as I was.

"It is nothing but an allergic reaction," said Viathol. "My eyes water from time to time, that is all." But his voice belied the words, and I looked oddly at him.

"Excuse me, please," he said to those around him, and left the lounge. I left shortly afterwards, and followed him to his quarters and pressed the entrance buzzer.

"Come in, cousin," said a muffled voice. Viathol thought that one of his royal friends had followed him; they always called each other 'cousin' even though unrelated. I entered and a look of shock passed over him.

"Can I sit down, Count?" I asked.

He half-heartedly waved a hand towards a chair.

After I sat, I said, "I would like us to make peace with each other. Otherwise it will be difficult for us to work together on the Bridge." Viathol shrugged.

"Will you hold my hand as a peace offering?" I asked.

Viathol shrugged again. I held it out to him, but I never really expected him to respond. However, the day was full of surprises and he took my hand and held onto it for rather longer than seemed necessary.

"I hope that your allergy improves soon, Count," I said, looking directly at him. I tried a smile, but failed as the pain in my mouth was getting to me.

He shrugged again in reply.

"Count, I should go now. It is my first duty period on the Bridge. I should not be late for it,' I said then, wondering how to retrieve my hand without causing too much embarrassment on both sides.

"My cousin, the Captain, will not mind overmuch if you are late considering what has occurred. I see that your lip is still bleeding. You should attend to it first in sickbay and obtain some painkillers." He handed me his handkerchief to wipe the blood from my face. It was his way of saying sorry. Now, he hid his reluctance at having to release my hand, but I sensed his feelings and wondered what was really troubling him. About a year later, I found out.

I left him then, but went to the Bridge to do my duty, although he was right, I should have gone to sickbay first. Captain Javrayin, seeing that I had not sorted myself out, sent me there directly, exchanging glances with Prince Evroshette. The elderly Healer in sickbay was a very pleasant, friendly man, and asked me about myself. I told him that, as well as being an *Isithanyi,* I was a *Davracha* too and had done part-time nursing. He asked me if he could put me on his list of paramedical workers who were able to help out in sickbay in times of crisis. I said that I would be happy to help as long as the Captain agreed, and so he contacted Captain Javrayin, then and there, and cleared it with him.

So I passed the first week aboard ship gaining a great deal of sympathy from the crew who had heard what had occurred with Count Viathol, and could see the livid bruises for themselves and my badly cut mouth which made eating rather difficult. So, I drank liquid nutrition packs through a straw and dunked my bread in my soup. Captain Javrayin insisted on putting me on light duties for that week and the next, but I did not think that it was really necessary. I believe he was trying to make amends for what Viathol had done. Navaronschyia and Avernyi were a great support to me, one or the other of them were always with me at off duty times, until I was well and truly recovered, and my usual buoyant spirits had returned.

During that time, Viathol stayed very quiet. I think that some of his clan cousins had words with him. Time passed and he began to come and watch the computer games that I played on the mess deck, along with Lierschvaan and Prince Evroshette. They always sat at the same table, arriving ten minutes or so before it was my turn to play and leaving just as I finished. Prince Evroshette always bought me a drink, together with Avernyi and Navaronschyia, who were also usually there to cheer me on. Everyone cheered whenever I moved up a level in the game. I thought that it was very amusing that they should want to do such a thing, but they were all so bored. At that time we were going through a very quiet period in the space war. I often wondered whether our enemies were having the same difficulties.

By the time I became Captain of the Flagship *'Voran',* Evroshette was *Darth Ishala* with me, a true friend, like Navaronschyia and Avernyi. Viathol was no longer spiteful and petty. He had become quite a pleasant person to know and extremely generous to any of the low clan crew who happened to be in obvious need. He had begun to enjoy giving. Over the years I had watched him change from a malicious and petty man, to an extremely kind hearted person. He never did stop his dallying with the female crew, of course. It was as much a part of his character as breathing, I believe.

Recently, when I met Count Viathol again here on the Naiobi colonies, I did ask him whether he had achieved his ambition to dally with all the female crew aboard the *'Voran'* before he left the ship, and he replied, "Now, that would be telling, wouldn't it, Marayshan?"

From the look in his eyes and the expression in his voice, I was given to understand that he really had achieved his goal. Viathol took pride in being known as a playboy aboard the *'Voran'*, but he had changed now, and he had a young Human wife. Her name was Sally Miles, a Healer's daughter. Her parents, Gary and Sarah, were very pleasant, deeply caring Humans. It was a source of pride for a Sikaran to marry into the family of a Healer, and I believe that Viathol was proud of his young wife, who was very intelligent and already has some of the skills and temperament of a Healer herself.

Since Viathol left the Flagship *'Voran'* he became a Space Fleet Captain as Lierschvaan and I had been, and he took over a class 'B' battle cruiser and maintained his captaincy for six years. Lierschvaan and I had actually spurred him on to work for the exams, and since that captaincy he had really matured in many ways. He no longer had temper tantrums, for one thing, and he had become quite a family man for another. Avernyi, Navaronschyia and I found these temper tantrums a really entertaining experience, along with many others in the officer lounge when they occurred. They did not happen often, but it was worth being there when they did. He does still get angry, but it is a much cooler anger, and much more measured. I think he must have made a very strong captain.

***Here is a warning. May I now suggest that if you are Human and have read this article so far, that you do not read any further, if you are not prepared to be unsettled by what you read and learn about the Sikaran way of life. ***

Now let me go on. Something else, which is very interesting about Count Viathol, is the fact that he has extremely powerful touch telepathic skills. With the exception of me he possessed one of the most powerful minds amongst the officers aboard the *'Voran'*. However, he kept the fact well hidden from all of us, even from me, though my mind is *Isithan* trained and I am equal to Viathol in such skills. How did we find out that Viathol was thus skilled? It was only after a serious crime was committed aboard ship.

I am going to write about this incident in order to highlight the main differences between Humans and Sikarans, also in order to highlight the strength of character which none suspected Viathol possessed. The crimes committed amongst Sikarans fall into two categories: everyday crimes such as burglary, street crime and so on, and much rarer mind crimes, unlike Humans who only have one category of crime in their society and that is everyday crime, as they are not telepaths through touch as we are. We have a special Court system to try everyday crimes and a separate Judiciary to try mind crimes, that is, crimes of telepathic origin such as violations committed through touch telepathy, by one Sikaran upon another. These offences are thankfully rare in our society, and those who commit them are electronically tagged as a sanction and exiled for a certain length of time in a city called Galthais on the 1st world of the Sikaran Empire.

Now, the crime that was committed aboard the Flagship *'Voran'* was of a particularly nasty nature, and was a telepathic crime, done by a senior officer named Kavril, upon a young crewman named Ilashon, who was devastated by it and unable to return to duty for two weeks. It was our Chief Engineer who committed the crime and it shocked all of us to such an extent that the sentence given to him reflected the intensity of our feelings of compassion for Ilashon.

The Court set up was drawn from fifteen crewmembers and five officers, as laid down in our Fleet laws. We were out in deep space and could not easily return to our home empire. Captain Javrayin felt that the trial could take place as fairly on board as it would in a civil court back home, and said that we should relay the verdict back to our empire and log it in the Central Court on the 1st World. As I stated before, the usual sentence for a mind crime was that of exile to the city of Galthais for a number of years. However, we were not within easy reach of Galthais, neither were we able to do without our Chief Engineer for several years. We were in a dilemma, and it was partly ethical.

Thousands of years ago, our society used to pay back mind crimes with mind punishments, but that was in the bad old days, and mind punishments could be dreadful. Then we became an enlightened society and began to send people into exile instead as a punishment for such crimes. Now, there was no way to exile our Chief Engineer, and so we had to decide to revert to ancient ways.

I was one of the officers asked to be a part of the Court who were being assembled to try the case and Captain Javrayin was the convenor. The verdict we came up with would have been frowned upon in the empire, had we not been in deep space. We decided upon our verdict, and in a way it reflected Fleet Law, because it was a flogging, but a telepathic one, not a physical one, so it was something of a compromise, and did not involve mind torture in any form, as many ancient court sentences would have done. It would be something that was a one off event, quickly over, not to be prolonged for a period of days.

The idea of it still sent a chill through me though, and I knew that, as I had one of the most powerful minds among the officers, I might be called upon by the Court to carry out the sentence. However, it was to my great relief that Captain Javrayin stated publicly that because I was a *Davracha*, even though in the *Isithan*, I was exempt from being one of the men who might be called upon to impose the sentence. Had I been asked however, I would have done my duty and obeyed the will of the Court. The next stage of the proceedings involved holding a series of mind competitions to establish who the best officer at mind wrestling was, and who had mind power enough to bind someone telepathically to himself in order to carry out the sentence.

Humans may find telepathic binding a difficult concept to grasp, and may consider that this is one of the greatest differences between Humans and Sikarans, and I suspect that it may be so. Because, apart from our violet skin colour, the shape of our ears and eyebrows, and certain inner functions we are no different to Humans or Gloshans. The officers of the *'Voran'* got really enthusiastic about the mind competitions, and seemed to overlook the unpleasant reason for having them in the first place, or they pretended to forget.

After a week of such competitions, the semi-finals and finals were held, and to the amazement of all, it was Viathol, who showed that he was the strongest, by winning the competition. He had even beaten Avernyi who was nearly as mind-strong as I was. He bowed and accepted the applause with regal graciousness, but he did not smile which was unusual for him, and I sensed that the sheer awfulness of his position had just hit him. I went to him later that evening, when he was in his quarters, and I offered to take the burden from him, saying that I would talk with the Captain and despite being a *Davracha* I would volunteer to stand in his place, as we were equally mind-strong.

Viathol thanked me for my thoughtfulness, but said he had already accepted the Court ruling and had legally agreed to be the servant of the Court and to carry out the sentence on their behalf. I suspected that this was not yet the case, but that he would not allow me to do such an unpleasant thing because I was a *Davracha*. I sat with him quietly for a while, and from time to time we would look at each other, and I tried to give him some of my strength.

Viathol smiled at me at last and said, "Do not be so concerned for me, Marayshan. I am well able to find it within myself to do this deed. Remember how I hit you when you first came aboard?"

"It is not the same, Viathol," I replied quietly. "You know it is not the same."

Viathol nodded a little, and replied, "I know it is not, Marayshan, but my mind is strong enough and I am skilled enough to be clear and focused in what I am going to have to do. There is no danger that I will hurt Kavril more than I have to and he will certainly not be able to hurt me. I have no personal grudge against him, or I would have declared it to the Court, and he is also free to declare it if he feels that such a grudge exists. There is none I assure you. You may see my mind, if you wish, to determine the truth of the matter. Perhaps you should do so."

Viathol took my hands and opened his mind to me, letting me see clearly his thoughts concerning the Chief Engineer. There was nothing untoward there concerning Kavril, and so I nodded, and said that I would swear an affidavit to that effect.

We continued to sit together for a while longer. Then, Viathol said he wanted a stiff drink, before he went to the cells to begin the slow process of drawing Kavril to himself, so that he could in three days time carry out the sentence of the court.

"It will be unpleasant of course," he said to me, lightly then, "but let us not speak of it further." We went to the officer lounge to have our drink together, but there was little chance of not speaking about it. Viathol's royal friends were keen to discuss it.

When the conversation was at its height, I took Viathol to one side and said, "I've decided that I'm going to visit Kavril as a *Davracha* and talk to him for a while. Give me an hour before you come to the cells, Viathol, please."

"Of course," Viathol replied and smiled at me.

I went to visit Kavril, and asked the guard to let me past the security screen and sat beside him.

"Don't tell me you're the one who has been chosen by the Court, Marayshan," he said.

"No, but I could have been. My mind is strong enough, Kavril," I replied.

"Yes, I guessed that, as you're in the *Isithan*," Kavril replied. "So why have you come to visit me?"

"I just thought you might be in need of a welfare worker," I replied. Kavril did not speak, but he began to look distressed.

Finally he said, "I know I shouldn't have done what I did and I don't need you to tell me that. I did it because I wanted to do it. Do you understand that?"

I did not reply.

"I wanted to do it!" he said again.

"Do you realize how much you hurt Ilashon?" I asked then but he did not reply.

At last he said, "I've waited for a long time to do that, ever since he came aboard, but then he got that protector of his, Avarin, and I couldn't get near him until Avarin died in action last week. My need for Ilashon has been driving me crazy."

"Why didn't you approach his protector and ask to join with Ilashon legally?" I said. "Why didn't you make yourself acceptable to Ilashon? Why didn't you try and get to know him? Why force yourself on him?"

"I never had the time to get to know him, damn it! You know what it's like working on this ship, where do senior officers get the time to get to know people in that way?"

"That's an excuse, Kavril," I said. "Our First Officer was recently married to a crewwoman on board this ship, you know that."

"You've got an answer for everything, haven't you, Marayshan?" he said.

"I've been to see Ilashon," I said, and looked at him accusingly.

"He was asking for it," Kavril replied. "He was leading me on. Every time he went past me, he would brush past me and touch me provocatively."

"Are you sure it wasn't the other way round?" I said. "I noticed the look on Ilashon's face once, after he'd been in a lift alone with you, soon after he came aboard. I want you to promise me that you won't go near him again."

"Are you his new protector then?" said Kavril.

"No, I'm not Ilashon's new protector."

"Then you have no right to say that," Kavril replied. "I suppose he has a new protector by now. Do you know who it is? Tell him I do want to approach Ilashon and tell him I want to marry him."

"Really?" I replied. "I don't think that it's marriage you have in mind, do you, even if you join legally with him."

"What does it matter what I have in mind if we're legally joined?" demanded Kavril.

"It matters to me," I replied. "A I am certain that it will matter to his new protector."

"Who is his new protector?" asked Kavril.

"I have asked the Court to appoint Commander Lierschvaan, and he has accepted the responsibility. As you know, he is not a man who likes other men more than is usual, Kavril. But, being in the *Isithan* like me, he will protect Ilashon from you, that is for certain."

"You bastard, you've chosen the one officer I wouldn't easily be able to get past, haven't you? You've chosen the most powerful man on this ship apart from the Captain. Bastard! Well, I've offered to do the decent thing, haven't I? I've offered to marry him."

I did not reply, not trusting myself to speak.

We were silent again.

"Who is going to carry out the Court sentence then?" he asked at last.

"You know I can't tell you that. He has to come here himself." I replied.

"You're such an honourable bastard, aren't you? Why don't you ever do anything wrong? Will you give me a clue as to who it is?" he replied.

"I don't have to. Here he is," I replied, as Viathol walked into the cell.

Kavril sat up in amazement, "Count Viathol! But you are a royal!" he said. "This is ridiculous! Royals never do anything to get their hands dirty surely there must be some mistake. The playboy of the *'Voran'* isn't that what people call you? What is the playboy of the *'Voran'* doing here?" He laughed then continued, "Besides, I cannot imagine you have a strong enough mind, Count. I see that I am going to have some fun with you. I doubt if you are going to manage to get to me. I have quite a strong mind, you know." Kavril laughed again then with great amusement. "This is ridiculous!" he said again.

"I am surprised my presence here induces such mirth. I never realized I was so amusing," said Viathol, pulling up a chair, and sitting near to Kavril where he lay on the bunk.

Kavril finally stopped laughing when Viathol took his hand and held it and began to rub his palm.

"Oh, come now, Count Viathol. You are not really going to try and go through with this travesty, are you?" said Kavril, looking at him.

"Your mind is surprisingly open to me," said Viathol. "I had thought you would fight me all the way."

"You may do as you please," Kavril replied. "You will not have any power to hurt me when we really get to the core of our interaction."

"You think not?" replied Viathol, and then said, "Marayshan, I would appreciate it if you would stay for a while. Do you have any objection, Kavril?"

"Why should I? 'Mr Honourable' may stay for as long as he pleases. All he will witness is you being subjected to my mind and my will, not you binding me, Count, believe me."

Viathol did not reply, but surreptitiously insinuated himself inside Kavril's mind while he had the chance to do so easily without any opposition.

"That is enough! You have gone far enough into my mind. You shall go no further!" said Kavril, suddenly, sitting up and confronting Viathol. "Your presence is not welcome, Count!"

"You know that I have been requested to do this by the Court, Kavril," Viathol replied.

"Is there any reason why I should co-operate and make it easy for you? You are only half way there, and you will get no further. I will make sure that you are dishonoured by this, because you will have to arrange for me to be sedated before you can do what is required, because I am too strong and will fight you all the way from here. I promise you."

"Please do not fight me," said Viathol quietly, surprising Kavril. "I am stronger than you and you will not win. If you fight me it will only be distressing for you. Kavril, please do not fight me, please." Viathol stopped speaking.

Kavril paused then looked at him.

"You are concerned that you may distress me, Count. I am touched," Kavril replied. "It is obvious that you have been spending too much time with Marayshan." Kavril laughed then and said, "I am not going to make it easy for you beyond this point, no matter what you say. No matter whether you are a royal or not or whether I like you or not. You have accepted the Court's work, and so now I have no feeling for you beyond the fact that you are a servant of the Court and sent to carry out my sentence, so I am going to fight you, and believe me, I can fight dirty, Count Viathol. I can fight in ways that a royal could never imagine."

Suddenly he attacked Viathol with his mind and Viathol reeled backwards, letting go of his hand. I took Viathol's hand to help him and to give him some strength. He shook his head.

"No, it is well, Marayshan, I can do what I have to do, it is well."

"Oh, 'Mr Honourable' Marayshan," said Kavril, with some sarcasm, smiling at me. "You are so truly kind and so nauseatingly understanding. I do so wish your positions had been reversed. I would so like to do you some serious damage. But of course I would never hurt you, would I, as you are a *Davracha*. It is a great pity, such a pity."

"You could not do either of us serious damage, Kavril," I replied. "You will only make it worse for yourself. Give way to Count Viathol. Come on. Why are you talking about such dishonourable things as having to be sedated before you will give way to the Count? You have allowed Viathol to reach the half way mark and the sentence of the Court is bad enough, Kavril. Why make it worse for yourself? Why? You know how bad it could get for you."

I spoke quietly to him and something seemed to get through to him. There was a silence and then he nodded, "All right, you have won, Marayshan," he said quietly and smiled at me a little. "I am sorry I said those things to you just now. Will you stay with me as a *Davracha* for the ordeal? Will you be with me in three days time when I endure what I must endure? Promise that you will be with me."

"I shall be with you, I promise," I replied quietly.

He reached for my hand and I gave it to him, and he made no attempt at a telepathic link. He wished only for comfort from me, nothing more. I held his hand for a long moment then passed it to Viathol.

I had never been involved in anything so dreadful before and I knew that neither had Viathol and he and I looked at each other, wishing that we were anywhere else but there. Viathol took both of the other man's hands and held them for a long moment, and I sensed that he too was comforting Kavril with his mind then and not continuing with the process. I saw the look of surprise in Kavril's face, as he gazed at Viathol.

"I do not like to do this, you know, Kavril," Viathol said quietly. "Please do not think that I shall enjoy it, but the Court has requisitioned me to do it. It is my duty to do it and I shall do my duty, at whatever the cost."

"I begin to see you in a new light," Kavril replied shakily. "I have done you an injustice. I never realized you were such a man of duty."

Viathol did not reply then after a few moments he said, "
'Kavril, we must continue."
Kavril nodded after a moment's hesitation.

Viathol carefully rested a hand on his face and took Kavril's hands together in his other hand and did not waste time. He did not wait for Kavril to change his mind. He finished the process so rapidly that Kavril lay stunned by the speed of it and trembled badly and became emotional.

"I am truly sorry. I shall go now and return tomorrow," Viathol said quietly at last. He nodded briefly at me and left the cell and I sat with Kavril for a further hour.

In that time I began to feel that Kavril would need more than just the support of my presence in three days time. So, the next evening I went to see Captain

Javrayin who had convened the Court and asked if he objected to my holding Kavril's hand during the ordeal.

"You are a *Davracha*, Marayshan," was all he replied. "You may do as you see fit." Then, he paused and after some thought said, "It will be unexpected I think what you have decided to do, but none will question you. Do whatever you feel is best."

I nodded and my face must have belied my feelings because he said then,
"It is a difficult time for all of us, Marayshan. None of us cares for the thought that by doing this, we slide backwards into ancient ways. It is abhorrent to all of us, not only to you. How do you think I feel, after my father did what he did to me through his telepathic link with me? I am the Captain of this ship and so I will have to be present. I have no choice, but do you think I will want to be there?"

He stopped speaking then and began to look through some work at his desk, and I took it to be the end of the meeting. As I got up to leave he said, "It will be a great relief to me if you do hold his hand, Marayshan."

"Yes, Captain," I replied and went to the officer lounge. There it once more became the topic of conversation amongst the royals, but when Viathol came into the room after his second visit to Kavril, he looked grim. There was none of the playboy about him, the lightness and laughter, none of the entertaining banter with the female officers that everyone enjoyed.

He poured himself a drink and sat where he usually sat among the royals, but he did not speak at first. There was a space at the table and he invited me over, saying,

"If none of you object, I would like to ask Marayshan to join us."

There were no objections, so I sat with the five royals, and drank my *iskari*. We were both silent and the other royals looked at us, then Prince Nostarra said,

"For goodness sake, do say something, either of you, say anything!"

"I have spent a harrowing hour with Kavril in the cells," said Viathol. "Is that what you wish to hear, cousin?"

"It is better than this silence, cousin. It grates on my nerves," replied Nostarra.

"Indeed," Viathol replied then said, "Marayshan, Kavril asks for you. Will you please visit him later? He says there is no urgency. You may go when it is convenient for you."

Two royals came over then and one said, "Cousin Viathol, do tell us what it feels like for you to do such a thing, to draw someone so tightly to you in a way that is usually so frowned upon. It must be rather exciting."

"Exciting?" Viathol said. "Young cousin, air jet racing is exciting, sailing a yacht around the 'Crest of Milvanyi' is exciting; spending an evening with a beautiful woman is exciting. This is not exciting. This is horror. Do you not realise what it involves? Perhaps you are too young or too thoughtless or both."

"Oh," replied Count Astathyi. "I did not realize, cousin Viathol. Please forgive me." He looked crestfallen. He had been hoping for some light-hearted interchange with Viathol, as many relied on him to be witty and cheerful when things became difficult.

"Tell me, cousin Viathol," said Prince Evroshette. "Now that you are more acquainted with Kavril, how do you think that he will stand up to the ordeal tomorrow?"

"How would any of us stand up to such an ordeal, cousin?" Viathol replied. "But my mind is strong enough and clear enough to ensure that he is not hurt beyond his level of endurance, for I am certain that none of us wishes that to happen. He has asked for Marayshan to be at his side as a *Davracha* during the time. Marayshan, may I ask a favour, if it seems that Kavril cannot go on, please speak, then I shall stop regardless of whether the sentence of the Court is fulfilled or not. It would be only right and proper to cease."

"Of course, Count Viathol," I replied. "And I will be able to gauge how he is feeling very easily, because I have decided that I am going to hold his hand throughout the ordeal."

Viathol nodded a little and smiled at me. "I am relieved that you will be doing that for him," he said quietly.

Prince Avalyin said then, "I wish all this were over. I cannot bear such talk, and I cannot think how I will cope with witnessing it."

"You will not be called upon to witness it, young cousin," Evroshette said. "Our Captain has said that all the younger members from among the officers and crew will be asked to go to recreation area 3, where you will stay while it is happening. It will be relayed to the rest of the ship, but not to that area."

Prince Avalyin did not look any happier and said then, "Cousin Viathol, how can you bring yourself to do such a thing?"

"Young cousin," Viathol replied. "The Court has asked me to do it. I am doing my duty that is all, however unpleasant it may be."

"But you are a royal!" said Astathyi. "Surely you could have refused the Court, cousin, surely?"

"Of course I could have refused," replied Viathol, with unusual sharpness. "And if I had refused, then what? The duty would pass to Marayshan, who is equal to me in mind strength. In fact, he offered to do the deed to save me from it, but he is a *Davracha*. Would you force him to do such a thing? I would not, and the next in line would be Avernyi, who is very nearly as kind and caring as his friend Marayshan. No! I have no justifiable reason to pass on this duty, young cousin, or I would bring shame upon the royal clan. Can you not see that?"

Astathyi was silent then, and scrutinized his feet saying, "Surely Commander Lierschvaan could have done it, cousin?"

"Astathyi, you are too young to understand," said Evroshette. "It has to be someone with a strong enough mind to focus clearly or it could be dangerous for Kavril. In ancient times, no one cared about such things, and criminals were often hurt beyond their levels of endurance and even mind-damaged by sentences from the Mind Courts. These days we are different, are we not? We do care about such things. We are restrained. We are more caring generally. We are not as our ancestors were, Astathyi, you know that. Surely I do not need to say this, young cousin?"

The next evening came too quickly for me and, before I knew it, I was leading Kavril up the platform steps in the main hall. There was a bunk and two chairs there. I sat and Kavril stretched out on the bunk. I held his hand. Through telepathy, I clearly sensed the change in mood as Viathol mounted the platform and took his place in the chair beside us.

He took Kavril's other hand then and began to massage his palm. The other officers came onto the platform, and sat in two rows. In the centre of the front row sat Captain Javrayin with Avernyi on one side and 1st Officer Astivan on the other. Then there was Evroshette and Lierschvaan and Devthanyi. Beginning the second row was Navaronschyia, and he was directly in my line of sight when Captain Javrayin gave the order for the proceedings to begin. He covered his face with his hands.

There was nothing to see, of course, except for Kavril flinching and crying when things became too difficult. Only once did he cry out towards the start, and so I held him more tightly and he succeeded in enduring until the end. It all took no more than twenty minutes, but it was the most dreadful twenty minutes I had ever experienced. At the end, Viathol looked pale. His face was expressionless as he stood and bowed to me, which was unusual. Then, he turned and saluted the Captain and began to look for a way out through the vast number of crew who were gathered in the main hall. A way opened for him suddenly, and many crewmen and women bowed their heads to him and crossed their hands at their chests, and there was complete silence.

Viathol surveyed them and stood with them until the silence had ended and they looked at him again.

One crewman came forward and said then, "May I speak, Count Viathol, Servant of the Court. We acknowledge that you have made a sacrifice and paid a price to serve the people. You have done your duty and done what had to be done. You have acted with great strength and courage and have not tried to pass on this terrible burden to another. You have won the respect of the people and we honour you."

Viathol clasped his hands to his chest and bowed to the crewman in acknowledgement of the honour.

Prince Evroshette and Avernyi came over to me then and helped me with Kavril. Between us, we got him up and slowly walked him to sickbay. We had agreed beforehand that we three would stay with him in sickbay and help relieve his pain and so we did until he was calm enough to eat and drink a little. At first, he was so distressed that he could not keep anything down, but gradually we calmed him, and he ate and drank by degrees. Then, we took it in turns to hold him until he drifted into sleep. I knew that later that evening, Viathol would have to break the binding between them, and I sensed it would be a difficult time for both of them. I did not realize how difficult.

When I felt Kavril had recovered enough, after he had awoken from his brief slumber, I called Viathol to sickbay on the intercom and told him that I thought it was a good time to distance himself from Kavril. I met him just outside sickbay so I could speak to him for a moment or two then brought him into the cubicle where Kavril lay. None of us four were expecting what happened next. There was such a scene that I have never forgotten it since. On seeing Viathol, Kavril began to cry out, and thrash around in the bed in an effort to get away from Viathol and Evroshette and Avernyi had to restrain him. It was a terrible moment. Kavril was almost screaming when Viathol went to sit beside him and took his hand. I succeeded in calming Kavril by holding his other hand tightly, and it quieted him.

It took Viathol nearly an hour to disentangle himself from Kavril. I believe that during that time it was only the presence of Evroshette, Avernyi and me that kept Kavril from becoming hysterical. As it was, he shuddered and tried again and again to push Viathol away.

Viathol worked slowly, so as not to hurt Kavril further, but at last he was finished and released the other man's hand. At which point, Kavril turned towards me and sighed heavily, then closed his eyes.

I looked at Viathol, he looked at me, and then at Avernyi and Evroshette. We all knew from that moment on, that we had changed inside, and that life aboard ship had changed for all of us, and that nothing would ever be the same again, certainly not for Kavril, and certainly not for Viathol. Shortly afterwards, Viathol was promoted to Commander, and no longer had the luxury to take things lightly as he used to do or to pretend that he was more foolish than he was. Neither I suspect, did he wish to do so any longer, for the experience had matured him more rapidly than anything else had done up to now. Now he was someone to be reckoned with and, when he spoke, people listened, and it was not because he was a royal.

Within a few days, Kavril publicly apologized to Ilashon. Six months later, he offered marriage but, to my relief, Ilashon did not accept as I do not feel that it would have been a good match for Ilashon or a positive start to a marriage.

End of Article 2.

Chapter Five: The Sikaran Court

When he was on Naiobi, Marayshan regularly kept in touch on a monthly basis with Captain Lawrence Grey, of the I.G.S. *McBride*. They talked for a time about general things, and then Marayshan said, "Lawrence, since I have been here on Naiobi, I have realized Gloria Kincade could have brought charges against Peter Grayson for his treatment of her. Don't you think that she should have done so?"

"I certainly do," said Grey. "He should never have been allowed to get away with it, but Gloria told me that she didn't want to do anything to jeopardize his career in the military, apart from the fact that she did not want to have to relate what had happened publicly in a Court of Law and to be cross-examined about it."

"Well, I think that would be still extremely difficult for her," Marayshan replied. "It is a pity we cannot convene a Sikaran telepathic court, then I could submit the details on Gloria's behalf through my telepathy, but Grayson is subject to Earth law."

"I have an idea," Grey said thoughtfully. "Why don't you ask the magistrates on Naiobi to make an amendment? They could validate a Sikaran telepathic court to supplement the human magistrate's court or if necessary to stand alone. Now that we are working so closely with your people, we are going to have to integrate your ways with our ways of doing things. I don't think the Earth president would object, do you? I'll have a word with him. Once you've sorted all that out, then you will have to discover the whereabouts of Peter Grayson."

"I know exactly where he is. He is in a hotel room just nearby, waiting to hear when he can collect his three-year visiting permit from me at the Civic Offices. He has left the Earth Special Forces temporarily and taken work on Naiobi for three years. I have not seen him yet on my own, as I cannot bring myself to do so or I might lose my temper with him. I will ask Captain Maitland to come to my office and be present while I issue his papers. Thank you for your advice, Lawrence, I will speak to the magistrates right away."

A few days later, Marayshan went to see his girlfriend Paula. "Paula, please move in with me," he said.

"Are you really that serious about us?" Paula replied. "We haven't been going out together for very long."

"I know that, but I also know that you are that serious about us, Paula, aren't you?" he said.

"I know you know, but I want you to be serious too," Paula replied.

"I am serious enough to say that I would like you to consider marrying me at some future point when I have prepared you enough."

"Prepared me? Oh, you mean a telepathic marriage link. It's the first time you've mentioned marriage in the context of you and me. Are you really sure? It would be a big step for you to marry a human woman. Are you *really* sure?"

"It will not be a big step for me if that human woman is you," he replied.

"My goodness," Paula said, "to be married to a Shield Lord of the *Isithan* would be a great honour, but to be married to the man sitting opposite me would be even more wonderful."

"Paula, you are a lovely person and I am going to take you to my home right now," he said. "I don't want to waste any more time."

"Oh really, and what about all the sorting I have to do here; all my things, my books, my papers, my furniture."

Marayshan held up a hand for silence looking suddenly very uptight and Paula stopped talking quickly. "You can come back and do that at the weekend and Chalek and Ilashon will help you. Just come with me now please, I need you."

"I'll do that of course, Marayshan. But is everything all right? Tell me what's wrong. Can you tell me about it or is it confidential?"

"Yes I can tell you, but later, not here. It is about Group Captain Peter Grayson, the Earth Special Forces officer who came here a few weeks ago. I mentioned him to you. I would like your opinion about this situation. I need to talk it through with you and to show you something with my telepathy. It is a very sensitive issue, to do with Grayson's ex-girlfriend, Gloria Kincade. I met and got to know her on the starship *McBride*. We had some fun together, for a few days, then I discovered something about Grayson through the surface telepathic link I had with Gloria. Gloria was in a very sad state and I cheered her up. She was having flashbacks about the last night that she spent with Grayson when he was very terrible to her."

"It sounds like a bad situation all round," Paula said.

"It is very bad. Through the link, I managed to help Gloria to cope with the flashbacks and, of course, I saw all that had happened between them on that night. Now it is disturbing my sleep, I want to bring this man to justice."

"Look, I won't be long," Paula said and kissed him and put some music on for him to listen to and went into the other room.

In half an hour she was ready and Marayshan took her to the Governor's residence and said to his men as was customary in Sikaran culture, "I have brought Paula into my home. She has become very special to me."

"I wish you joy at your merging," Avernyi said, bowing to him.

The rest of the Sikarans bowed and repeated the words to them both. Marayshan looked proud as he led Paula inside, showed her to a seat in the living room and brought her tea.

"Marayshan, this bringing me into your home, it's one of your customs, isn't it? Tell me more about it."

"Yes it is a custom," Marayshan replied. "It acknowledges the beginning of a special relationship. It means we are moving towards marriage. It is equivalent to becoming engaged for humans. It does not mean that we have to live together, but I wish you to live here with me, because I am impatient. You do not object, do you? I want your company very much."

"I don't have any objections. I want your company very much too," Paula replied then added, "Will we begin to prepare for a telepathic marriage link?"

"Yes, but it will take at least six months. It will be very tedious but there is no way around it."

"I wish I were Sikaran, so that you wouldn't have to wait for six months," Paula said.

"Well, you are not," he said pragmatically, "so we will just have to wait."

Paula kissed him and said, "Now I think you need to tell me about this business with Peter Grayson in detail."

"The best way to do that is to show you the images that were in Gloria's mind during the flashbacks," said Marayshan. He held her hands to transmit the thoughts.

Paula recoiled in horror as she witnessed the awful treatment that Gloria Kincade had endured from Peter Grayson.

"Stop, please, I can't see anymore, Marayshan. The poor woman, it's too dreadful for words." Paula wept as they hugged each other.

"Can you understand now why I feel this way about it?" Marayshan said.

"Yes of course I can," Paula replied. "You have to do something to make him account for behaviour like that. After all, he's a Group Captain now. He should not be allowed to get away with it. Why didn't Gloria Kincade tell someone about it, for goodness sake? Why didn't she go to her doctor or the welfare department or something?"

"Gloria was protecting his military career, apparently, and neither did she wish to speak about such personal things in an open court. So I have asked the Earth president to make an amendment to Earth law, to permit a Sikaran telepathic court to be convened here on Naiobi, so that my evidence can be presented and accepted on behalf of Gloria. Then, perhaps, there will be some justice for her."

"You know, I do think you're wonderful for helping her like this. You're a real knight in shining armour."

"Thank you, Paula," Marayshan replied.

Paula rested a hand on his face, but didn't speak, trying to send him a message in the hope that his telepathy would pick it up.

"Yes, I heard you," he said and kissed her.

"I hoped you would," Paula replied.

They rested against each other, forehead to forehead for a long moment.

"I am really looking forward to this telepathic merging," Paula said.

"Good, because I can't wait to get started," Marayshan replied.

"You're really keen, aren't you?"

"Of course I'm keen. You know that it's very much a part of how Sikarans make love."

"I know, you have mentioned it, let me see, at least ten thousand times, or perhaps it was twenty thousand. I lost count after the first thousand or so."

Marayshan laughed. "Paula, I am not as bad as that," he said.

"Oh yes you are," Paula said embracing him. "Farmers from the *Arakiarth* Valley obviously like their women, a lot."

"Well, yes, actually, that is true," Marayshan replied.

"I thought so. I got that feeling. Oh, starting so soon?" Paula said, as Marayshan casually slipped into her mind.

"Well, I am only using a little telepathy," he said.

"Hmmm," said Paula, "now, that is an interesting sensation, and that."

"Interesting? Is it not enjoyable?" Marayshan said, disconcerted.

Paula laughed and said, "I was only joking. I thought you could take a joke."

"Not when, well, not in these circumstances," he replied.

"Oh, I see. I do beg your pardon. You know, I don't think we should continue here in the living room. Shouldn't we, perhaps, retire for the night? I think we could use a bit of privacy, don't you?"

"Well, yes of course, but I was not going to go too far," Marayshan said.

"Oh, that's a pity," said Paula.

"In that case, we should go to my rooms, but are you sure? I thought you were tired," Marayshan replied smiling at her.

"If you think I'm moving in with one of the sexiest men in the colonies, and not going too far with him on the first night, then you're very much underestimating my human initiative."

"I had better not underestimate it again then," Marayshan replied laughing.

"Quite so," said Paula.

"I will just tell Deva that I'm going to spend the night with you. He will be very envious."

"Marayshan, I don't care who you tell, but I do want you all to myself. I do not want to share you with Avernyi, or Nava or Elaan or anyone else tonight. This is our special night."

Marayshan quickly told Deva not to disturb him for the rest of the night in his rooms, even if the entire Gloshan space fleet invaded the colony.

"Oh, I see," said Deva, "you know I'm very envious of you, Marayshan. You're beginning a very good relationship. It is exactly what you need. Be careful though, won't you? You know how carried away we can get when we use our telepathy to make love."

"Deva, you don't need to say that to me. Please ask Avernyi if he will sit in the next room in case I do need some help in restraining myself."

"Of course," Deva replied and bowed to him.

Avernyi quickly took up position in the room next door to Marayshan's bedroom, with a glass of brandy, some sandwiches and a book.

Paula had to walk past him to get to the bedroom with Marayshan and said,

"Avernyi, what on Earth are you doing here?"

"Marayshan asked me to stay here in case, well, just in case, you know, in case he needs me." Avernyi replied.

Paula sighed in exasperation.

They got into the bedroom and closed the door, then Paula said, "Marayshan, why is Avernyi just outside our door? Why?"

"Paula, he is there in case I get carried away with you. That is why."

"Marayshan, is that really likely? You are such a calm, controlled and careful sort of person."

"Paula, listen to me, there is something you don't realize about Sikarans. Our telepathy is very strong, and when we use it to make love, we can get really carried away. You may find it difficult to cope with the first few times. If either of us calls to Avernyi, he will come in and pull me off you."

"Oh honestly, I don't like the sound of that, Marayshan. I don't want anyone to pull you off me, for goodness sake. I love you. This is ridiculous."

"Paula, do you want to argue on our first night together after I have brought you into my home?" Marayshan said, with narrowing eyes, which Paula knew was a bad sign, because she had seen him get angry once or twice before with his men.

"No, no, I don't want us to argue, of course not. Besides I don't think I would be able to win. You know that I love you," Paula said hastily.

"And I love you too, otherwise we would not be here," Marayshan replied blandly.

"I'm sorry I've spoiled the moment. You know what I'm like. I usually speak my mind."

"That's why I wish to marry you," Marayshan replied, embracing her. "And you have not spoiled the moment."

Paula smiled and said, "Are you sure?"

"Yes, I am very sure," he replied, "But I am very on edge because I am concerned about starting to prepare you for the marriage link. It is making me anxious, together with this business about Peter Grayson. I will try to be very careful, I promise you."

Marayshan rested one of his hands on her chest and the other on her forehead and began drifting into her mind.

"That doesn't feel so bad, it's rather good actually," Paula said, trying not to flinch.

"I don't think you are telling the truth," Marayshan replied.

"Oh all right, it is a bit uncomfortable, but just a bit. Don't stop, for goodness sake, I have to get used to it sometime," Paula replied.

Marayshan pushed harder.

"Oh, it's getting a bit difficult now," Paula said and clung to him.

"So you see now why it's a good idea to have Avernyi outside the door. It would get a lot worse if I did get carried away," Marayshan replied.

Paula tried not to cry out.

Marayshan stopped abruptly and kissed her and Paula relaxed and said, "I'm all right, try again. Go on, just keep trying."

"Paula, I know you are trying to do this quickly for my sake, and I love you very much for doing that, but it will take time, and I am prepared to be patient, even though I am longing to join with you."

A few minutes later, Paula got more than she bargained for. Suddenly she felt him both in her mind and body.

"Oh, how is that possible? We're not; we're not doing anything. I mean how is it happening?" Paula tried desperately to stop herself from crying out because of the depth of the link and was suddenly afraid, as she felt Marayshan tremble and tighten his hold on her.

"Marayshan, wait," she said quickly, "don't go any further please. I'd appreciate it if you could stop now, just for a minute."

Wrestling with himself he reigned in his passion and withdrew back to the surface link, his breathing becoming ragged. He kissed her passionately and repeatedly.

Paula was not sure how to cope, and tried to catch her breath before he entered her mind again.

Suddenly he pulled away from her and said, "No, we have to stop now!" He broke the surface link, pushed Paula away from him and covered his face with his hands. Then, after a few moments, he embraced her and made love to her without the telepathy.

Paula felt exhausted by the telepathy and Marayshan realized how she was feeling. He made an effort to calm down and things became low key and relaxed. Paula heaved a sigh of relief.

After a while he caught her up tightly in his arms and said, "Paula, I love you so much," and entered her mind suddenly going down to the deep level.

Shall I scream now or can I wait for five minutes? Paula thought to herself anxiously, and tried counting to one hundred, then yelled, "Avernyi! Help! Avernyi! Help!"

Avernyi leapt to his feet and rushed into the room and succeeded in taking Marayshan's hands away from Paula's chest and forehead. This was not an easy task but somehow he managed it.

"Marayshan, Marayshan," he said quietly, "take a break, come on, calm down, you know you don't want to hurt Paula, come on." Slowly Marayshan came to himself.

"Paula, are you all right?" Avernyi asked.
Paula nodded, and said, "Yes, thank you for helping me out. I would appreciate a glass of water if you don't mind." Paula shut her eyes then trembling badly.

Marayshan kissed her hand then and she said, "Darling, let's take a break and just rest a bit, just calm down a bit. Let's take Avernyi's advice."

Marayshan nodded and talked to his friend for a while. Paula tried to think clearly then, but failed miserably and closed her eyes and went to sleep, not waking up until seven o'clock the next morning.

"Oh my head," Paula complained, as she awoke, "it feels as though herds of wild horses have been thundering through it. Oh, Marayshan."

"Paula, you're not complaining, are you?" Marayshan replied. "It's only the first time we've tried anything like this. If you're going to complain every time we do something, then it is going to get very irritating."

"I'm sorry, but I feel so wretched. I don't usually cry when I'm with you, do I? But I feel so miserable," Paula replied, tearfully.

Marayshan sighed and kissed her until she stopped crying.

"Thank you, thank you." Paula said quietly.

"*Var* preserve me from Earth women," he said.

"Marayshan, you don't mean that," Paula said.

"No, I don't mean that," Marayshan replied, "of course I don't mean that or we would not be here, you *gretch*."

"I take exception to being called that. Isn't a *gretch* a silly bird with very little brains?"

"A *gretch* is a very foolish bird, who cries because she feels neglected and has not yet realized how much I love her. Come here, *gretch*," he said.

"How is it you know me so well? We've only been going out for a short while," Paula replied.

"I got to know you on *Solus Beta 3* when we were on holiday together, remember? And I'm good at judging what other people are like, even aliens. I'm good at other things too, as you found out last night," Marayshan replied smiling.

"Well, yes, you are, awfully good, awfully, awfully good," Paula said closing her eyes and languishing in his arms.

"Listen, *gretch*, you know, you should not let me take so many liberties," he said.

Paula looked at him and smiled, "Why ever not?" she said. "You can take as many liberties as you like."

"Paula, you know you don't want to do anything today, you're exhausted."

"Well, yes, I must admit I am, but you're not. I don't want to stop you enjoying yourself."

"Last night was enough for the moment. We'll wait a few days before we try again. No. No arguments. You need a break to recover from everything."

Paula nodded. "I won't argue with that, I do need a rest."

"I will bring you breakfast in bed," Marayshan said, "You would like that, wouldn't you? Scrambled egg on toast."

"Yes, of course I would. I can't believe you remembered it was my favourite breakfast, from when we were on holiday together."

"I have remembered everything you have told me."

Paula touched his face and spoke silently to him, hoping that he was picking up her thoughts.

"Yes, *kirathie*, I heard you," he said.

"Some things aren't easy to say aloud, it's wonderful that you can hear what I want to say to you with your telepathy. I can never put things like that into words. I'm absolutely hopeless at it."
"You are not hopeless at anything. It is just circumstances that have caused you to lose your confidence. A lot of my men are like that," Marayshan replied.

"Are they? I didn't realize that. I was thinking you would take care of them the same way you take care of me. I've noticed you doing that with one or two of them, apart from Chalek, I mean. They're more than just soldiers to you, aren't they? You care about them as individuals, don't you? I'm sorry I've become so dependant on you so quickly. I'm usually such an independent person. Now everything has changed. It's because I know I can rely on you absolutely, and I trust you to do the right thing for us. Now I really *need* you in my life as well as love you."

"I have realized this too, Paula, but it is mutual, I need you too," Marayshan replied.

"I know you do, but not as much as I need you. I've never told you this before but there's no one left in my family that I can turn to when things go wrong. I lost them all in the space war. The only one I have now, apart from you, is my old friend Alan Panton. He helps me now and then and he's been good to me over the years. Marayshan, I would really like you to get to know him and his wife, Clara."

"Of course I will. Invite them to dinner with us one evening. Now I am going to make you scrambled egg on toast, just the way you like it." Paula's face lit up and Marayshan smiled at her. "We will do well together, you and I," he said. "I have a good feeling about it."

He went into the living room of the suite of rooms within the Governor's mansion that he had taken for himself and there was a kitchenette in it. And there he made breakfast for her.

Paula sat thinking happy thoughts and reading her book while she waited.

Marayshan returned with breakfast and they ate it together, enjoying each other's company.

Marayshan rapidly got the validation amendment passed and held a press conference to announce it. In that time, he avoided all contact with Peter Grayson, apart from when he had given him the visiting permit. At the first opportunity, he called together Captain Maitland, Deva, Joe Marsh and Dave Sanderson who were all Peace Officers now in Maitland's Police Division. He told them that he was going to confront Peter Grayson in his office and wanted them present when he did so together with the two colony lawyers, Mr. Henson and Mr. White. One usually took the prosecution and the other the defence. Marayshan sent Nava and Avernyi to collect Grayson from his workplace and bring him to the Civic Offices. Seriously annoyed by the interruption, Grayson took the rest of the day off from his work and he complained about Sikaran Governors most of the way to the Civic Offices. That is until Nava silenced him with an angry look and he stopped complaining soon enough.

"Grayson, I never thought I'd see you again," said Joe Marsh. "What's a bastard like you doing here on Naiobi?"

Grayson said, "Oh whining on again, are we, Marsh? Did Gloria go crawling to you bleating about me, did she?" Marsh coloured dangerously.

"Why did you treat Gloria like that?" Marsh said angrily.

"Well Marsh, she was such a pathetic woman, always complaining about nothing and crying for no reason. It got on my nerves, so sometimes I just gave her a little something to cry about. I never did too much. She's lying if that's what she said."

"Mr. Grayson," said Maitland, "Gloria Kincade, now Mrs Gareth Jones, is bringing charges against you. That is why you are here today."

"Sit down, Mr. Grayson," said Marayshan. "The charge is one of serious assault and prolonged emotional cruelty."

"Oh yes," said Grayson aggressively, "and how is she going to prove that, may I ask?"

"Gloria used to tell me things about you, Grayson," said Joe Marsh. "I'm prepared to testify against you in Court."

"Yes, well, Gloria was completely deluded," he said.

Dave Sanderson had to hold Marsh back from punching Grayson there and then in the Governor's office.

"Mr. Grayson," said Marayshan, "a lot of us are in the queue waiting to hit you, not just Joe. I am next, then Captain Maitland, then my two friends Nava and Avernyi. What do you think of that?"

"You're out of your mind, you Sikaran—"he was about to insult Marayshan, but stopped before saying too much, then continued, "how dare you disturb my work, just for this travesty. Gloria can't prove anything against me, not one thing!"

"Mr. Grayson, if you were to admit some of these charges, there would be some leniency for you," said Maitland.

"Admit them? Why should I? Gloria is lying! It's her word against my word. Look, I want legal representation! Legal representation, do you hear me, Mr. Sikaran Governor! I demand legal representation!"

"Stop shouting at me," Marayshan said calmly. "Nava, please ask Mr Henson and Mr White to join us. They are waiting in Room 3. Mr Grayson, they are the lawyers of this colony." Nava brought them in,

When Marayshan saw them, he said, "Mr Henson, Mr White, good morning. This is Mr Grayson. I believe that Captain Maitland has briefed you in detail about all this."

"Yes Governor, everything will be very clear cut now that the Sikaran Court is to be involved. Without it, proceedings would have been drawn out and extremely complicated."

"Why should there be a Sikaran Court involved?" demanded Grayson. "I am an Earth citizen and so is Gloria. What has this to do with Sikarans for God's sake? Tell me!"

Marayshan leaned forward on his desk and looked directly at Grayson.

"There is a Sikaran Court too because *I* am involved," he said.

"You? How? How could *you* possibly be involved?"

"On the Starship *McBride*, on the voyage here, I met and got to know Gloria Kincade, you know, fairly briefly. Gloria wished to have some fun with me, on the basis that anyone, even a Sikaran, is better than you!"

"Oh really," Greyson said eyeing him malevolently.

"Yes, really," Marayshan replied attempting to keep control of his temper.

"So, you gave her a good time, so what? What does this have to do with any Sikaran Court?"

"Mr. Grayson, it is a telepathic Court," said one of the lawyers. "Captain Marayshan has telepathic evidence against you. The Court has been validated by amendment from the Earth president. The evidence will be accepted. It has already been logged, passed to other Sikarans here who have sworn an oath that Captain Marayshan's evidence is true and entirely admissible."

"Oh, I know what is going on here," said Greyson. "This is all a huge bluff, isn't it, to get me to say something. Well then, Captain Maitland, perhaps, if there is some leniency, I suppose I will admit the charges."

The two lawyers began writing furiously in their case files.

"I admit that I was a bit over the top with Gloria."

"A bit over the top!" said Marayshan angrily. "What are you? A human or a monster! Which? Tell me. I want to know! I am interested in these things."

"Why is all this, such a big deal?" said Grayson, "Maybe I was a bit rough and inconsiderate with her now and then, but so what."

Marayshan made a supreme effort to control his anger, then said,
"Mr Henson, Mr White, may I be permitted to show my evidence to Mr Grayson?"

The lawyers conferred then Henson said, "As Mr Grayson has admitted to the charges, I see no reason why not. Mr. Grayson you were looking at five years in prison, but as you have admitted these charges, this will be reduced to three years."

"It's still a long time, I will have to leave my job, oh damn it! Gloria, damn it, look what you've done to me."

"Look what you've done to Gloria!" Marayshan said, grabbing his hands, concentrating and sending telepathic images to him.

"You really do know what happened then," he said quietly, looking completely deflated; then looking very ashamed he covered his face with his hands.

"Mr Grayson," said Henson, "as the Sikarans are involved, I believe that there is a Sikaran alternative to three years incarceration, which would mean you did not have to leave your job."

"Oh yes, yes please choose the Sikaran alternative, Mr Grayson, yes please," said Marayshan smiling unpleasantly at him.

"The alternative," said Henson "would be over in half an hour, Mr Grayson, it's a beating."

"No problem then, I'll choose the beating any day of course," Grayson replied, "I don't want to give up my job."

"Oh good, really, you have made my day," said Marayshan.

"I thought you were supposed to be a nice guy, that's what people say about you," said Grayson.

"Oh I am, I am, but not where you are concerned, Mr Grayson, not where you are concerned."

He paced the room now with his hands behind his back.

"As you are a military man, your punishment will be a military one. Deva will carry it out. Deva, you are to use the *Chora*."
Deva nodded.
Later when things got a little difficult for Grayson, during the appointed half hour, Marayshan said, "Hey! Shut up and put up with it!" using the same words that Grayson had used with Gloria. Although not the best half hour of his life, Grayson coped mostly due to the fact that Marayshan allowed him long pauses in between, so that he had the chance to recover. He kept his new job, and began to make a new life for himself on Naiobi, but Marayshan kept an eye on him, and went to visit him when he heard that Grayson had become engaged to be married.

Marayshan and Grayson faced each other when Grayson opened his front door.

"Good evening, Mr Grayson, may I come in and speak with you?" Marayshan began.

Grayson shrugged then said, "All right, if you have to. Are you thinking of interfering in my life yet again, Mr Sikaran Governor?" He made it sound like an insult.

They sat opposite each other in the living room and Marayshan said after a moment, "I have come to talk to you as one soldier to another, you know, man to man. There are issues we need to discuss here."

"You sound like one of those damn welfare workers from the *Interspace* Welfare Department. They came to see me a few days ago and I told them to get lost. Look, I've changed. I don't have battle stress anymore. That night I had just gotten back from one of the most difficult missions I had ever been on against Gloshans and it got to me, it just got to me, can't you understand that?"

"I am beginning to understand how some human men react under extreme stress. By the way, I have been doing welfare work with Dr. Ryland to help victims of the space war. I am a qualified *Davracha*, which is similar to a human welfare worker but not completely the same."

Marayshan replied. "I would like you to allow me to use my telepathy to check if what you are saying is true about your battle stress."

"All right, you might as well. What harm can it do?"

"No harm at all. I am very skilled now with humans, and if I find that there is a problem and any way that I can help, through using my telepathy, then I will do so as I helped Gloria."

"You'd do that for me? I thought you hated me because of what I did to Gloria. Why are you going to so much trouble to help me?"

"I don't hate you," Marayshan replied. "And I would like to understand why you behaved as you did. I have read your military record carefully and it is impressive. That is why I would like to try and help you if I can. I would not like things to go wrong again. It would be good for you if you could have a decent relationship this time, for your sake as well as your future wife's sake."

Marayshan held out his hands to initiate the telepathic link and Grayson took hold of them. Marayshan found that Grayson had been telling the truth, a combination of battle fatigue and anxiety had consumed him, and he had not known how to cope with it except by taking it out on Gloria.

"Close your eyes and I will try and help you," Marayshan said, reaching the place where the anxiety lay still tightly wound up like a coiled spring, waiting to be released. Grayson had tried to control it, but had not overcome it.

"Why don't you try and let it go, the battle is over," Marayshan said.

"I might be recalled to active service if the space war takes a turn for the worse," he replied.

"It will not do that. The Sikaran Space Fleet is containing it until the Gloshans are defeated which will probably be in about a year's time now. You must not be recalled into action. I will write a letter to your commander. Shall we continue? That was only surface telepathy I used just now, a light contact, but to really help you, I will need to use a deep link and you may not find it easy."

"I understand," Grayson replied.

After a time, he became emotional and trembled badly.

"I find it too hard to relive those battles. I can't show you those missions. I can't."

Greyson's levels of anxiety and aggression, at that point, were so high that he pulled his hands away and kicked the coffee table, then hit the cups so they went flying violently and smashed against the wall.

Marayshan quickly went and sat beside him and put an arm around his shoulders and said, "Stop, it's all right, those battles are over. Try and calm down."

Very gradually he calmed Grayson, mostly by holding him, and then Grayson began to cry. "I was the best special forces soldier in my unit," he said, "the best. I continually pushed myself to my limits. I got results. I made sure those Gloshan bastards never returned to their space ships."

"I know, I have spoken with your unit commander. You deserved all the medals you won, but now you need to distance yourself from all of that. I seriously don't think you should go on active duty again. It would be too damaging for you. Your unit commander would very much like to recall you, you know, but I told him I would have to talk with you first and that you had developed some problems because of the war. He said to me that his whole Special Forces Unit was crazy. 'The crazier the better,' he said to me."

Grayson laughed despite how he was feeling.

"That sounds like my unit commander, 'old mad dog', that was our nickname for him. He's a guy you knew you could trust to be at your back in a bad situation. I think you would be like that too, wouldn't you?"

"Of course, I am a Shield Lord of the *Isithan*. I'm a very experienced soldier just like 'old mad dog.'"

"Thanks for helping me, I really appreciate it," said Grayson then.

"You know, you human men are really strange. You are so complicated. It took me quite a while to grasp what was really wrong with you. I think I know now."

"I suppose we are kind of strange," said Grayson, smiling at the Sikaran. "I must seem to you like a really objectionable person after what I did to Gloria. Sorry. Now you've seen the things I've done on missions, too, through the telepathy. You must think I'm pretty awful."

"I have been in many battles too. I can take it," Marayshan replied.

They tried the telepathic link again, and this time Marayshan was bombarded by violence. Each time the violence surfaced, he subdued it, and calmed Grayson. This time he attempted to reach the centre of the aggression to try and release it, but Grayson pulled away and shouted, "No! I can't take anymore! I can't! I can't! I can't!"

Marayshan sat calmly with him for a long while and then made them some tea.

"You know, you are going to have to let me continue," he said. "I can almost see a way to help you."

Grayson drank the tea in silence then said, "All right, all right, you can continue if you want to, but I don't know why you want to be bothered with me." Marayshan had realized that shame and guilt were partly responsible for consuming Grayson because of some of the things he had to do to the enemy in combat situations.

"Grayson, you will have to let go of the past, or it will never give you a moment's peace or happiness," Marayshan said, taking his hands again.

"What is that music?" Grayson asked, hearing it through the telepathic link.

"It is my memory of some Sikaran music I used to enjoy at home. It is very soothing, isn't it?"

"It is beautiful music," Grayson said, closing his eyes and resting back on the settee.

"You are in the midst of the worst battle you ever fought," Marayshan said quietly. "Can you still hear the music?"

Grayson nodded.

"Concentrate on it, and feel the beauty of it inside you. You are moving beyond the fury of the battle, you are leaving it behind, it is not important anymore. Leave it behind so that only the beauty of the music matters now."

"I lost my best friend in that battle, his name was Matthew." Grayson said, crying again.

"Your friend is resting now. He has gone across the sea in a silver ship, to a new shore, and is awaiting you, and when it is your time to fade, you will be reunited with him. That is what Sikarans believe."

Grayson thought then of the peaceful requiem music that had been played at his friend's funeral and Marayshan heard it in the link.

"That is beautiful music too," he said.

"It was played at Matthew's funeral. I asked for a copy of it afterwards. It's all I've got left to remind me of him," he said. "I have lost so many friends, look at all of them. Can you see them in my mind?"

"Yes, I can see their faces alive in your memory of them," Marayshan replied calmly. "Why don't you let them rest? You will meet them again one day. Why don't you say goodbye to them now and let them rest."

Marayshan had realized now that, at the heart of all of Grayson's fury, was his unresolved grief at the loss of so many comrades.

"I have lost many dear friends in battle too," Marayshan said sympathetically.

Grayson looked at him for a long moment, then took courage and said, "I *will* say goodbye to them now. It is time, isn't it?"

Marayshan nodded and said, "Yes, I think you should. It is long overdue."

"I could light some candles for them in the church, and give a list of their names to the minister so that they can be remembered in his prayers," Grayson said.

"Good," Marayshan replied calmly, "you are finally letting them rest."

Grayson nodded then said, "Will you come with me when I go to the church to light the candles? Please?"

"Of course, of course," Marayshan replied.

"I would really like you to meet my fiancée Sarah Kendrick too," Grayson said.

"That's fine you must also meet *my* fiancée Paula Watson."

"Your fiancée, I didn't realize you were thinking of getting married to a human woman."

"Yes, we love each other very much, but before we can be married, there are issues. Earth women! I don't know! There are always issues with humans. This time it is issues about my telepathy that have to be resolved. Sikaran men have to work through all kinds of issues with Earth women, because our telepathy is so strong, and unless we practice it a lot with the woman we love, it would be difficult for her in a marriage situation, when we want to make a marriage link. It is all very tedious, but this preparation just has to be done." Marayshan shrugged and sighed, then looked up at the ceiling.

Grayson smiled at him.
"You really are one of the good guys, aren't you?" was all Grayson said.

***

A few months later, the minister invited all the soldiers on Naiobi to a service of remembrance for their comrades who had died in the space war. He invited the Sikaran soldiers, too, to take part. The service was open to anyone in the colonies who wished to attend, and so it was held in the arena. The minister asked the soldiers if they would march into the arena, to the music of a military band. Many of them readily accepted, wanting to do something to acknowledge comrades who had gone. Marayshan had a call from Grayson, telling him about the remembrance service and asking him if he would attend with Grayson, as Grayson did not feel he could go on his own, but really wanted to be there.

Marayshan told him that he and his men were all attending and that they would be marching alongside the human soldiers in the arena and Grayson was pleased to hear it. He thanked Marayshan and said he would see him there.

Paula sat in the arena seats with Sonja Harding and all her friends, who were teachers from both the Naiobi schools. Captain Maitland was there, too, with many of the Naiobi police, who were ex-soldiers. Lierschvaan was there, too, in uniform, marching alongside Marayshan. They all made an impressive site. Later when they stood in silence, Grayson broke down, unable to cope with his grief, and Marayshan went to stand beside him.

"Grayson, all is well, 'old mad dog' is here," he said, then put an arm around the other man's shoulders which helped him to calm down. Marayshan stood with him for the rest of the service.

"Shouldn't you be with your own men?" Grayson asked quietly.

"They already know I care about them, they will not object to my helping you." Marayshan replied.

"Thanks, I mean it, thanks a lot." He took Marayshan's hand and held it for a long moment.

"No problem," said Marayshan, "that's what we 'old mad dogs' are here for. How are you getting on with Sarah?"

Grayson smiled. "Fine, we're getting on just fine. We're going to be married in six months time. I hope that you and Paula will be at the wedding."

"Of course we will," Marayshan replied.

At the end of the service, when everyone was leaving, Grayson suddenly flung his arms around Marayshan, and said, "Thanks, thanks again."

Marayshan held him in return and then patted his shoulder and said, "All is well now," and kissed him on both sides of his face.

Grayson went to find Sarah while Marayshan took Lierschvaan with him to where Sonja and Paula were seated.

"Paula, Sonja, shall we get something to eat in one of the Mall cafés?" Paula nodded looking sad.

"That sounds very nice," Sonja replied. "Why don't we go to *The Tea Shop*, Paula. I want to show off with you both; you look so smart in your uniforms. We're very proud of you." Lierschvaan looked both extremely pleased and extremely embarrassed all at the same time.

Sonja took his arm and Marayshan held out a hand to Paula. She took it and said, "It was a very moving service. I was thinking of all the people in my family who died in the space war. Still, best not dwell on the past, one has to look forward, that's the thing. Let's go to *The Tea Shop*. And Marayshan, please walk slowly, I want everyone to see you with me beside you."

Marayshan smiled at her and bowed to her as she stood. "Lee and I want to talk to you both, we have a favour to ask of you," he said, "shall we talk about it in *The Tea Shop?*"

"Yes, of course, that would be fine," said Paula exchanging glances with Sonja.

They sat in the warm, welcoming *Tea Shop* and decided what they wanted, then, after the waitress had taken their orders, Marayshan said, "Now that Lee and I are the two High Commanders of the Sikaran Space Fleet, we need two human Aides, one for each of us and the posts will be paid for by the Sikaran High Council."

All the other humans in *The Tea Shop* were eves-dropping and riveted to the conversation.

"And you would like Sonja and me to make some suggestions as to who might be suitable. Well, let me see, I could instantly suggest Captain Maitland," Paula said.

"And I would like to suggest the headmasters of each of the schools here, Alan Panton or Dai Reece," Sonja interjected.

"Thank you, but Lee and I would like you and Sonja to have the posts," said Marayshan, "because we seek to honour you both. Paula, you have gone through a lot to marry me, because of the issues about telepathy, and Sonja, you are just about to start going through it all with Lee. Lee and I are proud that you have chosen us to be your husbands. We think that you are very intelligent, well educated and assertive enough to do this work. We need you to liaise with the Earth media and the media here on Naiobi and to hold Press Conferences on our behalf. We also will expect you to scrutinize our space initiatives, our battle plans and to give your opinions of them and to pull them apart, to criticise them fully if you feel it is necessary. We would like you both to be our aides because, apart from the fact that we think you are capable of the work, we would like to share our ideas with you at any time of the day or the night. We would expect you to keep a record of our ideas as we develop them. We are hoping to bring the space war to a close within the year, rather than to draw it out over the next two years, but the Gloshan Space Fleet is incredibly strong and so for this we need now to concentrate carefully, to be focused and to be creative in our thinking. It would also be your job to keep us focused. The most important thing for Lee and I is that we know that we can trust both of you."

"Good gracious, that sounds like an amazingly responsible job for us. Marayshan, Sonja and I are going to have to be very serious about this, aren't we?" Paula said.

"You and Sonja are always serious about everything, Paula," said Lierschvaan.

"Yes, I suppose we are, but a job like this? Good heavens, Sonja, it's a bit scary. Don't you think?"

"Yes, very, but I am prepared to have a go if you are," Sonja replied, smiling at her friend.

"Well, I'll give it a try of course. It is quite an honour to be asked. Don't you think though that the High Council might object, because each of us is in a relationship with each of you?"

"No, they do not worry about that kind of thing," said Lierschvaan. "It is entirely up to us who we choose to be our Aides."

"Goodness," said Sonja, "what a challenge, how exciting."

Chapter Six: Sikaran Telepathy

Captain Maitland showed Joe Marsh the newspaper article from the *Beta-Naiobi Chronicle* in the police archives:

Renegade Special Forces Earth Soldier runs riot on Beta-Naiobi.
Human soldier terrorises the Naiobi colony's community of humans, Ringulians and Kalesians. Conrad Weissner does not seem to mind who he attacks, be they human, Ringulian or Kalesian. However the Ringulian and Kalesian women are fighting back. They have taken to carrying baseball bats to protect themselves whenever they go out. This disturbed human soldier remains free to wreak havoc, defying Naiobi police. An expert combatant, he is effortlessly able to blend in with his surroundings. There have been fifteen assaults and twenty-eight attempted assaults so far. Seriously folks, it's a bad situation. Captain Geoffrey Maitland, you need to do something about this. Three months is too long: a resignation may be called for.

***

After they arrived on beta-Naiobi, it did not take Marayshan and his men many days to track down the renegade soldier, Conrad Weissner, for Police Chief Maitland, and he did not have to resign his post as Chief of Police, for which he was extremely grateful. Unfortunately living in fear for so many months had taken its toll on the community and the human women were in a constant state of nervousness, jumping at shadows, but the Kalesian and Ringulian women were made of sterner stuff.

Molly Kelshaw was particularly affected because her friend Karen had been assaulted, and it seemed to have left psychological scars on Molly. Molly began to withdraw from the company of men whenever she could, and went out of her way to avoid having physical contact with them at her work in the Civic Offices. Her parents became concerned and went to talk about it to Dr. Mark Ryland, the resident psychiatrist.

"I don't think it's anything lasting," he said, "but you'll have to help her to snap out of it. Take her with you to as many social functions as you can and I am sure it will all come right in the end."

The night of the dance arrived, and it began on a high note, full of excitement, music, lights and laughter. After a short time, the dance was in full swing, being enjoyed by Sikarans and humans alike. Geoffrey Maitland watched everyone enjoying the dancing with relief. Since Marayshan's elite group of *Isithan* soldiers had arrived, the anxiety and dread of Gloshan attack had diminished and especially as they had captured the renegade Earth soldier, Conrad Weissner. Everyone was happier now because they felt safer and more secure. The Sikarans were extremely pleasant men to socialize with and they made an effort to join in as many social functions as they could.

Marayshan went up to Molly Kelshaw and said, "Will you do me the honour of being my partner in the next dance, *kirathie*?"

Molly Kelshaw was both flattered and pleased to be asked to dance by the Sikaran Governor of the colony. He was a very attractive man, personable, had a great sense of humour and was a military hero. Molly, an over-imaginative young woman, could not think of a better man to idolize than the new Governor. But most of all, for her, it was his rescue of prisoners from the hands of Gloshan torturers in Camp *K'Taak* that was the thing that impressed her most about him, and he became her dream knight in shining armour. To the surprise of her parents, Molly was happy to be spun round and lifted and held close by the Sikaran Governor, despite all her present inhibitions. To their continued surprise, when she and the Governor were presented with the trophy for the best dancers of the evening, Molly hugged and kissed Marayshan with enthusiasm and he hugged and kissed her in return.

Late in the evening, however, the mood changed for Molly, after she had danced with her boyfriend, who really loved her, and wanted to marry her. He persuaded her to go for a walk outside with him and within moments there were the sounds of screams and Molly dashed back into the hall in floods of tears.

"*Kirathie*, what has happened?" Marayshan said, rushing up to her with her parents and Maitland.

Molly flung herself at Marayshan and clung to him, shaking like a leaf.

The young man rushed in after her and said in anguished tones, "I didn't *do anything!* All I did was kiss Molly. I swear it!"

"Molly, tell me, did your boyfriend just kiss you?" Marayshan asked.

"Yes, but I got scared. I got scared, I'm really sorry. I'm so sorry. It's because that Earth Special Forces soldier assaulted my friend Karen a few months ago. It terrified me and I'm a bundle of nerves. Peter, I'm so sorry. I'm so sorry."

"It doesn't matter, Molly," Peter replied, "but I just wish you would get over it soon! I would really like to marry you some time, you know."

"I know, Peter, I know. I just don't know what is happening to me anymore. I can't control it, I can't." Molly wept on Marayshan's shoulder.

"Oh *kirathie*, don't cry," Marayshan said gently and succeeded in quietening her. Everyone was interested in the new Sikaran Governor and so they watched him now as he comforted Molly.

"You have a real talent for doing that, Marayshan," said Geoffrey Maitland, smiling at him. "It's good to see and to know that the galaxy is not as awful a place as it might otherwise be."

Marayshan thanked him for the compliment, then led Molly back to her seat. Peter went for a long walk with Molly's father.

"Marayshan, you're feeling sorry for Molly, aren't you? I can tell," Nava said shortly after.

Marayshan smiled at his friend.

"How is it that you know me so well, Nava?" he said. "I'm sad for Molly. She is such a lovely human woman. I sense her fear of men runs deep and she may never be able to marry Peter."

"That is very sad," Nava replied. "So why don't you help her?"

"In what way can I help her?"

"She trusts you. That is obvious. She trusts you a huge amount."

"Oh, I see. So she trusts me. So?"

"Help her to lose her fear of men."

They looked at each other.

"It would not be easy," said Marayshan.

"Is there anything easy that is worthwhile in this life?" said Nava.

"No, nothing."

"So, help her. Go and talk to her parents in a few weeks time. Tell them you would like to help her if you can. You know as much about human women as I do. They're just the same as Gloshan women."

Marayshan didn't need to make the offer of help. Both Matthew Kelshaw and his wife, Linda, were both magistrates in the Civic Centre. The Kelshaws knocked on the door of his office in the Civic Offices a week later. Mrs. Kelshaw opened the conversation.

"Governor, we have come to thank you for being so kind to our daughter Molly in the dance last week. We have been talking to Dr. Ryland. He thinks we need to find a man she really trusts to help her get over all this. It's ruining her life and that of her boyfriend, Peter. Molly will never be able to marry Peter or anyone else unless she can get over this awful psychological problem that she has developed."

Her husband spoke now. "Dr. Ryland suggested to Molly that you might be able to help her and she was happy with his choice. That's why we are here, to ask you if you would possibly consider helping Molly again. We would be so grateful. It is, however, asking rather a lot from you on a personal level and we would quite understand if you chose not to get involved."

"I will try to help, but I don't know how easy it will be. I would offer to use a little telepathy, but it would only be a temporary measure, not lasting, but I will try to help."

"We're not expecting you to work any miracles, Governor, but Dr. Ryland thinks it would set Molly on the road to recovery. He doesn't think it will be a pleasant experience for you because, despite trusting you, she is likely to be still very frightened. Dr Ryland would like you to do things like massage and aroma therapy with her," said Matthew Kelshaw.

Marayshan then said, "When does Dr Ryland wish me to start working with Molly?"
"Oh it's up to you entirely, Governor; whenever you feel able to leave work for a few days. The committee are happy for you to do that, I checked with them."
"I never feel able to leave my work, but we will start tomorrow. I will ask Devthanyi to take over leadership of my *Isithan* group while I am otherwise engaged."
"It is really very good of you to help Molly like this, Governor. We'll see you tomorrow then. Come in time to have lunch with us, say twelve thirty."
"Thank you, I will bring my two friends, Avernyi and Navaronschyia."

They arrived at the house the next day, and Molly welcomed them.
Marayshan said, "Molly! Hello! It is good to see you." He embraced her and kissed her on both sides of her face.

"Hello. Thank you so much for taking the time out to help me. I'm so grateful, but nothing might be able to help me, not ever and then I'll lose Peter."

"Why don't you wait and see. Let us begin by enjoying lunch together." Matthew and Linda Kelshaw welcomed him together with Peter and Dr

Ryland: who shook hands with the three Sikaran soldiers; over lunch, Dr Ryland said,
"Molly, what would you think of lots of massages with wonderful scented oils, wouldn't it be heavenly? Marayshan could give you a massage every day for two weeks, how does that sound?"
"Rather embarrassing actually," Molly replied. "I really haven't thought about things like that." Molly looked very uncomfortable.
"Now come on, Molly, for heaven's sake," said her father sounding exasperated.
"Well, I suppose there's no harm in it, is there? Except that, well, that …" Molly went silent, blushing.

Nava said something in Sikaran to Marayshan. "Molly, look, when we were dancing together, I was holding you and you were holding me. We were very close."
"That was different. We were dancing," Molly replied. "In a massage, you would have to, well touch me, over other parts of me, I mean."
"Molly is very sensitive I think," said Avernyi, smiling at her.
Molly nodded and said, "It's awful being so sensitive about everything. That's why I'm in this state. After my friend Karen was assaulted, I went to see her in hospital. It was terrible, really terrible."
"Yes, but Marayshan is not like that Earth soldier, *kirathie*, he is very trustworthy."
"Yes, I'm sure that he is, Avernyi," Molly replied smiling at him. "I know it's me just being stupid, but I can't help feeling the way I do."

Marayshan reached over and took her hand and said, "Everyone is entitled to be stupid at least once in their lives, *kirathie.* I am here to help you get over those feelings and fears. Poor old Peter, he is really very keen to marry you. I can see it in his eyes. He loves you very much. You know you cannot keep him waiting forever. You cannot go on like this forever. I have heard human men at the Civic Offices commenting because you shy away from them and you get emotional, even if they touch you by accident. It is not fair on them. You cannot blame all human men for the deeds of one. Mostly the human men here on Naiobi are family men. They are good men. Actually Molly, you are treating them very badly."

"I hadn't thought of it that way, Governor, but now you've said it, I do see what you mean," Molly replied.

"Good. You know, I think you will be able to control these feelings, Molly, when you start to be able to distinguish between different kinds of men. There is a huge difference between Peter and that Earth soldier Conrad Weissner who assaulted your friend. Peter does not do things like that. He has never done them and I never think that he will. This is a fantasy you have built up in your mind. You are seeing the image of Conrad superimposed on the image of Peter and you cannot separate the two. You are doing a great injustice to Peter and seriously, I mean seriously questioning his honour. It is wrong, Molly. See how unhappy you have made him?"

Molly became tearful and said, "Peter, I'm so sorry. I do love you. You know that, don't you?"

"Just sort yourself out, Molly. That is all I am asking," said Peter. "Please, sort yourself out and do it soon. Just follow Dr Ryland's advice and do whatever it takes."

"Peter, dear, this must be so difficult for you," Linda said sighing.

"Dr Ryland, what is your programme? Shall we get started? The sooner the better I would say." Marayshan said.

"Yes. Molly, would you please leave us for a few minutes."

Molly went out of the room.

"Marayshan," Ryland said, "I've already talked to Peter about this. As a fallback position, if nothing that we do on the programme succeeds Peter has agreed that you should have a go at making love to Molly."

"And suppose Molly objects?" said Avernyi.

"Well, I would like Marayshan to use his powers of persuasion. That is my considered recommendation."

"Do you mean he should seduce Molly?" demanded Avernyi. "Marayshan could not do that. It would be extremely dishonourable. You cannot ask him to do such a thing! He is *Ivthalyin Isithan*!"

"It might be the only thing that works in the end, and I would not ask anyone else, but Marayshan, to do such a thing with Molly. Whether or not he is *Ivthalyin Isithan*! I have a very high regard for your friend, Avernyi. I have had many excellent reports about him from the officers and crew of the starship *McBride*," Ryland replied.

"I cannot understand your reasoning, doctor, I am sorry," said Avernyi.

"I think I can understand it, Avernyi," said Nava. "Molly is gripped by this fear and doesn't know what to do. But part of it is her own inexperience; the fear of the unknown because she is so sensitive. Now if Marayshan, being an older man, can persuade her to let him make love to her that is fine. It will change everything. It all depends on the fact that Molly trusts him to do the right thing to help her. Now, if he tells her that before he begins and says, 'Trust me, no matter what happens,' I think it will have the same effect, because it is Marayshan who does it."

Dr Ryland looked surprised at Nava, and said, "You have got it absolutely right, Nava. It all hinges on Molly's feelings of trust for Marayshan and, having spoken at length to her, I have discovered that Molly trusts him at the deepest level of her consciousness."

"I have sensed this also, doctor," said Nava, "and I think that, handled carefully, it will work. I am confident that Marayshan will be able to bring success out of this for Molly."

Peter suddenly coloured and said, "I really don't think I can go through with this. I'm out of here! I'm sorry, Mr and Mrs Kelshaw, I have had ten months of it and I cannot take much more. I am going and I won't be coming back!" Peter got up angrily and left the house.

"I thought that would happen," Ryland said. "I'll talk to Peter tomorrow. He's become very jealous of Marayshan."

"I have no feelings for Molly other than a wish to help," Marayshan said.

"Well, with or without Peter in the picture, we still have to help Molly," Ryland said. "So I think we should give it our best shot. I wonder if you could use small amounts of telepathy with Molly to reassure her, if you have no objection to doing that. I heard from Captain Grey that you and your men used your telepathy very positively in a number of situations, especially with a soldier named Lance Dayton. You aided his recovery, didn't you? So I have every confidence in you, Marayshan."

"I will not let you down," Marayshan replied.

"Well, I had better return to my afternoon clinic. Goodbye one and all," Ryland said.

When he had gone, Matthew said, "Would anyone like a brandy? I know I could use one."

"Yes please, we all drink brandy, it is one of our favourite drinks," replied Avernyi.

Marayshan drank his brandy in one mouthful and Kelshaw looked at him in surprise. He stood. "I will see you all later," he said and went to find Molly who was in the garden looking very forlorn.

"I heard what Peter shouted about going away and not coming back. Actually, I heard everything Dr Ryland said. I was listening behind the door."
"You should not have been listening, Molly," Marayshan said.
"You're right, I shouldn't have been, but I did hear. I do trust you. I do trust you to do the best for me, whatever that is." Molly sounded very sad.

Marayshan went with her to her room. As he carried her, Molly closed her eyes and he became her knight in shining armour. Marayshan sat holding her for a long time quietly. Molly would smile at him now and then and close her eyes and lean against him.

Finally she said, "I'm so lucky to have found you to help me. I wish that I were different and didn't feel so deeply about everything."
"There is nothing wrong with being so sensitive. It makes you aware of other people's feelings and that is a good thing not a bad thing. It means you can help them."
"Yes, I suppose it does, but I identify with them too much. The way I identified with Karen. My friend died you know. It was awful. She didn't last the night."
"I am so sorry, *kirathie*. I didn't realize," Marayshan said.

Molly wanted to weep but stopped herself, "I've spent too long crying for Karen these past ten months. I don't think I can cry anymore," Molly said.

Marayshan kissed her hand. "You're going to an awful amount of trouble to help me, I don't know how I can ever repay you," Molly said, smiling at him.
"You can thank me by smiling again. You are feeling too sad, Molly. You are feeling too sad." He kissed each of her hands.
"I like that. I really do, do it again, please." Molly said, smiling at him. He did the same again. "You know I have a feeling that everything is going to turn out right for you," he said.
"How can you say that? Everything is dreadful. I scream whenever Peter tries to kiss me. The men in the Civic Offices are fed up with me. They only put up

with me now because of my father being a senior magistrate. Peter wants to make love to me, but he can't get near me. I become hysterical. My father ... I can't even let him kiss me. You're the only one I feel safe with now."

"It is a good thing there is someone you feel safe with, or what would happen to you?"

"I would never marry and always be lonely. No husband, no children. I would grow old on my own and grow bitter. No, probably not that, not bitter, but I wouldn't be very happy, I shouldn't think."

"Listen to me. You are too good a person for that to happen to you. I am not going to let it happen to you. I am going to do whatever it takes to help you."

Molly put her arms around his waist and squeezed him and said, "You are so wonderful for helping me like this."

Marayshan lit an oil burner after a while and covered his hands with scented oils and began to give her a massage. "Why are you so quiet?" he said.

"I am trying to control my feelings. I don't want to behave badly and hurt you the way I hurt Peter."

"You will not hurt me," Marayshan replied, embracing her again.

Molly remained passive, submitting to whatever he did.

Marayshan frowned, concerned about her. "We are getting on much better than I thought we would, Molly," he said, trying to cheer her up.

"I am determined to try and keep ... control ... of myself. I am not going to stop you from doing anything." Molly touched his face looking into his eyes then rested against him feeling warm and reassured.

"You've done something with your telepathy, haven't you?" she said. "I sensed you. I felt you in my mind like soft falling rain on my face. I really liked the feeling. Please do it again."

"It was a very light touch. You are extremely sensitive to have felt it in that way."

He touched her mind again and Molly whispered, "Please don't stop, I love it. I really love it."

Marayshan had to reign in his passion suddenly as it caught him unawares. Molly was beginning to call him to her, beginning to desire him, or so he thought.

"Molly, please don't call me in that way in your mind. I am becoming too aroused. Oh *hai cheh*! This is seriously not good news." He pulled away from her and calmed himself down, trying to control his breathing.

"I'm sorry. I didn't mean to do anything wrong," Molly replied.

Marayshan got up quickly and dashed out of the room.

"Avernyi, Avernyi!" he called and spoke at length in Sikaran.

"Oh *hai cheh*," Avernyi said, groaning. "Marayshan, this is not good news for Molly. Just calm down, will you. You've been working too hard since we got to Naiobi. Show me what happened in your mind."

Marayshan let him see, and Avernyi said, "This is not a call to you for sexual merging. It is a call to you, yes, a call of wanting, but not in that way. It is a very mixed message because Molly is human. Part of it was a sexual call, yes, but it was not genuine. Look at the rest of the message now that you are calmer and can distance yourself from the situation. Molly is pretending, she is trying to engage you, appealing to what she thinks will hold you. Molly needs your friendship and support and is looking to the future. I think she thinks this is the only way she can see that will engage you enough to want to return to her at a later stage to be a friend to her. I think it is a human way of a woman; engaging a man's friendship if she needs him. I noticed that happening on the human starship with a few other human women. It seems difficult for them to make straightforward friendship ties to human men, probably because the men are the way they are. But we are different, so you will have to show Molly that she does not have to pretend to call you in a sexual way, to guarantee your friendship in the future, or your assistance at this difficult time in her life."

Matthew poured another brandy for everyone and Marayshan knocked it back in one go, much to Kelshaw's admiration. He listened to the conversation, fascinated by the insightfulness of the Sikaran men. He had never expected alien special-forces soldiers to be in any way like that. He had never expected them to give a damn about anyone's feelings, especially not the feelings of humans.

It had come as a shock and a revelation and he knew that other humans in the colony were beginning to look upon these Sikaran soldiers in a new light. They all had the stereotype fixed in their minds of the typical Earth special-forces soldier: violent, aggressive and deadly in battle and sometimes out of it. After the experience with the renegade Earth soldier, they were more than worried about what an elite group of the toughest Sikaran soldiers was going to be like.

Matthew remembered his high level of anxiety as he waited for the Sikarans to arrive in the market square from the transport that had brought them to *Naiobi* from the starship *McBride*. He could see the fear and expectancy in the faces of the people around him. He could sense terror in a few people. He could … He stopped thinking abruptly as he realiszd that the three Sikarans were watching him intently.

"What's wrong? What's the matter?" he said, alarmed.
"Your thoughts have reached us," said Nava, "that has never happened with a human before. They are clear, not just feelings. They are clear thoughts. You have telepathic ability. We picked up your thoughts because they were focused on us. Ah. That would explain what is happening to Marayshan. Molly must have inherited this telepathic ability from you. It is submerged. Marayshan, we should tell the Sikaran High Council."

"Tell them what?" Matthew asked.

"About your telepathic ability, even though it is submerged," Avernyi said.

"Are you sure they would be even remotely interested?" Matthew said.

"Yes, I think they would," Marayshan replied. "I think they would. That would explain completely what just happened with Molly. That is why I reacted the way I did. Even though, as you say, Nava, the telepathy is submerged, it is nevertheless there. This is amazing. You must be very unusual humans, you and Molly."

"Yes, I suppose we are, Molly and I," Matthew replied. "Though my wife isn't the same; over the centuries on Earth, people like me were persecuted for the smallest reasons. We were thought to have supernatural powers. We can trace persecutions back a long time in my family tree to a place called Salem. That was the worst place for my ancestors. Other humans used to be frightened and suspicious of people like Molly and me. They blamed everything bad that happened on my ancestors: if crops failed, if cows didn't give enough milk, if it rained too much. Now it is different of course, the humans on Earth are much more tolerant. Mind you, I am glad we moved to Naiobi, because I have had the opportunity to meet the three of you, and so has Molly."

"Touch my hand," Nava said. "Can you hear me in your mind?"

"Of course I can hear you, quite clearly actually. Can you hear me?"

"Yes, it is quite amazing." Nava smiled and transferred the thoughts to his friends by touching their chests.

"You are coming over loud and clear, Matthew," said Avernyi. "I like the song you are singing in your mind, where is it from?"

"It is from a place called England on Earth; a very ancient song. I thought you might like to hear it. My ancestors came from England. You stopped there for a few days when you first arrived on Earth, remember?"

"Yes, Matthew, we must talk again," said Marayshan, "but I think I should go back to Molly now. Give me another brandy before I go, will you."

"Certainly, I know how you feel," said Matthew.

Marayshan drank it again in one mouthful and left the room.

"How does he do that? I wish I could," said Matthew in admiration.

"Marayshan is the toughest of us," said Nava shrugging.

"Good Lord, I would never have thought that, he seems such a nice person. I know that he is your leader, but that wouldn't necessarily mean that he'd have to be the toughest of you."

"That is true, of course, and he is all you said of him, and very caring too," said Nava. "Yet he is still the toughest of our group, believe me."

"Yes, believe him," said Avernyi. "People have sometimes forgotten that and underestimated Marayshan, to their cost."

"Good Lord," said Matthew shaking his head again.

Marayshan found Molly looking very unhappy.
"I got it wrong again, didn't I?" she said.
"You got nothing wrong," Marayshan replied, embracing her and speaking to her in her mind.
"Your father told us about the telepathy," he said.
"Oh I see," Molly replied, putting her arms around him.
"Yes, and I'm very happy about this, because now I can use much more telepathy than I thought, in order that I might help you."
"Will it make so much difference to anything?" Molly asked, hugging him to her.

"Yes, I think it will, wait and see." Marayshan replied. "You know, Molly, you can have my friendship in future years without feeling you need to offer me anything else. You don't need to pretend to desire me, you know."

"Well, I wasn't pretending exactly. You're a very attractive man, you know, but it's Peter I love."

Marayshan concentrated for a few moments then, in the best tradition of farmers from the Arakiarth Valley, he said, "Hey, lose your eyes. Lie back and enjoy it!"

Molly laughed then did as he said. Time passed and Molly began to feel wonderful, invigorated by the sensations that Marayshan was passing to her through the telepathic link. Suddenly they translated to her body and she gasped, caught up in an ecstasy. Marayshan smiled to himself and kissed her.

"I think that you will be happy with Peter now," he said afterwards. "But we can do this a few more times just to be on the safe side.

"It would be really good practice for me wouldn't it," Molly said. "The trouble is, Peter isn't telepathic, so you will have to help me in the other way too. I would like to be really confident in every way. I really would, otherwise I just might start screaming again."

"Well, we cannot have that, *kirathie*, but it will take some time to accustom you to the other way of doing things, you know, because you are so inexperienced. Your packaging has not yet been removed, if you see what I mean."

Molly blushed vividly and giggled.

"You have gone a very funny colour, *kirathie*," he said.

Molly cleared her throat and said, "Good lord, is that the time?"

"What else have you got to do today?" Marayshan asked bemused.

"Oh nothing," Molly said. "I was just doing an impression of my father when he gets embarrassed. He always says, 'Good lord, is that the time?' and clears his throat."

Marayshan laughed this time.

"Are you sure you shouldn't just let Peter undo your packaging. I think he will go crazy if I do any more than I have done already with you."

"Well, I suppose I could, but I am still not completely happy about everything. Seriously, my nerves are still jangling. Peter is over-keen, especially about making love. He's desperate and he'll never control himself enough, you know what I mean?"

"Well, I can appreciate his feelings. You are very beautiful, really, extremely beautiful."

Molly blushed again, quite vividly. "Could you tell me something please? I am sure you've had experience of these things. Will undoing my packaging be really difficult?"

"No, it will not be difficult for me at all," Marayshan replied, making a joke of it.

"I meant me! Will it be difficult for me?" Molly replied, laughing.

Marayshan shrugged. "Oh, it will be nothing to worry about, *kirathie.* It is life. It just happens. It is of no importance. All people I have met do it you know." He shrugged again.

"I do worry about it, though. That's my problem, that's my problem!" Molly said emphatically.

Marayshan reassured her through the telepathic link.

"It will no longer be a problem when Peter returns," he said. "And once it is no longer a problem, what will you find to worry about next?"

"I suppose I'll think of something," Molly replied.

Peter did not however return to Molly. The following day, he signed up as an officer on a space cargo ship and left Naiobi, sending a message to Matthew Kelshaw to tell him that he no longer wanted to marry Molly.

"Are you upset about it, Molly?" Marayshan asked.

"No, not really, for the past few months I have been expecting it," Molly replied.

"You know, when you feel that you have got over all this, there is one of my men I would very much like to introduce you to. His name is Ilvaren, from the *Gira* Clan. He would very much like to settle down here on Naiobi and get married. I said that I would help arrange a marriage for him now that we are staying on Naiobi for the foreseeable future. I cannot think of a better person than you, Molly."

"I would love to meet Ilvaren. I would so like to marry someone who is telepathic like me. It would be really wonderful," Molly replied.

"Ilvaren is a very kind and understanding man and would take good care of you," Marayshan said.

Molly embraced him to thank him.

He then spoke to Molly's parents, telling them her wishes and saying that he would ask Ilvaren to come and meet them all.

The next day, Marayshan called the police station on the direct communicator he had in his office and asked Police Chief Maitland if he could send Ilvaren to him as soon as possible as it was important.

Geoffrey Maitland replied, "Of course, Governor. He is here doing some admin work. Ilvaren, Governor Marayshan wants to see you in his office now," Maitland called over to him.

Ilvaren stood, looking concerned at Avernyi. "Var, I must be in trouble, Avernyi," he said. "Thank you, Captain Maitland. I will go right over." Ilvaren straightened his police uniform jacket and adjusted his collar.

"Wait, you have some dust on your sleeve, Ilvaren," Nava said, and removed it for him. "There now you look smart."

"Oh hai cheh!" said Ilvaren. "I must be in a lot of trouble for the *Ivthalyin* to call me to his office like this in the middle of the day."

"Be brave, Ilvaren, be brave," said Nava, patting him on the back.

Maitland was surprised by the exchange, thinking that there must be a sterner side to Marayshan that he had yet to see.

Ilvaren walked across the way to the Civic Offices and tentatively knocked on Marayshan's door.

"Enter," Marayshan called out abruptly in military fashion then said, "Ah. Ilvaren."

Ilvaren stood smartly to attention, saluted and bowed. "Shield Lord: am I in a lot of trouble?" he asked, not daring to look at Marayshan.

"No, you're not in any trouble at all, Ilvaren. Please be seated. Do you remember at the dance two weeks ago, I was dancing with a charming human woman named Molly Kelshaw, the daughter of the senior magistrate here?"

"Yes, Shield Lord, we all thought you very fortunate to be dancing with the most beautiful woman there. We were very envious."

Marayshan paused for a moment then said, "Do you remember, Ilvaren, just before we came here, you asked me to help you to find a suitable wife? Well I think I have found her."

Ilvaren looked at the Shield Lord in astonishment.

"You don't mean Molly Kelshaw, Shield Lord. How can I marry a woman from her high social background? I am from Clan *Gira*, the lowest clan on *Sarcharie*. I have nothing to offer her except myself."

"That will be enough for her, Ilvaren. Humans don't really seem to care about clan status. There are a few who do but Molly and her parents are not like that, and I have discovered something about Molly. She is a very special human and so is her father. They both have telepathic ability although it is submerged. It seems to be activated in the presence of Sikarans. There must be some vibes we emit that are compatible with their telepathy. Apparently telepathy runs in Matthew Kelshaw's family from many generations back."

"This is truly marvellous, Shield Lord. What a discovery, but wouldn't you wish to marry Molly yourself?" Marayshan paused.

"Well, that had occurred to me, but I feel she's too young for me really. You are a more suitable age for her. I have also been in a true marriage already, twice if you count my relationship with Triatha in the Gloshan camps. One way or another, I've had a lot of experience with marriage and I'm not ready to marry again. I want a break for a while, whereas you have never been married. Now I know that you are a kind and understanding man, because you have been picked as many times as I have to take part in the ritual '*Darath kiathar*'. Molly is a woman who needs a great deal of patience and understanding. She's very sensitive. Molly is also kind and caring to others, as you are. Molly has said that she would very much like to marry a Sikaran man and so I thought instantly of you, Ilvaren."

"You do me great honour, Shield Lord, I am sure I don't deserve such honour."
"Yes you do, Ilvaren." Marayshan replied, "You haven't been very fortunate in the past have you." He paused then continued. "You are one of my best soldiers, you know."

Ilvaren looked extremely happy and proud at the compliment.
"If you would like me to, I will arrange for you to have dinner with Molly and her parents in their home. I could be there, too, if you like, with Nava and Avernyi."

"I would appreciate that, Shield Lord," he replied. "I cannot believe that this is happening to me."

"Well, believe it, Ilvaren, it's time something nice happened to you," Marayshan replied smiling at him. "But Ilvaren, although I will be at the meal with you, after that you're on your own. You will have to make a good impression on Molly. But that will not be too difficult for you, I am sure."

"But for me to marry such a woman of high status and so beautiful, Shield Lord, how can I? It would be such a great honour."

"Why shouldn't *you* have such an honour? Why should it always be the High Clans? Now go. Leave me. I am busy. I will let you know when I have arranged the dinner."

"Shield Lord, thank you. One day I will pay you back for your kindness. I will not forget this day." Ilvaren knelt on one knee to him for a moment.

"I do not want any payment from you. What I do want is to see you and Molly happy together. Now go!"

Ilvaren left the office, scarcely daring to believe what had just happened. He dashed across the road into the police station, and grabbed Nava and hugged him and spoke in Sikaran, looking overjoyed.

"Ilvaren, come along, tell me what's happened, I would like to know too," said Captain Maitland.

"Oh sir, it is the most wonderful day of my life. *Ivthalyin* Marayshan is arranging for me to have dinner with Molly Kelshaw in the home of her parents!"

"Lucky you, Molly is incredibly beautiful and very charming with it," Maitland replied.

"Oh yes, oh yes, Molly is so beautiful." The young man said dreamily. "Because she is telepathic like us, Molly has asked the *Ivthalyin* if he would find her a Sikaran man to marry and he has chosen me. He has chosen *me*. Avernyi! He has chosen *me*!"

"Nava and I already knew that, Ilvaren. You and Molly will do well together," Avernyi replied smiling at him.

"Avernyi, does Marayshan do a lot of matchmaking like this?" Maitland asked.

"Well, not really, just from time to time Chief," said Avernyi. "He is good at it, actually. Why do you ask?"

"Oh no reason really, well, I have a daughter who could do with some extra help to find a good husband. She wouldn't mind if he was human, Sikaran, Ringulian or Kalesian, as long as he was a good man; I'll have a talk to Marayshan about it."

"Captain, it would be very good if your daughter were to marry a Sikaran," said Nava. "One of us would make her a good husband."

"Yes, I believe that you would," Geoffrey Maitland replied thoughtfully. "I believe that you would. Things have been a bit difficult for her lately."

***

A few days later Deva sat at the desk in his office in the police station, having just contacted Andrea, the Human scientist whose company he had enjoyed so much on the starship *McBride*. He kept her picture on his computer screen as a screen default image and was gazing at it. Nava came in and saw the screen. "Oh, Andrea," he said knowingly.

"Andrea is coming to see me, Navaronschyia," Deva replied smiling at him.

"Oh, Andrea is coming to see you. I like the sound of that. I think she's serious about you. I told you at the time I thought she was."

"But what about all that panicking she did when I tried to merge just a little bit with her? It was only a very small amount, Nava, just a tiny, little bit of merging."

"It was just nerves. You shouldn't have taken it so seriously. Human women are very nervous about everything in my experience, especially anything to do with their clothes. I am not sure why. You just have to help them to get over their nerves. Play some music to her. Give her a massage. Sing to her, all that sort of thing. Tell her a joke. Recite poetry. Distract her from the telepathy."

"All right, thank you, I'll try your advice, Navaronschyia. You've had a fair bit of experience with human women by now, haven't you?"

"I should say so," said Nava, "they're so warm and friendly to me. Mind you, Deva, you're right actually. Most of them can't cope with our way of doing things. Some of my girlfriends really try to last for an hour with me, but they just can't manage it and they leave me. There is only one actually who has managed it, but she fainted three times. Mind you, the Gloshan women were always fainting too. I sense that she really likes me though. Her name is Elsa. I think that I may try to build up a relationship with her. It's all very well, Marayshan saying that we should use only surface bonds and empathy to get some pleasure for ourselves, but I'm longing to do a lot more than that. Aren't you? I really want to get right inside Elsa's mind, you know what I mean? Right inside. I know that they're human women, but they are like our women in many ways. It is just so tempting to go all the way."

"Navaronschyia, you must not do that," said Deva. "You will have to build up to that slowly with a human woman, or you'll hurt her badly. You see how some of them, like Andrea, panic over even surface bonding. I know it would not do any lasting damage to them, but still, we shouldn't do it, and Marayshan has forbidden it."

"I know, Deva, I know. He's a real spoilsport," said Nava.

"Navaronschyia, if something like that were to happen, Marayshan would be seriously unhappy about it. You couldn't rely on his friendship then. You would be in a lot of trouble with him. You know that he's threatened us with a public flogging or the *Chora* if ever we did that, without preparing the human woman first. I think I need to remind you of that."

"He wouldn't really do anything, Deva, surely? He's no different to the rest of us. He really wants to do it too," Nava replied.

"Navaronschyia take a step back from him. You are too close. He's our group leader and the head of the whole *Isithan*. I think you're forgetting that, because you've been friends with him for such a long time. Avernyi is able to make the distinction, but I don't think you are. You need to slow down and think. He will not hesitate to discipline you, either with a flogging or with the *Chora*, whichever way you will be devastated. Because he is our leader, he won't be able to support you. Now I would be very unhappy if I had to flog you, and secondly he would be very unhappy if he had to administer the *Chora*. You would not care much about how I feel, I'm sure, but you would care about how Marayshan feels, wouldn't you, wouldn't you?"

"Deva, stop frightening and depressing me all at the same time; you always seem to be able to do that," Nava replied.

"Someone has to bring you to your senses. Take a break for a while from your girlfriends. Slow down. Just concentrate on Elsa. Bring her to socialize with the rest of us, so she can get to know Avernyi and Marayshan. If Elsa is serious about you, then she will want to get to know your friends and we will explain to her about not allowing you to do too much of anything until you've practiced enough telepathy with her. If she has feelings for you, then she won't want to see you get into trouble and, over time, you can gradually deepen your bonding. How does that sound?"

"It sounds fine, Deva," he said miserably, "just fine, and I was having such a good time too."

In the end, with Deva's help, things worked out well for Nava with Elsa and he didn't get into any trouble at all. However it was one of the younger members of the *Isithan* group, whose name was Ilashon, who surprisingly did the thing that they were all trying to avoid doing: using their telepathy to enter deep inside a human woman's mind. It was the most unlikely person in the group to do such a thing.

Chapter Seven: The End of the Space War

Police Chief Geoffrey Maitland took a call one morning, a few days later, from a Mr. Mark Anstey, a property magnate. He said that Ilashon had done something unpleasant to his daughter, Ellen, in some way, although he wasn't quite sure how as she seemed to be physically unhurt, except that she had been screaming and crying for several minutes.

Captain Maitland turned to Deva and Avernyi and said, "We have an incident between police cadet Ilashon and a young woman by the name of Ellen Anstey. This is the first Sikaran-Human incident that we've ever had on Naiobi. It's so rare that I'm going to come with you to see what's going on."

"Ellen is Ilashon's girlfriend, Chief," said Avernyi.

"Right, Mr Anstey said that his daughter was alone with Ilashon in her bedroom. It looked as though they had been listening to music together."

The Sikarans exchanged glances.

"Chief, I am calling Marayshan," said Avernyi, "he will want to see what's happened himself."

"Of course," said Maitland. "It is so unusual, for anything to happen like this between a Human woman and a Sikaran man. I wonder what's going on with Ilashon. He's such a promising young cadet, just like Chalek."

"Yes, chief, he is, but we can all go off the rails at times," said Deva.

"Well, let's find out what's going on, shall we?" said Maitland.

They all reached the Anstey residence more or less together; Marayshan and Maitland, Deva, Nava, Avernyi and Elaan.

"Governor Marayshan, what on earth are you doing here?" said Mark Anstey, Ellen's father. "Captain Maitland too, look, all of you, I am so embarrassed for wasting police time like this. There doesn't seem to be anything wrong with Ellen now. She's stopped crying and is almost back to normal. Do come in, all of you, and you can see for yourselves. Ellen, Mary, we have a lot of visitors," Anstey said as he showed them into the living room.

"Where is Ilashon?" Deva asked.

"I left him upstairs in Ellen's bedroom. He's very upset," said Mary Anstey.

"I'll go and see him," said Deva, "come on Avernyi."

Marayshan went then and sat with Ellen and took her hand. "*Kirathie*, how do you feel?" he asked.

"Governor, it's good to see you," Ellen said. "I am so sorry I made such a fuss. I feel all right now."

"Tell me what happened," he said.

"Well, I was sitting beside Ilashon, and we were listening to some wonderful music together. He had his arms around me and suddenly he pushed his hand under my blouse about here on my chest, and held me really tightly and suddenly I felt this terrible pain all over me. It only lasted a few seconds, but it was unbearable. I didn't know what on earth had happened. It was agony and I screamed and screamed and my parents thought that Ilashon had molested me, but he hadn't. We haven't done anything yet. I wanted to wait until we got married. You see, we got engaged yesterday and we hope to marry in a year from today."

Nava and Elaan exchanged uncomfortable glances with Marayshan.

"Kirathie, I think that Ilashon has done something to you with his telepathy. May I use my telepathy to see how badly you were hurt? It will only be a surface link, so you need not fear it."

"I'm not afraid of you, Governor, of course I'm not," Ellen replied, "please go ahead."

Marayshan rested one hand on her forehead and the other on her chest and flinched.

"Elaan, go and bring Ilashon and the others here. This is really bad."

When they came in Marayshan said, "Deva and the rest of you, come and take Ellen's feelings from me and give me your opinion about what happened. I think she has been badly hurt."

After they had touched Marayshan's hand, Deva said, "Yes I agree with you," and the rest nodded assent.

"So you don't think that I am overreacting then?" he said.

"No, it's bad, Marayshan," said Avernyi quietly.

"Governor, what's wrong?" asked Mark Anstey, "What has Ilashon done with his telepathy?"

"He has attempted to make a marriage link with Ellen, but he has done so too quickly, and too strongly, without preparing her. He should have spent at least six months, using small amounts of telepathy with her, so she could become accustomed to linking with him. The marriage link is difficult enough for a Sikaran woman to cope with because it runs so deep, but for a Human woman, without any kind of preparation, it would be very bad. I am so sorry, *kirathie*, that you were hurt so much. May I help you with my mind?"

Ellen nodded. "Yes please, it's still rather painful actually, but bearable," she said and then sighed after a moment, relaxing back on the settee. "Thank you so much." She said. "That has really helped." She hugged Marayshan and kissed him.

Marayshan turned and looked intently at Ilashon for a moment, his eyes narrowing, then said, "Geoffrey, when we first came here to *Naiobi*, my men and I, I told them, and all the other Sikaran soldiers here, that under no circumstances were they to make such a link with a human woman without at least six months preparation. I said that if something like this did happen the man responsible would be severely disciplined."

Ellen looked concerned and said, "Governor, I'm all right now, really. You don't need to discipline Ilashon on my account."

"Ellen, this should never have happened," Marayshan said, standing up. "I specifically said to all of them that this should not happen. Ilashon has gone against my wishes." He put his hands behind his back.

"So Ilashon, speak. Tell me why this has happened."

"Ivthalyin, please forgive me, please, it is not like me but I got carried away. Ellen is such a wonderful person." He sounded very frightened of Marayshan now, which surprised Maitland and the other humans considerably as they had only ever seen the nice side of Marayshan.

"Yes I agree with you absolutely, Ilashon. Ellen is a wonderful young woman and you are a very fortunate young man. It therefore follows, does it not, that Ellen definitely does not deserve to be treated in this way. Ilashon! How dare you! You have shocked me by your behaviour here today and you have deeply disappointed me. I thought better of you." Marayshan paced the room now.

"Let me tell you, Ilashon," Marayshan continued, "that you are this close to being publicly flogged by Deva. Do you hear me? You are this close!" He held up his finger and thumb with hardly any space between them.

"Now I am giving you a chance to give me a better explanation of what happened. If your explanation is good enough, your punishment will be reduced and will happen in private." To Maitland's surprise Ilashon began to cry.

"Ilashon, you know, it is usually only Gloshan ground troops who are dishonourable enough to inflict pain on alien women. Sikaran soldiers do not do that. *We do not do that*, especially if we are in the *Isithan*! Do we, Ilashon?"

"It is not the same, Ivthalyin! I am not like a Gloshan soldier! How can you say that! Please don't say that, please."

"Ah, I have touched a sensitive area, haven't I, Ilashon."

"Ivthalyin, please may I speak?" Elaan said.

Marayshan nodded.

"Ilashon is my friend and he is a very good person. He is not anything like a Gloshan soldier. He is a young man, and young men often make mistakes. Please don't have him flogged in public, please. It would be terrible for him, and such a disgrace."

"Elaan, what he has done is a disgrace. Do you understand that? It is a disgrace! It is very dishonourable. Do you understand that? It is dishonour!"

"Marayshan please, he is a young man," said Nava. "I can understand a public flogging if Avernyi or I or Deva had done such a thing, but not Ilashon, please, not Ilashon. I am asking you as my friend. If our friendship means anything to you, do not do this."

"All right, Nava, all right. If you put it like that, there will be no flogging in public." There was an audible sigh of relief from all the Sikarans, especially from Elaan who was supporting his friend.

Ilashon rushed to Marayshan and bowed to him and said, "Ivthalyin, I am so grateful, I am truly grateful." Marayshan nodded and glanced at his friend Nava.

"Ilashon, you have not yet heard what the alternative is to be. I am going to temporarily break my bond with you." Ilashon's eyes shot to the Shield Lord's face.

"Yes," said Marayshan, "now you know what I am thinking of as the alternative." He grasped Ilashon's hand and put a hand on Ilashon's chest.

"Ivthalyin, please don't do this," Ilashon said, beginning to cry again.

"Be quiet, Ilashon, be quiet." Marayshan said. "One way or other you are going to be disciplined."

There was a tense silence and then Marayshan released him.

"Elaan, take Ilashon into another room and talk to him. He will need your support in a few days." Marayshan said.

Avernyi came to stand beside Ilashon too.

"I will support him too if you have no objection, Marayshan," Avernyi said.

"I have no objection, Avernyi." Marayshan replied.

Ilashon turned and clung to Avernyi.

Marayshan went and sat down with Mark and Mary Anstey to drink some of his tea.

"Deva, dismiss them," he said.

Deva nodded.

"Yes, Ivthalyin," he replied, and they all saluted Marayshan.

Mark Anstey exchanged glances with Maitland.

"Marayshan," said Maitland, "I didn't realize you have authority over all the Sikaran soldiers here on Naiobi."

"Yes, Geoffrey," Marayshan replied, "all the soldiers here are from the Sikaran Special Forces. The *Isithan* is an elite group within the Special Forces. I am *Ivthalyin Isithan*, and also the Head of the Special Forces."

Mary Anstey exchanged glances with her husband and Maitland and said, "Would you like some cake, Governor? Do have some, it is home made."

"I made it," Ellen said.

Marayshan took some and ate it and said, "It is very good, Ellen. Ilashon is a very fortunate young man. I hope that you two marry and are happy together for many years to come. I wish you both a good future together."

"Governor, what alerted you that there might be problems like this in relationships between humans and Sikarans?" Ellen asked.

"I realized that there might well be problems when we were on the Human starship *McBride,* the vessel that transported us here. While we were living among Gloshans, relationships were not really an issue."

"Why weren't they an issue with Gloshans?" Mary asked.

"Well, my group and I were so revolted by Gloshan women, most Gloshan women, except a very few, that we did not ever consider relationships, except for Avernyi, but he was very sensible about everything. That is what he is like. When we first got to know human women aboard the starship *McBride*, the one that transported us here, we, er, um, found them very acceptable to us, and they seemed to like us also, so it was a two-way thing you know. My men, how you say, just freaked out. It was the best thing that had happened to them in ages, so I warned them to be restrained and when we arrived here I made it an order. Human women are so like our women in many ways. It was a natural extension to assume that once one of my men was in a relationship with a human woman: he was going to want to use his telepathy to make a marriage link, sooner or later, especially as the human women we have encountered have been so warm towards us." He sounded a little embarrassed.

Nava came and sat with them. "Marayshan you are in a very bad mood today," he said.

"No, I'm not, Nava," Marayshan replied.

"You know, Ilashon really looks up to you. He hero-worships you. He has no father now and you are a father figure to him."

"Nava, what are you trying to do? Make me feel guilty?" Marayshan replied.

"I am trying to find out how long you plan to leave him without a bond to you. You shouldn't have taken his bond away, Marayshan. It has devastated him."

"Nava, when I want your opinion I will ask for it!" Marayshan said sharply.

"You know, sometimes, I just don't like being your friend. Most of the time I do, but at times like this it is difficult for me."

"And you think it is not difficult for me, to be in this position with so much responsibility?" Marayshan said angrily.

"Marayshan, you are very good at handling responsibility, that's why people keep giving you more. You are a natural leader."

"Fine, then why are you questioning my judgement concerning Ilashon, Nava?"

"I am not questioning your judgement. I am just saying that Ilashon looks up to you as a father figure, that's all."

Ellen spoke then. "It is true, Governor. Ilashon told me how he feels about you. He really does look up to you, you know. You really are a father figure to him."

"Marayshan, come on, lighten up," Nava said. "For Var's sake, I cannot take this atmosphere between us."

"All right, Nava," Marayshan replied and took his friend's hand for a moment, "I will go and talk to Ilashon for a while."

"Thank you." Nava replied and Marayshan went into the next room.

"Nava, it's so nice of you to try and help Ilashon," Ellen said.

"It's no problem. I have known Marayshan for years. We grew up together on neighbouring farms with Avernyi. We have stayed together all these years and Avernyi and I have watched our friend being promoted in the Space Fleet and the military world, until now he has become extremely powerful. We thought the power would change him and make him arrogant, but it has not. He is still as he ever was."

"He's quite special, your friend, isn't he?" said Mark Anstey. "He has an enviable talent for communicating with people and sorting out all kinds of problems."

"Yes, he is very special, and Avernyi and I take good care of him as we love him very much. Soon he may be promoted again. There is a job about to become vacant, in our Space Fleet Command. There are two High Commanders who command all space war operations from wherever they happen to be at the time. One of these is to finish her term of five years and to retire. Her name is High Commander Princess Alina. She is a really brilliant tactician. We think that Marayshan will be given the job to replace her."

"Is one of your High Commanders a woman? My goodness, that's impressive." Ellen said.

"Yes, I know her from Fleet days and, believe me, she is impressive, and also makes marvellous cakes, just like you, *kirathie*. Have you recovered fully now?"

"No, not entirely, Nava, would you be able to help me the way that Marayshan did?"

"Yes, of course, it is basic telepathy." Nava replied, and rested one hand on her forehead and the other flat on her chest.

Ellen sighed again in relief.

"You know, I didn't realize, at first, how bad you are feeling, Ellen. There is a Sikaran man on Naiobi who could really help you, you know. His name is Viathol, Count Viathol. I think I should call him to come here."

"If you think it would help Ellen, please call him, Nava," Mary said.

Count Viathol arrived and bowed to everyone in the room. He was dressed immaculately as usual and very proud of his good looks and full of himself. He was quite a character and the media reporters just loved him. He had a reputation for being a playboy.

"Viathol," said Nava, "Ilashon has attempted to make a marriage link with Ellen here, but he did it without preparing her at all and Marayshan is furious, absolutely furious."

"I am not surprised," Viathol replied, "what was Ilashon thinking of, my poor, dear young woman. Give me your hands. I must orientate myself to your mind and your feelings. You are quite, quite charming."

Viathol closed his eyes for a long moment and then opened them again and drew Ellen into his arms and rested his hand on her chest.

"I really don't think you should be holding me like this, Count Viathol," Ellen said uncomfortably, suddenly very embarrassed.

"It is necessary," Viathol replied, "close your eyes and relax, relax, relax." He spoke very quietly.

"Where am I?" Ellen murmured with her eyes closed.

"You are in a far away place, and you have moved beyond your discomfort. You are dreaming of warmth and beautiful things. There are flowers surrounding you. Look at their bright colours and inhale their scent. Let go of your discomfort and drift and think only of Ilashon and your love for him."

"I do love him so much, why isn't he here with me? I want to be in his arms, not yours." Ellen became tearful.

"He will be with you soon. Stay here with me. Do not return to the discomfort. You are drifting and dreaming. Don't be afraid, I will soothe you."

"No ... please don't, I only love Ilashon," Ellen whispered trying to push him away.

"I must follow the path that Ilashon took in order to ease your discomfort. Don't be afraid, all is well, *kirathie*, all is well." Viathol spoke softly.

Ellen sighed in relief after a while and closed her eyes and slept whilst Viathol held her.

"How could Ilashon have done this, Navaronschyia?" Viathol said. "This young woman is too nice a person to deserve such a thing. I have sensed her goodness, it is almost tangible."

"He is young, Viathol. It was a mistake that is all, it was just a mistake."

"This is his future wife, is it not? The memory of this day will be one of misery for her, much as she loves him. It will be a sad memory. That is no way to prepare for a marriage to such a lovely person."

"What's done is done, Viathol. We cannot change that, no matter how much we would wish to do so," Nava said. "They love each other very much and I believe that their love will see them through this difficult time."

Viathol nodded then said, "Ilashon has been a very foolish young man. If I did not know him so well I would have said that this was an act of sheer wickedness, to do this to a human woman without preparation, sheer wickedness. But Ilashon is not like that at all. It must have been his inexperience of life that has led him astray. Do you realize Nava that it will take days for Ellen to recover?"

"Viathol, for Var's sake, don't tell Marayshan. He has been speaking of a public flogging for Ilashon."

"I am sorry Nava, but I will tell Marayshan. It took Ilashon nothing but a few moments to cause this. It is outrageous, Nava, it is outrageous!" Viathol said intensely. "All right, a public flogging would be too much for Ilashon, he does not deserve that and he would never cope with it, but I think that he deserves the *Chora*. Don't you? Be honest Nava."

Nava nodded after a few moments. "Yes, I don't want to admit it, Viathol, but I do agree, much as I don't want to."

Marayshan came back in at that moment and said in surprise, "Viathol, hello – what are you doing here?"

"Marayshan, I had to call Viathol," said Nava. "Ellen is having real difficulties. He's helped her for the moment."

"Marayshan, it will take days for her to recover. Ilashon has made a dreadful mistake. I was just saying that if it had been anyone but Ilashon I would have suspected the man of malice and condemned him to Galthais. Is it possible that Ilashon's personality has somehow changed without any of us noticing it?"

"Viathol, every single one of my men developed psychological problems while we were living among Gloshans, with the possible exception of Deva. I have told you that. Ilashon is no different to the rest. I suppose it could have been deliberate."

Marayshan paused then said, "Viathol, what are you trying to tell me?"
"Take my hands and I will tell you in the silence," Viathol replied.

After a long moment they released hands, and Marayshan looked pale and grim.

"Marayshan, are you all right?" Maitland asked, concerned. "Can you tell us what's going on? Can you explain what's wrong?"

Marayshan took Maitland's hands and held them tightly for a moment but still did not speak.

"Marayshan, if you tell us what's wrong, we could all try to help, but you have to tell us first," Maitland said.

"Viathol thinks that Ilashon has developed severe psychiatric problems. He fears that the attack was deliberate. He feels that Ilashon may need help before he can marry Ellen."

"Then let's start helping him," said Maitland. "I vote we call Dr Mark Ryland to come here now and talk to him."

Ilashon was brought back into the living room, and Dr Ryland, the resident psychiatrist on Naiobi, sat and had a friendly chat with him.

After a time he said, "Ilashon, tell me how you are feeling now."

"I feel very good, because Ellen and I are married now and I am a part of her. Now I cannot lose her. I am deep inside her and it feels so good."

"Ilashon, Ellen is experiencing a lot of discomfort because of you, have you realized that?" Ryland said.

"That is not true!" Ilashon said angrily. "Ellen is fine, I made a marriage link with her and she is fine and beautiful and she is mine! I long for her. I yearn for her." He reached out to touch her and Viathol blocked him quickly.

"Why do you stop me, Viathol?" he asked, sounding confused.

"Ilashon, Ellen is very tired and is sleeping, do not disturb her now," Viathol replied.

"Oh, I see, I will let her sleep of course. Viathol, she is so beautiful, and she is in your arms. Why is this? Why is *my* Ellen in *your* arms?" Ilashon's voice shook with anger.

"You know, if Ilashon were not so young, I would say that the first stages of *Kirra-shoth* were upon him," said Nava.

"Actually, Nava, I agree," said Viathol, "but that is ridiculous, because it is ten years too soon for him. It is impossible. Mind you, it would not be impossible at his age if someone had given him some of the sex hormone, *Drotha*, without him realizing it. I sense treachery, Marayshan."

"Do you really think that one of your men would do that, Marayshan? They're usually all so honourable," said Maitland.

"Yes, I do think it is possible, Geoffrey. It could be someone who is jealous of Ilashon and wants Ellen for himself, or—" he went quiet.

"You suspect someone, don't you?" Maitland said.

Marayshan nodded.

"Yes, another young man who may be jealous of Ilashon for other reasons. A few weeks ago, I praised Ilashon for doing a really good job with something, I can't remember what, but I noticed a fleeting look from Chalek in Ilashon's direction. Chalek has been becoming very difficult lately, I'm not sure why. Up until we arrived here, I have always spent a lot of time with Chalek, as I promised his parents that I would look after him. But now he's older, and I am busier being Governor here. I've started giving more time to Ilashon whom I neglected because of Chalek. Dr. Ryland, could you possibly test for *Drotha* in Ilashon's circulation and, if it is there, could you work out whether his body is producing it, or whether it has been introduced from outside?"

"Yes, it wouldn't take me any time at all to do that," Ryland replied, finding a small machine in his case, and connecting it up to Ilashon's arm. Ilashon flinched as he moved switches until he was satisfied with the readings.

"There is a *huge* amount of *Drotha* surging through his system, but it isn't being produced by him. It was definitely given to him from an external source. I am going to flush it out of his system as quickly as I can." He grabbed two fluid packs from the case and attached them to the machine.

"Ouu!" Ilashon said, pulling his arm away, "Leave me alone!"

"Ilashon, he is only trying to help," said Marayshan, "look, let me restore my bond with you and that will make you feel better." He did so and Ilashon looked much happier.

"I still don't understand why Count Viathol has *my* Ellen in his arms," Ilashon said, sounding confused. "Please, tell me why, somebody."

Ryland spoke then, "Ilashon, something bad has happened to Ellen, something to do with her mind and to do with telepathy. Count Viathol is helping to heal her, so that you and Ellen can be together again soon. Do you understand?"

Ilashon nodded vaguely.

"I thought, perhaps I dreamt it, but I thought that I had made a marriage bond with Ellen."

"No, Ilashon," Viathol said, "I think you dreamt it, because you love her so much. Someone has unfortunately violated her and Captain Maitland doesn't want any of us to say who that person is. Only Marayshan, Captain Maitland and I know who it is. Ellen is going to be all right in a few days, but you will need to be patient."

"But I really wanted to talk to Ellen today. It's my day off and I wanted to spend all day just talking to her. We were going to walk in the park."

"I'm giving you some time off, Ilashon, to get fit again," Maitland said. "You have three days and then, when Ellen feels better, you can spend another three days here with her. How would you like that?"

Ilashon smiled and nodded, and said, "Thank you, sir." He looked exhausted. "Have I been ill? I don't remember," he said.

"Don't try and remember anything now, there's a good chap," said Ryland, "everything's going to be all right, you'll see."

Ilashon closed his eyes and yawned.

Ryland checked the machine carefully and rested a hand on Ilashon's forehead and Ilashon smiled. "Mr and Mrs Anstey, could I ask you please to look after Ilashon here for the next few days? He needs rest, good food and basically someone to cheer him up."

"Of course we'll look after our future son-in-law, Dr Ryland," Mrs Anstey said.

"Marayshan, what's wrong now?" Maitland asked.

"Oh, Geoffrey, I am just concerned, because it is such an awful mess now that Chalek may be involved. Deva, take Avernyi and confront Chalek with all this. Should we get Lierschvaan involved, do you think? I want your opinions. Nava?"

After a long moment he shook his head. "Viathol, what do you think?"
"Ask Deva first," said Viathol.
"Deva?"
"Yes, I think that we should," Deva replied.
"Avernyi?"
"No, I don't think we should."
"Viathol?" Marayshan came back to him.
"Lierschvaan would be too intimidating for Chalek," Viathol said.
"Then it falls to me," said Deva.

"No Deva, Marayshan should be the one," Viathol said.

"Oh thank you, Viathol. That has really made my day!" said Marayshan, "Chalek and I are too close. He has been like a son to me."

"Exactly," said Viathol.

"What do you mean by 'exactly'?"

"I mean, *you* will not intimidate him, for Var's sake. He is even younger than Ilashon. You cannot let Lierschvaan loose on Chalek, not in an *Isithan* capacity. You know what Lierschvaan is like. As Principal of the school, he is fine, but as an officer in the *Isithan* he turns into a monster. No, it would be a big mistake. If Chalek is having personal problems that have driven him to do this to Ilashon, you need to use your relationship with him to find out what it is all about. In fact you do need to treat him as though he were a son despite everything that has happened."

"He has a point, Marayshan," said Deva. "You are probably the only one of us who could sort all this out. Chalek has never done anything wrong before, it is really out of character."

"Fine, all right, fine." Marayshan replied. "Thank you all for letting me know what you think about the situation."

Sounding more alert now, Ilashon said, "Navaronschyia, can you please buy some flowers for me to give to Ellen when she awakes? Ellen loves roses. Could you use your money to buy three red roses for her and I will pay you back at the end of the month. They are so expensive I couldn't afford more than three."

"Ilashon, let me buy them please," Viathol said. "Nava, here, take fifty credits, buy twelve roses for Ilashon to give to Ellen, and spend the rest to buy Ilashon some home entertainment movies that he will enjoy watching while he is recovering, something that will cheer him."

"Thank you, Viathol, that's kind of you," Nava said. "Ilashon, how would you like to watch the '*Earth versus Ringul*' baseball championships?"

"Oh yes, Nava, yes!" Ilashon replied, showing enthusiasm. "I would really enjoy that!"

"Good I'll go and buy everything now," Nava replied.

"Ilashon, I'd quite like to watch those championships myself, shall we see them together?" said Mark Anstey.

"Oh yes, I would like that very much, sir," said Ilashon smiling.

There was a pause then Marayshan said, "You know, Ilashon, you are very lucky to have Ellen for your girlfriend. We all think so, and we are wondering how you beat us all to it. We are very envious."

Ilashon smiled again.

"Marayshan, surely it is obvious to you," said Viathol. "Ilashon and Ellen were made for each other."

"Do you think so sir?" said Ilashon.

"Of course," Viathol replied. "There is absolutely no doubt in my mind. You are both so alike, both wonderful people. You will do well together."

"I agree totally," said Mary. "They seem to be perfect together, bless them."

"May their love last forever," said Avernyi.

Marayshan crossed his hands at his chest and said, "Ilashon, I wish you joy in your merging with Ellen. May you both know happiness: always."

"Thank you, sir," Ilashon said, suddenly tearful.

Deva was the next to repeat the words, followed by Avernyi and then Viathol.

Ilashon looked at the people around him and glowed with pleasure, "This is the best moment of my life," he whispered.

Mary Anstey went over to him and kissed him.

"This is an official welcome to our family, Ilashon. I hope you never have reason to leave us, or to regret anything in any way after you have married Ellen."

"I second that, Mary," said Mark Anstey.

Ilashon hugged his future mother-in-law and cried on her shoulder, not wanting to let her go.

"I know it's been such a difficult day for you, dear. I'm going to get you your favourite meal and, when you've eaten, you'll feel a lot better."

Mary went and brought out a tray with cold stew and bread and butter. "I don't know how you can eat that, Ilashon," said Mark Anstey. "Wouldn't you like it heated up? Please let us heat it up for you."

"When I was a boy, my mother could never afford to heat up our food, sir, so I became accustomed to it like that," Ilashon replied quietly.

Mark Anstey shook his head in dismay and looked at Dr. Ryland.

Viathol spoke then. "Marayshan and I met Ilashon on the Flagship *Voran*. He joined as a crewman at the youngest possible age to earn money for his mother and younger brother and sister. We realized that he needed a great deal of help and so we took care of him, Marayshan and I. He arrived aboard ship in a state of deep distress. Something dreadful had happened at home. His father was away and his mother was in real difficulties. They are from Clan *Gira* of course; it is the lowest Clan on *Sikarus* and some of the poorest people are from that Clan. That is how we know Ilashon so well and know, too, that he is a very good person. Do you remember, Marayshan, when we first met him?"

Marayshan nodded and looked pensive and sad.

Mary Anstey put an arm around his shoulders. "You look as though you have the weight of the galaxy on your shoulders, Marayshan," she said.

"Marayshan has a huge amount of responsibility and he is a man of duty and takes it all seriously. He is very special and I admire him greatly. I feel it is a privilege to call him my friend." Viathol said.

"Viathol, please, you are embarrassing me," Marayshan replied looking at the other man.

"That's as may be, but it is nevertheless true," Viathol said, bowing to him from where he sat.

"We think our Governor is very special too," said Mary Anstey, "and we don't want to lose him either. You won't have to go back into the Space Fleet if you get this post as High Commander, will you? We'd all be very sorry to lose you from the civic offices."

"No, I can do the work from here. It involves strategic planning of space battles that is all, Mary," Marayshan said dismissing it as though it were deeply insignificant.

Maitland and Anstey exchanged glances.

It took another day for Ellen to recover, although this was still sooner than expected, due to Viathol's careful handling of her and she enjoyed looking at the roses and, in between that, gazing into Ilashon's eyes. Nava had bought a flower basket covered in tiny hearts for the roses to sit in, and Ellen thought that it was wonderful, and Ilashon thought she was wonderful, and so the romantic pair carried on as if they were doves building a nest together.

Mr and Mrs Anstey doted on them and spoiled them abominably and Ilashon lapped it up, loving every minute of the attention he received. He watched the '*Earth versus Ringul*' baseball championships with Mark Anstey, Avernyi and Nava and laughed until he cried at the comedy antics of some of the Human and Ringulian players, in the 'behind the scenes' clips from the second half of the movie.

Later the next day, Geoffrey Maitland went into the Civic Offices at lunch time and asked Marayshan if he wanted to go for a walk with him.

"I need some fresh air, and I would like to carry on talking from where we left off yesterday, if you've no objection, Marayshan," Maitland said.

"You know I like to be outside also, Geoffrey," Marayshan replied, put on his cloak as the outside air was quite chilly that day and went with the Police Chief.

As they walked, Maitland said, "You know, I do admire the way you handled that incredibly difficult situation with Ilashon and Chalek, Marayshan, I really do. It could have turned into something truly dreadful, but you managed to contain it. I have a friend in the *Interspace* Welfare department. His name is Sanjay Khan. I wonder if you would object to my telling him about this and how you coped with it. I know he is very interested to meet and talk to you about a group of fifty humans he has found very difficult to do anything constructive with. Sanjay is the head of *Interspace* Welfare, by the way. The names of these fifty people have been referred to him from all over Earth from juvenile detention centres. These fifty young men seem to be hopeless cases and the detention centres want to be rid of them and are pressing Sanjay to open an off-world detention facility here on Naiobi to accommodate them. Sanjay and I have discussed this for quite a while and considered carefully who we would want to involve in the project. We feel that it would do these young men good to get a different perspective on things, by getting to know and work with Sikarans as we do. I thought of asking you, Deva and Lierschvaan to be involved, because of all the successful youth work you three have been doing here on Naiobi. We have the finance now to build the secure facility from scratch, but we would need your help in fundraising for equipment to furnish the facility. You could have as little or as much involvement in the day-to-day running of the facility as suited your civic programme. It wouldn't be an extra burden for you, please don't think that, we would expect you to take time off *in lieu* of the youth work. We feel that it is at this moment much more important than your civic work. To help you, we are appointing a deputy for you who will pick up the civic programme when you are in the facility. Marayshan, Sanjay and I are really hoping that your ability to be creative in difficult situations will help the life and work of this project. All the units these youths have attended up to now have failed them, in one way or another. They are habitual offenders. A lot of units on Earth have bad reputations. No one seems to care. I am afraid that the detention sector has been pushed to the bottom of the financial heap ever since the last world war on Earth. People who really care like Sanjay and I and some others have formed a pressure group to petition the Earth President for better resources. Of course, the Earth President doesn't care either, because he's so uptight about the space war. No one can blame him for that, but none of this helps the situation, and we were hoping that you, as you're quite a celebrity now, would give the project the kudos needed to raise the profile in the mind of the Earth President. Marayshan, Sanjay and I really need you for this venture. Please will you try and help us? Will you please consider it?"

Marayshan was silent for a moment then said, "You do me a great honour by asking me. I will help you of course, why should I not? My men and I came to live among your people to be of assistance in whatever way we could. The Sikaran High Council sent us specifically to do that now that we are allies with Earth, Ringul and Kalesia. I know that we are soldiers, but it does not only have to be military or police help that we are prepared to offer. We have other skills too as you know."

"Thank you, I am so grateful and relieved," Maitland said. "I think now that the project has half a chance, just half a chance of success."

"Geoffrey, I will do my best for you, and I am sure that Deva and Lierschvaan will say the same. It is an honour for us that you ask us to help in this way."

Epilogue.

The space war reached its greatest intensity six months later. The planet *Gloshos* was attacked by the massed forces of the Sikaran Space Fleet and was captured. Sikaran ground forces were placed on the planet surface. All Gloshan space vessels were impounded. The Sikarans put many Gloshan soldiers onto re-education programmes. The independent movement of all Gloshan nationals across the galaxy was restricted for one Galactic year, which was equivalent to ten Earth years, unless Sikarans escorted them.

Warlord Shtol was tried for war crimes by a galactic tribunal and found guilty of infringing the *Treaty of Naforek* several hundred times. Captain Kaleen was never tried, but remained within the Central Temple of Sikarus where he was looked after and where Marayshan visited him once. Kaleen never left the Temple as his mental condition did not stabilize, but deteriorated instead and he became generally infirm and, within two years, he passed away. Shtol was permitted to attend his funeral. Marayshan was there too together with his men although neither he nor they really felt that they wanted to be there, but they had known Kaleen for so many years, for better or worse, that they went.

It felt like the end of a bad dream for Marayshan and his men with the passing of Kaleen and the detention of Warlord Shtol. Now the hard work would begin for all the Sikarans in an attempt to build a better future for the ordinary men and women of *Gloshos*. A Sikaran King from the Royal Clan was put in place to rule *Gloshos* for the foreseeable future, until a new Gloshan leader could be found who would improve the lot of the ordinary people of *Gloshos*. The Sikaran King's name was Javrayin, ex-Captain of the Flagship *Voran* and old comrade and friend of Shield Lord Marayshan.

Peace broke out in the galaxy and the Sikarans who made a pact that they would patrol the galactic rim for five Galactic years maintained it. They kept to their promise, and slowly, very slowly, a good feeling of serenity spread from place to place and people began to feel that, at last, they could be happy without worrying about the war.

The crew of the Starship *McBride* stood down and most of them went home, except for Commander Baillie and the Security Team who turned up one fine day on Naiobi and rushed into the Civic Offices and knocked on Marayshan's office door. Marayshan was delighted to see them and welcomed them to Naiobi. Heinrich flung himself at Marayshan, embraced him and said, "Geeze, we've all missed you, Marayshan."

There were tears in Marayshan's eyes as he said, "Heinrich, it is great to see you, I have missed you all too."

Heinrich said, "You know I got married to Chiret last year."

"I am very pleased," said Marayshan, "and I am married now also, to a wonderful Earth woman named Paula. You must all come to my home and meet her. Commander Baillie, it is very good to see you again."

Baillie saluted him and Marayshan returned the salute.

"The first time I met you, I kind of knew there was something special about you," Baillie said, "and I was right. Dang me, but I was right."

The End.